Get Your
Coventry Romances
Home Subscription NOW

And Get These
4 Best-Selling Novels
FREE:

LACEY
by Claudette Williams

THE ROMANTIC WIDOW
by Mollie Chappell

HELENE
by Leonora Blythe

THE HEARTBREAK TRIANGLE
by Nora Hampton

AURORA

Joan Smith

FAWCETT COVENTRY • NEW YORK

AURORA

This book contains the complete text of the original hardcover edition.

Published by Fawcett Coventry Books, a unit of CBS Publications, the Consumer Publishing Division of CBS Inc., by arrangement with Walker and Company, Inc.

ISBN: 0-449-50160-4

Printed in the United States of America

First Fawcett Coventry printing: February 1981

10 9 8 7 6 5 4 3 2 1

For my son, Robin-Joe

Chapter One

"What I ought to do is *steal* it," Lady Raiker said, with an angry glint in her blue eyes.

Her sister, sitting with her in the garden, hunched her shoulders and smiled. "She'd only steal it back. She has magnetic fingers that attract gold and jewels."

It was Lady Raiker's diamond engagement ring being discussed, a gift from her late husband, and not entailed, as Clare claimed, but her very own, a part of her widow's paraphernalia, bought by dear Bernard. "Not only gold and jewels." Lady Raiker took up this favourite theme of the rapacity of the dowager Lady Raiker. "The firescreen that I worked with my own fingers sits beside her grate; the little Wedgwood tea service that I bought with my own allowance sits in her dining room, and a dozen other things she is not entitled to in the least."

"But then she has given you a title that rightly belongs to her," Rorie pointed out, with a mischievous twinkle in her eyes. "I heard her call you the dowager the other day."

"That is a new stunt she has come up with," Marnie declared, her pretty little face colouring to an alarming degree. "If either of us must be known as a dowager, it is herself. After all, she was my father-in-law's wife, even if she was young enough to be his daughter. Her husband is dead, and she became the dowager Lady Raiker the day Charles died, whether she likes it or not."

7

"Society was presented with a novel dilemma when your husband died," Rorie said, with some intention of calming down her sister, and some less noble notion too of getting a rise out of her. "It left the world with two widowed Ladies Raiker, of more or less the same age." She did not add, but knew perfectly well, that both the widows were determined not to be styled dowager.

"Clare was Bernard's father's wife. Her husband is dead these many years, and there is no problem in the matter. Till her son marries and produces another Lady Raiker, *Clare* is the dowager, and *I* am Lady Raiker. She knows it perfectly well, and as her son is only eleven, I trust that will not occur for a good ten or fifteen years."

"How did old Lord Raiker come to marry a girl young enough to be his daughter?" Rorie asked. "A widower for ten years and father of a grown family. He should have known better."

"He was always susceptible to young girls. His past is not, shall we say, pristine? We prefer not to speak of it, but there were episodes that are best forgotten. He met her at Tunbridge Wells, where he went to recover from the gout, and she went to recover from being poor and an old maid. Both cures proved effective. They left together a bare month after their separate arrivals, and it seems to me they must have made an extremely odd-looking couple. Of course she would have been taken for his daughter by anyone who didn't know them. She used to tease old Charles and say he had robbed the cradle, but it was she who plundered the grave. He didn't last more than two years. He was old enough to know better, but Clare soon convinced him she cared not a straw for any gentleman under fifty—they were mere striplings to her ripe twenty years."

"I take it he had second thoughts when he got her home to Raiker Hall and presented her to Bernard—a sprig of twenty-five."

"Oh, she was right after Bernard, he told me so. Indeed even his younger brother Kenelm—and he was only fifteen then, you know—she regarded with an unmaternal eye. She cordially invited them both to call her Clare. Well, Bernard could hardly call her Mama, and he five years her senior, but Charles could not but feel uneasy

8

when she took to calling her stepsons 'dear' and 'darling,' and batting her lashes at them in a wanton way."

"Quite a Grecian situation," Rorie said, trying to envisage the dashing Clare's ever bothering her head with Bernard, who, despite his good looks, was an old stick.

"Something had to be done. Charles had severe doubts by then regarding her preference for old age, and that is when he shipped Bernard off to London as a member of Parliament, and I met him and married him."

"What about his brother, Kenelm? You implied she had an eye for him, too."

"For anything in trousers, my dear. The grooms, the footmen, and most especially the neighbours. It was shocking. But Kenelm was away at school most of the year, and came home only for the holidays. Even that proved a terrible mistake, of course."

"But Clare and old Lord Raiker must have got on well enough. She gave him a son in any case, and from the looks of little Charles, there can be no doubt regarding his paternity."

"She spared us that indignity, at least. Charles is legitimate, of course. It wouldn't have mattered to us if only Bernard and I could have had a son too, for Bernard was the eldest, and *his* son must have taken precedence. But it was not to be. We had only the one daughter." She looked with a rueful sigh to where her one offspring played under the tree with a striped kitten. Bernard, like all the Raikers, had been tall, dark and handsome. Marnie was short, blond and pretty. Their daughter, Mimi, was medium, mousey and plain.

"Pity," Rorie said, and so it was. If only her sister could have produced a son, she might have remained at Raiker Hall with him, where she had gone after old Lord Raiker's death. She and Bernard had lived there for nine years, till Bernard had been struck down with a mysterious ear ailment in the prime of life, only thirty-five. Whoever would have thought he would go so young, and he as hale and hearty as could be.

"We ought to be glad Clare did give the family another son, or heaven only knows what would have happened to Raiker Hall. The estate would have gone into escheat or something horrid."

"Wouldn't it be nice if young Charles and Mimi could

9

make a match?" Rorie asked, feeling just a little sorry for Mimi. So terribly plain. She knew well the difficulties of making a good match. She herself was not so pretty as her older sister. She had been trying for several seasons in Devonshire to land a husband, without success, and when her sister had suddenly been widowed, she had been very happy to come and stay with her and try her luck in Kent.

"My dear, Charles would not be at all eligible! He is her half uncle."

"Oh, is he? How confusing it is, with all these widows and stepchildren and half this and half thats." .

"It is not confusing in the least. Charles is Bernard's half brother, and he is Mimi's half uncle. You have only to split everything in two, and it is as clear as glass."

"A pity you and Clare couldn't both call yourselves half a baroness, and have done with it," Rorie said archly.

"We are both Lady Raiker, and I do not begrudge her the full title. She is welcome to it, if only she would give me back my ring. It is not so much to ask. She has Raiker Hall back. She didn't get to stay long the first time around with Charles dying on her so early, and she only married him to get a respectable roof over her head, and of course the title. How she hated to leave when he died! But we finally got her sent off here, to the Dower House. Still close enough to pester the daylights out of us, but at least not under our roof. She tried a dozen times to inveigle her way in, but Bernard wouldn't hear of it."

"*You* would have welcomed her, I suppose?" Rorie asked with a teasing look.

"I had no fears she would steal Bernard on me, if that's what you mean. He despised her. She claimed the Dower House was too drafty in winter. Not that she minded, but little Charles was subject to some imaginary lung trouble. Then the roof was leaking, and a dozen other things. Well, I expect she is very happy now. She has her little Charles to secure things for her. As the baron's mama, she has undisputed right to reign supreme at Raiker Hall, as the *dowager* Lady Raiker."

"What about Kenelm?" Rorie enquired. "Little Charles is only the third son. Kenelm is really next in line for the title. He was never reported as dead, so far as I know."

"Oh, Kenelm! She makes no effort to find him. *He* it is

10

who should be Lord Raiker now with Bernard's death. I'd give anything to know what happened to him."

"How is it *possible* for him to vanish into thin air?" Aurora asked, wondering anew at the odd doings of this whole family. "When did it happen, anyway?"

"About eleven years ago, not too long after little Charles was born. Kenelm was home from school on holiday, or so we heard, for of course Bernard and I were in London at the time. We made only very short and infrequent visits home. He had a row of some sort with his father. I wouldn't be a bit surprised if the dowager was the cause," Marnie said, with a very significant lift of her brows.

"Surely not! He was only a child, and she must have been . . ." Aurora came to a halt, frowning with the effort to remember ages and calculate the years.

"She was twenty-one, she *says*, and he was sixteen then."

"She was too old surely to be interested in a boy."

"You don't know her. He was old enough to wear trousers, and shared a little his papa's susceptibility to the fair sex. Already one was beginning to hear a few stories about Kennie. I'm afraid I would not put it past him, and of course it is exactly what one would expect of *her*."

"He sounds a bit of a rare bird."

"He was, and I wish he would come back. If anyone in this world could handle Clare, it is Kenelm."

"Why do you think so? You hardly knew him. You only met him at your wedding, and a few times in London when he was a boy."

"But what a boy!" Marnie tossed back her blond curls and laughed.

"What was he like?"

Marnie put her chin in her hands and smiled nostalgically. "Like a corsair," she said. "Dark as a gypsy—black hair, black eyes, full of the devil. Tall, wide shoulders, a flamboyant way about him—so very animated always. A little more so than Bernard, actually. It was his youthful exuberance, I suppose, that lent him that sparkle. Still a boy, but giving every evidence of growing up into a full-fledged corsair. I wonder what ever became of him."

"He ran away, did he?"

"He was *sent* away, I believe."

"Sent where? His father would not have turned him

11

from the door with no destination in mind. Even a rene-
gade son has some provision made for him, some effort
made to reclaim him."

"Bernard's father refused to speak of it. He told Bernard
he had only two sons—meaning Bernard and Charles. You
may be sure Clare induced him to take such a course. She
is certainly mixed up in it. Kennie was always her favourite stepson, yet from the day he disappeared she has said
not a word, ostensibly in obedience to her husband's wish.
But his other wishes were not so assiduously followed. The
portrait of Charles's first wife, for instance, was removed
from the gallery within a week of her return to the Hall. I
asked her for it a dozen times—by Gainsborough, and very
valuable, but she says it is mildewed. I haven't a doubt in
the world she sold it."

"Did Bernard try to find him?"

"My dear, we did everything imaginable! Had men out
scouring the countryside for him far and wide, called in
the Bow Street Runners, ran ads in the papers—nothing.
He vanished."

"Wasn't there some story about the gypsies taking him?"

"Pooh—that was all a faradiddle. Clare's story to the
neighbours to try to make the thing look respectable.
There were gypsies camped here in the woods at the time,
but they do not steal young men, you know, only babies.
And as far as that goes, I daresay they have never stolen a
baby in their lives. What would they want with babies?
Anyway, Bernard had the gypsies followed, and Kenelm
was not with them. They didn't know a thing about it.
They were frightened out of their wits, Bernard said."

"I wonder if they would have killed him."

Marnie shrugged her shoulders. "Who knows?" Perhaps
they caught him *in flagrante delicto* with one of their
gypsy girls and stuck a knife between his shoulders.
Bernard didn't have the woods scoured for new graves.
But if that is what happened to him, it is as well that it not
be known; like a few other family items, it is best left in a
dark closet."

"He must be dead," Aurora decided sadly. It was this
mysterious member of her sister's family that most in-
trigued her. Perhaps because he was the one she had
never met. She had been sick with measles at the time of
the wedding, and as the match had been made in London,

12

the groom's family had been unknown to her till she had made her first visit to them. She sat musing, her deep-blue eyes taking on a faraway, dreamy look. As Marnie observed her, she thought it strange her young sister hadn't any beaux, for she was really very pretty. Not so pretty as herself, it was generally said—the hair darker, the face more round than heart-shaped like her own, but pretty.

"If he *were* alive," Aurora went on, rousing herself from her dream, "how old would he be now? That was eleven years ago, and he was sixteen. He would be twenty-seven. Just a good age for me."

"Or *me*," her sister replied with a coquettish look. "Oh, I know I am thirty, but could pass for being in my twenties still, and Kenelm preferred older women."

"Did he like you?"

"He was too discreet to let on if he did, but he used to flirt a little when Bernard was not around."

"You will do better to stick to Mr. Berrigan," Rorie replied. "Bernard is dead only a year, but I notice your crepe has dwindled to dark gloves, and I suppose they will go too now that spring is come."

"My dear sister—how can you be so unjust! You will notice I wear a mauve gown, half mourning."

"I notice too that Mr. Berrigan likes you in mauve. You will be married a second time before I make one match. It isn't fair."

"You're only twenty-one, but *I* am in no hurry either. In another year or so I may remarry. Meanwhile I shall sit back and pray for Kenelm's return."

"The Lord helps those who help themselves," her sister reminded her, thinking this a lackadaisical way of finding the rightful heir. But either way it would make little difference to Marnie whether it was little Charles or Kenelm at the Hall, she would still be the widow, living in the Dower House. She mentioned this.

"True, but it rankles—the speed with which Clare bolted off to London to present Charles's claim to the title and estate the very week of Bernard's death, as though she couldn't wait to be rid of us. She got herself a sharp lawyer and convinced the judge, or chancellor or whoever she saw, that an absence of eleven years more than fulfilled the seven-years waiting period, and had the new baron installed before anyone knew what she was up to."

"You knew. God knows she showed you that nisi decree often enough. I feel I know it by heart."

"In my distracted state after Bernard's death I hardly knew what was going on. 'For the time being,' she kept saying, and all I really wanted was peace and quiet. She pestered me into it. If I had had my wits about me, I would have fought it. I should have insisted on staying there till some effort was made to find Kenelm. I wonder what would happen if he were to turn up now?"

"He would have to prove his claim, I suppose. It shouldn't be difficult for him," Rorie said, happy to revert to the possibility of his being still alive.

"She'd make it difficult. Say he was an impostor and go demanding he produce papers and certificates that she, very likely, has burned. She'd put up a good fight. She likes very well being the baron's mama, and lording it over everyone from the Hall. You may be certain she wouldn't give up her glory without a good fight. And Kenelm is the very one who would give her a battle."

"Why don't you start advertising again? He may be about the countryside somewhere. He may not have heard of Bernard's death, and not realize he is now Lord Raiker."

"What, roaming the countryside for eleven years? Hardly. One would have heard of Kenelm, I am convinced. I sometimes wonder if he went to America. We are practically on the coast. I wouldn't have a notion how to go about advertising in America."

"You would hire an agent, I expect."

The word "hiring" had the immediate effect of lessening Lady Raiker's interest in finding her brother-in-law. She was not precisely purse-pinched, but she had a certain natural tendency to behave as though she were, and her interest was diverted to the roses, where she discovered some slugs that sent her looking for her gardener.

Chapter Two

Lady Raiker returned to her chair, complaining that she had found the gardener under a tree, smoking a pipe if you please, while the slugs ate up every petal on her roses. "What is it?" she asked in alarm, as she observed that her sister was staring toward the shrubbery, and pointing.

"Oh, the gypsies are back," Marnie said, unperturbed. But the swarthy-faced hag that smiled at them through broken teeth looked dangerous to the younger lady.

"Quick, get Mimi!" Aurora said.

"They won't *eat* you, you know," her sister scoffed. "They come annually, usually about this time, in the spring. No doubt we will find a few chickens missing in the morning, but you need not worry about a slit throat. This one is the matron of the crew. She tells fortunes. How it brings it all back! She foretold Bernard's death last year—she told me there was a dark cloud on my horizon, and within two weeks he was gone. Already he was complaining of the earache. Let us hear what she has to say this time."

"Fortune, missie?" the old hag asked, advancing from the shrubbery when Marnie beckoned her. "Gypsy tell your fortune, yes?"

"Yes, please," Marnie replied, and held her hand out. Aurora flinched to see her sister's dainty white fingers

15

taken in that disreputable brown hand, and kept looking to Mimi, who had released the kitten and was coming closer, staring in fascination at the woman. While the old lady traced along the palm's lines and muttered to herself, Aurora regarded her closely. The hair sticking out from the front of her bright kerchief was grizzled, once black, now iron-gray. The face, the colour of café au lait, was lined and the eyes cunning.

"Tall gentleman friend coming," the gypsy said, smiling and shaking her head for emphasis. "Coming mighty soon, yes, missie. Good friend coming. Big dark man—handsome. He got troubles too. You got troubles. Big dark man and little gold lady help the troubles go away." She peered slyly up to Marnie's gold curls and blue eyes to see how this prophecy went down. As the lady was smiling in girlish delight to hear of a handsome gentleman coming her way, the gypsy went on. "Here's death going away, and life coming," she chanted, tracing some lines on the palm. The memory of Bernard seemed to fade into the distant past as she spoke. "Happiness in your future." She added a few details regarding watching out for dark moons and such obscure mumbo jumbo as left her listeners quite at sea, then she turned to Aurora.

"Tell the fortune, missie?" she asked. Aurora was repelled by the woman, but still some curiosity compelled her forward, and she held out her hand. The old gypsy shook her head doubtfully. One would think there wasn't a line to be seen from the look of uninterest the hand evoked. "Life is slow coming," she said at last. "No good here—no bad too. Long time no husband for missie. One day he comes. One long day from now." Intercepting an angry glance from her client, she added a little good news, hoping to increase her reward. "The dark clouds have gold linings. Yes, missie."

"What dark clouds? You saw no bad in my future."

"Not bad. Dark clouds—gold linings."

"I guess a dark cloud is better than nothing," Rorie decided after considering the matter a moment. The woman was right about the past, at least. Life had been slow getting started. No real bad in her past—no serious illness or tragedy, but no good either. No romance or adventure. Strange how she felt a tingle of excitement at the old woman's touch. Almost as though some energy, some

16

exotic adventure, clung to those brown fingers and transmitted traces of itself to her.

"No handsome, dark stranger for me?" she asked, becoming more comfortable with time.

"She is the one who requires a tall, dark stranger, you know," Marnie said, laughing lightly.

"She not the one he comes to," the gypsy said firmly. "He comes to gold missie. Soon he come. You help, yes?"

"Yes, I am very particular about helping all tall handsome strangers who come to my door." Marnie said, making a joke of the whole, but the gypsy was not laughing.

"Yes, missie. You help big man. You help!"

The smile faded from Marnie's face. She stared closely at the old woman as she reached in her pocket for a piece of change. "Go now. Run along," she said. The gypsy bobbed her head, snatched the money and left.

"What do you make of that?" Aurora asked.

"I don't believe it's the same one who told me about Bernard last year. They all look alike to me, and it was over a year ago. Tall dark strangers and happy futures are their stock in trade. When they start that, you know it is nonsense."

"A pity she couldn't have found one for me, then," Rorie answered ruefully.

"I'll let you have mine, in the unlikely event that he materializes." In her mind a vision of Mr. Berrigan—no dark stranger but a blond friend—arose and was an acceptable substitute for a faceless phantom.

Before more could be said, a termagant more terrible than the gypsy hag descended on them from their own doorway. She was Miss Malone, their . . . everything. Her duties were too large to be confined in one title. By a will stronger than steel and a love broader than the ocean she had risen to such a position of dominance over the girls that their own mother took second place, and the woman was only a servant. A junior servant too, according to rights, for she had been their nursemaid when they were small themselves, and had been brought to Raiker Hall to fill the same position for Mimi upon the child's birth. She had little education, had only learned to read when she was eighteen, though that had been perhaps thirty years ago, and she had ploughed through several cheap romances since then.

17

It was Bernard who was responsible for her rise to preeminence at Raiker Hall. Mimi had taken a terrible cold and fever in the first year of her life. The doctor as much as said she was done for, but Malone sat by her side, bathing her face with cold water, urging bits of liquid down her throat, tending her for days and nights on end till the nurse grew to a shadow of her former self. She had also prayed, and made the family do likewise. Mimi recovered, and Malone took the cure for her own miracle, as well she might. Bernard declared flatly, "The woman is a saint," and from that day onward she bowed to no one. Her way with the butler and uppity housekeeper was a sight to behold. With her fractured grammar and atrociously mispronounced vocabulary she bearled them all. She felt that upon coming into the home of a peer her plain old Irish English was not good enough, and took on a grand new language carelessly adapted from her readings. After the remove to the Dower House she had really no menials worth her talents, but still she was the real mistress of the small establishment. Mimi had now a governess, but Malone would let the poor child be pestered with this creature only for short periods at a stretch. Once an invalid, always an invalid. She was bound to find the girl looking pulled after an hour in the classroom learning those nasty numbers or putting together the map, and would usher her out for a "breath of air"—which was frequently taken in her own room, with the window carefully closed.

Wisps of reddish-gray hair flying from under her cap, her white apron flapping, she descended on them, pink-faced, green eyes sparkling. "What are you doing, talking to the likes of that old gypsy? You'll catch fleas or worse. Get into the house this minute. She'll have the rings off your fingers and her hands in your pockets rifling them."

"You mistake her for Clare," Marnie replied.

"Another she-devil! The world is infected with them entirely. But we'll not be spoiling our appetites with talk of that mallifluous woman, for there's a dainty tea waiting for you inside. Sides beyond, the wind's blowing chilly, and I don't want my Mimi taking another inhalation of the lungs, as she'll do if I let her sit out here. Come along, then."

The lady of the house obediently arose to do as she was

18

told, but Aurora said, "Tyrant!" and ducked to escape having her ear pulled. This little trick had been carried over from nursery days, no longer perpetrated on Lady Raiker, but still used to bring the younger sister into line.

"What did the old gypsy say?" Malone demanded as she herded them in to their tea.

"She said Marnie is to get a new beau, and I am not," Aurora told her.

"Never mind the likes of her. We'll find you a very good fellow, an indelible *parti* as you might say."

"I hope so. I wouldn't want him to fade away on me," Aurora replied.

"Aye, they're good at that. Only let them get a whiff of the minister and they bolt for the hills. But you worry too much about it. You're only twenty-one, and with the exterminating circumstances of us being in mourning for a year we couldn't make a proper push at all. There's young Lord Hanley would give his eyeteeth for a kind word from you I'm sure. If it's a stranger you want, I'll read the leaves for you after your tea, and won't be holding my hand out for pay neither. What did she charge you?"

"A shilling," Marnie said, and received a blighting stare. "Well, they have to live, you know."

"You're too soft by a mile, and so's the government. With the whole world taking the attitude that everyone deserves to live whether he ever does a stroke of work or not, it's no wonder the place is full of thieves and gypsies. The cook relieving us of a loaf a day and a half dozen of eggs, the laundress whisking the sheets home as rags before you can see a sign of light through them, and *that woman* buying muslin for dust cloths, we'll be lucky we don't have the bailey down our necks for debts before the year's out." *That woman,* never referred to by name, was Mrs. Higgins, the housekeeper, an insolent person who dared to stand up to Malone upon occasion.

"Never a body to open the door for a lady, and us with a butler being paid a fat salary," she grumbled as they entered. She pushed her charges into the saloon and went to jaw at the butler for not having the tea on the table. Had it been there waiting, he would have had his ears burned for putting it out early to get stone cold before the ladies were ready. She was a hard taskmaster, Malone.

"Here, this came while you were out talking to the

19

gypsy," Malone told them, chucking a letter into Lady Raiker's hands and standing at her elbow to read over her shoulder.

"I have been summoned to Raiker Hall," Marnie announced.

"Summoned! I'll summons her," Malone said fiercely, taking it for an insult, though she had only a hazy idea what it meant.

"When?" Aurora asked.

"Tomorrow morning at ten. It must be urgent to get Clare out of bed before noon."

"Does she want me to go too?" Aurora asked.

"She doesn't say."

"You go if you have a mind to," Malone ordered, the summons suddenly a thing to be desired. "Don't let that underbred hussy deprive you of your just deserts."

"Speaking of desserts, may I have a slice of that plum cake, Marnie?"

Marnie was not allowed to lift a finger. Malone cut off a wedge four inches wide and passed it along. She often remained in the room when the ladies were together, and though she refused totally to ever take a seat, she likewise refused to leave. The only way to be rid of her was to hint that Mimi had need of her.

The hint was dropped by the child's mother, and Malone was off in an angry rustle of starched aprons, with a Parthian shot tossed over her shoulder. "I'll be back to read your leaves. A gypsy ain't the only one can conjure up a beau. There's more beaux in a teacup than ever came out of one."

"That explains why I have had such poor luck in finding one," Aurora said to her sister. "I never thought to look in my teacup." She did so now, but to no avail.

Chapter Three

Aurora, Miss Falkner, decided to accompany her sister to Raiker Hall in the morning. It was not home to her as it had been to her sister, since she had not come to stay till after the death of Bernard, but she had visited there during Marnie's marriage and had often been to call in the year she had been staying at the Dower House. She was familiar with the elegant Blue Saloon into which they were shown, and she had ample time to become familiar again, since Lady Raiker kept them waiting ten minutes. She glanced around at the white-painted walls with embossed designs, the handsome blue velvet drapes, the Persian carpets and polished mahogany furniture, and regretted that her sister had had so soon to part with all this finery. The Dower House was nothing to it, the saloon a panelled room less than a third the size of this one, and the window hangings there were of faded brocade, somewhat the worse for wear. Marnie's eyes were only on the firescreen, worked by her own hands, and a constant source of irritation to her. She felt strongly about keeping what belonged to her. She was nearly as adamant as the elder Lady Raiker in that respect, but was less cunning, and less successful.

At the end of ten minutes there was the whisper of a silken skirt in the hallway, accompanied by a musky scent, and followed by the dramatic entrance of the dowager Lady Raiker. She was now in her early thirties, but held tenaciously to the accoutrements of youth. Her hair, blond like Marnie's, was short and worn in a careful tousle suggesting that a brush had been drawn through it, no more. Her audience knew well enough that it took half an hour to achieve this casual effect. Her cheeks were shell-pink and unflawed by day, a shade less pink but still unflawed when she retired to her bed. Her eyes were large and lustrous and her teeth in good repair. Her figure too was still good, not the sylphlike frame that had first attracted old Charles, but not full enough to allow of the term "full-blown." She carried a trailing wisp of heavily laced handkerchief in one hand, and entered smiling graciously, as became the chatelaine of Raiker Hall.

"So kind of you to come, my dear," she said in a failing voice, wafting herself forward to take up a seat beside them. "Dear little Charles is abed with a fever. I was up with him half the night." Her clear eyes belied this motherly statement, but no one argued with it. Polite enquiries elicited the information that there was no real fear—merely Mama's concern had caused her to exaggerate the danger. "I feel it is my own fault. I had him posing for me in the garden yesterday. I am taking his likeness to hang in my own room." It was a bit of a relief to hear that the latest rendition would be put away from public view. Since Charles had come into his dignities and titles, Mama had executed a score of likenesses, one of which she stared at now across the room, wearing a wistful smile. The visitors' eyes followed hers, to gaze on a handsome young fellow posed with a dog at his heels. It was well done. Clare was a talented painter.

"The doctor has been to see him, and assures me there is no danger." The concerned mother face vanished, and a calculating look took its place. "So I have decided to consult with you about the manner in which we should announce little Charles's accession. I thought some sort of a quiet do, to introduce him to everyone."

"Everyone knows him. He has been declared the baron for nearly a year now. What do you mean, Clare?" Marnie asked.

"A little fête of some sort—a garden party or tea. It cannot be a ball; he is too young. Now that the year is up

22

since your dear Bernard's passing, we shall begin to go out a little again. Not that one looks forward to it in the least, but people in our position, you know, are not expected to keep entirely to ourselves."

As Lady Raiker had made not the slightest move to keep to herself during the past year, this modest speech was greeted with open derision. "You are going to have a party, in other words?" the other Lady Raiker asked baldly.

"Some token gesture must be made to honour the occasion. The nisi decree has come down that Charles is now Lord Raiker, and it would be too backward not to acknowledge it. What do you feel—an outdoor party, or a rather more formal tea?"

"I expect Charles would prefer an outdoor party," Aurora suggested, being so naive as to think Charles's happiness was involved in the matter.

"Just what I thought myself," the mother took it up. "But then the weather is unreliable. To erect Japanese lanterns and tents and a pavilion for dancing outdoors and have the whole spoiled by rain . . ."

Marnie's brows rose to hear the extent of the modest celebration planned. "Very true," she said, "and people do make such a mess of the lawns at an outdoor party too. The place was always a shambles after public day."

"Had I had the foresight to redo the saloon, I would not hesitate a moment to do it inside," Clare said, casting a condemnatory look at the opulence around her. "Really, the place was allowed to go to rack and ruin while you . . ." Then she stopped discreetly. "But then I know you never cared at all for keeping up Raiker Hall, my dear Marnie. I do not say it in a reproving way, I assure you. I know your interests lay elsewhere, with your daughter and your charity work. Quite proper, I'm sure, but then we who are placed by chance in these old stately homes have a duty to keep them in good repair. Now that the court has finally placed some of Charles's income at my disposal, I shall do what I can to repair the ravages of time. The party, however, I wish to hold immediately, as soon as it can be arranged. I am inclined to hold it here, despite the looks of the place. It is a great nuisance preparing the outside, and then if we should be rained out . . ."

"I cannot think the place so tatty you need be ashamed
23

of it in the least," Marnie said hotly. "I kept it up a good deal better than *you* did the Dower House."

"Oh my dear, I have offended you! It is not at all *tatty*—it is only that I should like it to be seen at its best, as it used to be. But you are right; it is nothing to be ashamed of, and I'll have a tea indoors. Now, I wonder if you would be kind enough to help me with this list I am working up. The Dougalls of course must be asked, and the St. Albanses, the Spencers and the Brewsters." She went on to name off the illustrious of the parish, who were by no means her own set, and to omit all those persons with whom she generally consorted. Her intention was soon discovered. As the mother of the baron, she wished to ingratiate herself with the proper people, and felt the likeliest way of achieving it was to show the world she had the support of the younger Lady Raiker. Bernard and Marnie had moved in the first circles; Clare had not. As a young widow at the Dower House, she had been befriended by the raffish, and been very happy too, but now she was above the rich cits and wished to take her rightful place as the mistress of Raiker Hall. Marnie was under no misapprehension as to the use to which she was being put, but she felt it proper that Clare raise the *ton* of the callers at Raiker Hall, and was willing to abet her.

It was decided that Clare would "just scribble off the cards," and Marnie would drop them off at the designated homes, adding her own personal entreaties that they be accepted. She had no other function except to attend the party herself and show her approval. All the planning and redecorating would be done by Clare; she would not be pestering dear Marnie in the least. As a reward, Clare said at the end, "I have been thinking, why do you not take that lovely little firescreen you made home with you? It would look well by your grate, and I have seen an appliqué one in the village that would suit me better."

"I would like to have it," Marnie said at once. "And the Wedgwood tea service in the—"

"Oh my dear! Don't quite strip the place bare on poor little Charles!" Clare laughed.

Marnie held her tongue, but she thought that future help might bring not only her tea service but even her engagement ring back to her.

"By the way, Clare, the gypsies are back," Aurora said

before they left. "One came to tell our fortune yesterday. You must make sure Charles is not let out alone."

"Are they indeed?" Clare asked, with a frightened look, the first genuine emotion she had shown. "I'll have them run off."

"They are harmless. Bernard never bothered with them," Marnie said.

"Harmless? They are thieves and worse. You know the Raiker necklace was stolen by them."

This was a piece of family legend that had not arisen till the death of Clare's husband. When it had come time to turn over the heirlooms, the fabulous Raiker emeralds had been missing, and then it was revealed that it had vanished at the last visit of the gypsies. No public clamour had arisen, as the departure of the gypsies had also seen the departure of Kenelm, and there was just enough doubt in everyone's mind that it was he and not the gypsies who had taken the necklace that it had not been officially reported as missing. Bernard, the heir, was the logical one to raise a fuss, but he had never done so.

"We don't know they took it," Marnie pointed out.

"We don't know they didn't. Still, they are full of mischief. One trembles to think what they might do if one treated them harshly. Charles will not be out alone, you may be sure. Indeed, I never let him outside alone; he is too precious to me. He is all I have left." The wisp of lace was raised to her eyes.

The ladies took their leave, and as they travelled down the road with the firescreen bobbing precariously behind them, Aurora asked, "Do you think Kenelm stole the necklace?"

Marnie regarded her shrewdly. "She stole it herself. She knew her husband was dying and her days as a rich woman were numbered. It would make a good nest egg for her."

"Why didn't Bernard do something about it?"

"How could it be proved? Besides, she intimated in her own sweet way what a pity it would be for her to have to point out to the officials that it had vanished at the same time as Bernard's brother. Blackmail is what it amounted to. I didn't bother changing his mind. Emeralds don't suit me, and it was entailed. I mean, I could only wear it while

25

Bernard was alive. It's not as though it would ever be really my own."

This blatant self-interest did not surprise Aurora. She loved Marnie dearly, and accepted her little flaws with philosophy. Marnie continued, "I wouldn't be a bit surprised if the necklace turned up any day now. She would have the use of it while Charles is still a boy, and while it wouldn't suit her either, she would like to sport it, I think. The return of the gypsies might make an excellent excuse. She could say she got it back from them somehow. If it reappears, we shall know very well she stole it. Not that we could do a thing about it."

"She's horrid," Aurora decided.

"Indeed she is, but at least I got back my firescreen, and she is welcome to the necklace."

When they returned home, Malone demanded to know what the summons had been all about, and was told. "She hopes to trod her toe into decent society, does she?" she said, undeceived as to Charles's being involved in any other capacity than an excuse. "Down dancing with the gypsies is where she belongs. Oh, I must warn you, there was one of them spying around this morning. A handsome rascal he was. Halter ran him off from the chicken coop. Empty-handed. He didn't steal any. There's none missing *yet*. I'll keep my Mimi tied to my apron strings while they're about, vicious brutes. At the far end of the woods is where they're camped, down at the stream. What they'd want with water I can't imagine, for it's plain as a pikestaff it never touches their hides, and it's not water they drink, or I'm a living saint. Heathen creatures.

"Come on and eat, then," she continued. "Cook has made you up a mess of potash that he calls ragoot. Well named too—smells like boiled eggs. What a lady would want to be eating such glue for when there's good ham and mutton in her larder is above and beyond me. I like to know what I'm eating. But the Frenchies are all alike, they don't know a thing about cooking, but only that old French kweezeen. You made a big mistake to hire that foreigner, missie. Eats his weight in toadstools every day. I never saw such a man for stuffing hisself with toadstools, as though he was a fowl to grace the table. At least they're free. He tossed some of them into your ragoot, but you just pluck them out. Don't go sullying your insides with parasites." She was off to rescue Mimi from her governess, and see that *that woman* didn't go feeding the child toadstools.

Mr. Berrigan came to call in the afternoon. He had been a friend of Bernard's, and had begun his calls as a friend and business adviser to the widow. By the time the business was settled, he had grown into a suitor, and before many months it was assumed he would escalate into a husband. Malone had not accepted him as a suitor for her mistress yet. He smoked nasty cigars and occasionally ruined his appearance by a Belcher kerchief, but on the other hand he knuckled under to her very mildly, and called her Mrs. Malone, which she rather liked. She had never had a husband nor wanted one, but liked the dignity of being called Mrs.

Aurora felt a bit out of place when Mr. Berrigan came. It was quite plain he desired privacy with her sister, and lately she thought Marnie wanted a little privacy with him too. After she had chaperoned them for fifteen minutes, she said, "I think I'll go for a walk in the meadow."

"Remember the gypsies are in the forest," Marnie reminded her.

"They are at the far end, where the stream widens. I might just go in a little and pick some wild flowers. There are some lovely bluebells there."

She did as she had mentioned, walking slowly through the grass that was already hip-high, soaking up the sun. She picked a few random flowers as she went, and when she got to the edge of the forest, she stopped, undecided. The gypsy camp was three miles away. She would enter just a little. The gray walls of the Dower House were still visible behind her. The gypsies would not be brazen enough to come this close, and wouldn't harm her, one of the ladies of the place, in any case. Yet as she glanced down at her plain blue dimity gown, she realized she didn't look so very like a lady. Malone was supervising a washing that afternoon, and had commanded her into this old frock.

Peering in at the edge of the forest, there was no sound but the cooing of a pair of doves and the soft stirring of the leaves. She saw the patch of bluebells in the near distance and walked quickly toward them. It was cool and sweet-smelling in here, with the slippery bed of fallen pine needles under her feet. A black squirrel sat on his haunches nibbling at a nut. He was tame enough that he didn't dart off at her approach. She hoped she might be allowed to touch him, but at the last minute he took fright and scampered to a branch to guard his dropped nut jealously. She went on toward the flowers growing in profusion by the stream's edge, and suddenly heard some noise—the rattle of a harness and the soft thud of horse hooves in the distance. She was a little alarmed, but thought it was very likely the game warden. Clare would have him out today to keep an eye on the gypsies. As a precaution, she ducked behind a tree to determine who the intruder was before showing herself.

She was glad she had taken the precaution, for it was no game warden, but one of the gypsies. He sat on a sleek black horse, which seemed the proper mount for him. He too was dark and sleek. He stopped at the edge of the stream and stood up in the saddle, throwing both arms out wide. Aurora became alarmed. She thought he was about to go into some gypsy ritual, possibly religious or mystical, but he only yawned, then hopped down from his mount and advanced to the stream. He walked with a soft, silent stride, like a red Indian. There was something furtive, almost feral, about him. He looked about on all sides before he bent down to the stream and lifted a handful of water. He wasn't drinking it. Malone was right about that. He smelled it, it seemed, then let it out of his hand. Before Aurora could move, he began to strip off his shirt. He wore a dark shirt and no jacket, nor any hat either. He soon stood revealed before her, naked to the waist, with a broad tanned chest, and golden shoulders, well muscled. A black shock of hair fell across his forehead as he knelt down to splash water on his face, arms and chest. The horse, untethered, came forward and began drinking from the stream.

"Do you mind, Baron?" the man said, and shooed the animal away. "What do you think this is, the Ganges?"

She was surprised he was so well-spoken. A gypsy, she thought he would have a strange accent. Her impulse was to run, but her exit would not be silent, and what if he should chase her? No, best to stay concealed and make not a sound.

The horse nuzzled forward again, apparently thirsty. "You have neither manners nor breeding, commoner," the gypsy said, looking at the horse askance. "Can't you let a gentleman bathe in peace? And as to drinking my bathwater, don't think to impress me with that self-abasement."

Undismayed, the horse drank on. The man leaned forward and immersed his whole head in the cool water. For a minute it seemed he had run mad and was drowning himself. Aurora stared, wondering what to do, but then he raised his head suddenly and shook it like a dog coming out of the water. He brushed the excess from his face with his hands, then turned swiftly to look behind him. His ears must have been excellent, for Aurora heard nothing, but in a few seconds a girl came forward through the trees. She too was gypsy—black hair held in a red kerchief, with golden earrings and a blouse that didn't seem much to care whether it stayed on or not, but kept shucking off one shoulder. She was young, strikingly attractive in a jungle sort of way. She said some words to the man, while her bold black eyes wandered over his bare torso. She spoke in low tones, her words indistinguishable, but the sound of them not so English as the man's. Soon she was running her fingers over his chest, looking up at him through her lashes with her head tossed back. *Hussy!* Aurora thought. What a brazen hussy. But perhaps he was her husband. It would take a marriage between them at least to account for such forward behaviour in the young lady's opinion. When the man put his two bare arms around the girl's waist and began embracing her quite passionately, Aurora felt sure they were man and wife, and was petrified lest they begin further intimacies. He was muttering softly in her ears, kissing her shoulders, his hands caressing her sides and, oh dear! She turned her head quickly and calculated the distance to the meadow and safety. When she looked back, the man had stopped and was telling the girl to go. She pulled off her kerchief and tossed her black tangle of curls back, running her fingers through them while regarding him with a challenging smile.

"Go on, before I forget I'm a gentleman," he said, and gave her a pat on the derrière.

Gentleman! Some gentleman! The girl tossed her shoulders, shaking the blouse loose over one, and left, her hips swaying provocatively. The man looked after her with open admiration at her performance. One last inviting

29

'glance was cast over the retreating shoulder. The man took a single pace after her, then stopped and returned to his toilette, shaking his head and muttering something. He fumbled in his pocket for a comb, combed his hair, put on his shirt and began stuffing the shirttails into his trousers. He then grabbed the reins of his mount, and Aurora breathed a great sigh of relief. He was going. Her relief was short-lived. A dog, a mutt of no discernible breed, came trotting from the woods, barking strenuously.

"Shut up, Rags. Do you want to announce to the world we're here?" the man said.

It seemed rather a game the mutt had in mind. He picked up a stick and presented it, tail wagging, to his master. The man took it and tossed it across the stream, where it landed not three yards from Aurora's feet. The mutt bounded joyfully into the water, out the other side, and retrieved the stick. Then his keen sense of smell sent his ears perking up. He sniffed the ground and spotted her, cowering behind the tree.

The man on the other side of the stream whistled. "Come on, Rags," he said.

The dog stayed where he was, the stick forgotten, his tail wagging wildly. He emitted a sharp yap in the direction of his quarry, dropping his stick in his excitement.

"What is it? Cornered a rabbit? Too bad I don't have my guns with me." This was at least a relief. She wouldn't have been a bit surprised if death was to be her fate. Her heart was in her throat, and she risked a peep from behind the tree. The gypsy was staring hard at her, and in a flash he was bounding across the stream.

"Well, well. What have we here?" he asked in a playful way, while his black eyes raked her from head to toe. "My lucky day. Girls popping out at me from all sides." She didn't say a word, but stood frozen while the dog yapped delightedly at his find.

"Lucky I just made my toilette," he continued, rather enjoying her fright, she thought. He looked around carefully and shushed the dog. Privacy, concealment, was his wish, and she trembled to consider why this should be. In her dismay the flowers fell on the ground in a heap.

The gypsy looked at them and laughed. "All your labour wasted. But then you had a free show, so your afternoon was not entirely in vain. I usually charge a fee for

30

performing, you know," he said, and put his fingers on her chin. "What's the matter? Cat got your tongue? She couldn't get a single syllable out of her constricted throat.

"Before you succumb to an apoplexy, my girl, let me tell you I have just passed up a more appetizing armful than you will ever be, and am not about to ravish you. Where do you come from?"

She pointed to the west, unable to speak.

"Where? The Dower House?"

She nodded. "Do you work there?" he asked.

"No," she squeaked out.

He regarded her dimity frock. "Not Lady Raiker, by any chance?" he asked ironically.

"Yes!" she said, knowing, or feeling at least, that he would not dare molest Lady Raiker.

"Isn't that a coincidence, for *I* am Lord Raiker," he said, and threw back his head and laughed. "I was going to let you go free, but for that plumper you will pay a forfeit." He then pulled her into his arms and kissed her soundly on the lips. She was too stunned to speak, too frightened to move. She was like a stone statue in his arms.

After a brief moment he let her go. "I strongly recommend you never take up lovemaking as a profession, miss. You haven't the knack for it," he said bluntly, and released her. "Now, tell me who you really are, and never mind pretending to be Lady Raiker. Do you live at the Dower House?" It was suddenly business, no more, no less, and her terror lessened.

"Yes."

"Who lives there now?"

"Lady Raiker."

"Which one?"

"The younger one."

"And Clare, the dowager?" he asked, with a strange smile.

"At Raiker Hall."

"I thought so! Her son—he lives with her?"

"Yes."

"How do they get on?"

"What do you mean?"

"Do they live in a high style? Has she availed herself of the baron's income?"

"Certainly. She is the baron's mother."

31

"I see. You can go now, but I don't suggest you go gathering flowers while we gypsies are about. They are not all so well behaved as I am."

She checked his face for signs of irony, and decided he meant to let her off this easily. She took one step, then he reached out and grabbed her arm. "Before you dash off, who are you? What do you do at the Dower House?"

"I'm Miss Falkner, Lady Raiker's sister. I keep her company."

"Good God!" he said, and dropped her arm as though it had burned him. "You can't be! Though there is a resemblance. . . ." He looked at her face closely, examining it, and appeared to be convinced

I beg your pardon, ma'am. I mistook you for one of the house girls. So you are Marnie's sister."

"Who are you?" she was emboldened enough to ask, but in a shaking voice.

"You'll learn soon enough. I shall be seeing you again. And Miss Falkner—now how shall I phrase it? I would appreciate it if our little meeting could be forgotten, if *I* could be forgotten for a few days. If you would assume a polite uninterest when next we meet."

The dog became impatient with this conversation and began demanding attention. "All right, I'm coming," the gypsy said. Aurora stood staring after his broad, straight back, and was still looking in fascination as he hopped up on his mount and turned it around. With a wave, he nudged the horse with his heels and clattered off into the forest. The woods fell silent again, as man, horse and dog vanished from her view. The doves, she noticed, were still cooing.

She didn't wait to gather up her flowers, but dashed quickly from the forest into the broad daylight of the meadow. The whole episode seemed like a dream. She walked home slowly, pondering it all. The gypsy so well-spoken, so curious about the family, so knowledgeable, knowing Clare's name, and that she had a son. Hadn't he also used Marnie's name? "So you are Marnie's sister." Marnie said they came every year. It was their custom perhaps to discover what they could of the places they stopped. For the fortune-tellers, so they could make their palm reading to the point? If they knew Marnie was a widow, for instance, they might provide her with a hand-

32

some stranger, to please her. That must be it. But why had he said he would see her again? And why asked her to be silent about their meeting? She must tell, of course. Certainly the family must be warned how close the gypsies came to the house.

She ran the last part of the way home, and told her sister and Berrigan of the encounter. Told them she had seen a gypsy man and woman at the stream, but found herself unable to tell the whole tale. That he had stripped and bathed before her eyes—how could she tell it? And that he had kissed the gypsy girl was bad enough, but that he had also kissed herself was enough to put her in disgrace. That he had found her unattractive was a source of shame even to herself. How demoralizing that the first man ever to embrace her should tell her to her face she hadn't the knack for it! And he would know. He had the knack for it pretty well himself. She remembered vividly the manner in which he had embraced the gypsy girl, with passion and the keenest interest. Pooh—what did she care for a gypsy who had the temerity to call himself a gentleman? Yet she found him difficult to forget, with his dark eyes and broad brown shoulders.

"How would he know our names?" Marnie pondered.

"Been coming for years and years. Imagine they know all about you," Berrigan said stolidly. "Maybe the fortune-teller overheard Rorie use the name."

"Ah, that would account for it," Marnie decided, and the matter was dropped.

Chapter Four

Charles's formal tea was set for one week hence, and the interval was a busy one for the Raiker ladies. The dowager had time to get her carpets and drapes torn off and cleaned, and the younger lady had ample time to deliver the invitations and encourage a favourable response. The acceptances were all given, with various degrees of pleasure, but one could not like to offend poor Bernard's widow, and if *she* wanted it, it would be done. Such a degree of amicability sprang up between the two that the Wedgwood tea service found its way to the Dower House. This was achieved on the day Lord Dougall and his lady were induced to attend the party. Their acceptance was a major coup, one Clare could not have hoped to pull off by herself. The earl would have been happy enough to go to her at any time, but his wife was a high stickler. It had taken a deal of flattery to gain her acceptance. The engagement ring was still lacking, but there were tantalizing hints being let drop that even it might become unentailed if the do went well. Charles's sole part in the preparation was to be measured for a new suit, in blue to match Mama's eyes and look pretty beside her white gown with blue ribbons.

The day for the party dawned so fair and warm that it seemed the tents and pavilion might have been erected outdoors without any disastrous results. At the last minute

Clare had a striped awning flung up over the rose garden that abutted the morning parlour, and the wicker furniture was washed down and put out beneath it. It proved an excellent idea, a place to shoo the heir and infant guests off to with their ices, so that the guest of honour not get in the way of the hostess. The dowager was immensely pleased with her conquest. Everyone had come. They arrived at four, and by five had thawed sufficiently that nearly every one of them had had a few words with her. Lady Spencer had even made a tentative mention of dinner one evening. She couldn't be lured into making it a firm date. "Soon" was the best that could be rung out of her.

The younger baroness enjoyed her day too. Mr. Berrigan, as a very rich squire, was not left off the list by any means. He not only came, but he came with Marnie, Aurora and Mimi, as a sort of hint of what the future might hold. As prophesied by her sister, Marnie left off her gray gloves for the occasion and appeared in a very pretty mauve gown that did not at all resemble half mourning. Indeed, as she sat in a corner looking over the guests, Aurora saw her sister did well to encourage Mr. Berrigan. Really there was not another gentleman in the room to equal him for looks or eligibility. Kent was even thinner than Devonshire for suitable mates. The only prospects open to herself to make a match were the two gentlemen with whom she sat, neither of whom she cared for the least bit. One was a younger son of Lord Dougall, the Honourable Hanley McBain, and the other a country gentleman of good family and expectations, but very little conversation. She never gave either one a thought unless she should happen to meet him somewhere such as this. Malone was a strong advocate of McBain, but it was only his father's title that attracted her. She couldn't like to see both her girls sink utterly from the peerage after their brief noble glory, and it was becoming clear Marnie was going to have John Berrigan.

The only man Rorie had given much thought to the past week was the gypsy. She couldn't seem to get him out of her mind. He really was excessively handsome. And he had kissed her. One's first kiss must make some lasting impression, she told herself. Whether it should make as strong an impression as it had was questionable, but then there was a mystery hanging around him, and that was what she thought of mostly. Malone had said one of the kitchen girls was seeing a gypsy in the woods. Aurora had not a doubt in the world that it was *her* gypsy, and very little doubt that there was more than "seeing" involved in the meetings.

"It'll be a wonder if we haven't got a black-eyed baby in the basket before the year's out," Malone prophesied hopefully, "and to rub salt in the womb, the chit is bringing it on herself. Once she may have met him by accident, but she slips out by choice each night after dinner. She's bringing her destruction down on her own head."

Aurora had not gone into the woods again. She stayed clear of the meadow as well. Her destruction would have to come after her. She listened with half an ear to Hanley McBain's story of some bit of blood he was buying, which called up a memory of the gypsy's black mount, so sleek and strong. While she sat half listening and thinking, the butler walked to the doorway and announced in unctuous tones, and with a perfectly impassive face, "Lord Raiker."

Charles had not yet been formally presented, and Aurora assumed it was this dramatic means Clare had chosen to present him officially to society as the new baron. She looked to the doorway, and nearly fell off her chair. Into the still room stepped her gypsy, wearing no dark shirt on this occasion, but a very well-cut dark jacket and sparkling linens. His hair had been cropped to a shorter length, but the black eyes and tan cheeks were the same. He stood a moment at the door, looking around him with bland interest, then, as no one made a move or said a word, he began advancing toward Clare, who sat in a state of rigid fixation, staring at him.

"Forgive my unexpected arrival at your party, Mama," he said in a silken voice, while some wicked flash lit his eyes, "but as I am the guest of honour, I feel my presence is not totally inappropriate."

Clare did not faint, but she looked as though she would like to. Her face blanched, and she went on staring at the gypsy, for that he was anything other than a gypsy did not for one moment occur to Aurora.

"You!" the dowager whispered, then her voice deserted her. She could do no more than look.

A wall of men began to close in around the pair, looking questions amongst themselves, wondering what should be done. "Throw this person out!" Clare said, when she had recovered her wits.

There was just a little something about the person, perhaps the width of his shoulders, perhaps the gleam of anticipation in his eyes, or perhaps the aristocratic sneer on his face, that made the men hesitate.

"And *I* am delighted to see *you* again too, Mama," the gypsy said. He then bowed formally and glanced around the room. Next he advanced to Marnie and bowed to her. "My other relative; I hope you are less distraught to see me. Being mother to a daughter only, your dismay will be less acute than Clare's. How are you, my dear?"

Marnie bit her lips and examined him. "Kenelm, is it *you*?" she asked.

"Ah, good, you have remembered my name at least. It is indeed I, returned to take my rightful place. Is it proper for me to commiserate with you on the loss of Bernard? I expect that you were even sorrier than I was myself at his passing, but I too was grieved to hear the news."

Still the men continued looking, wondering, and finally turning to Clare for instructions. "Throw him out! That is not Kenelm!" she stated in a voice becoming not only strong but strident.

"Better make sure," one of the men said, in a tentative tone.

"By Jove, looks like the old baron," another suggested.

"I was thought to favour Papa," the gypsy said boldly, then walked to a vacant chair and sat down. No one made a move to stop him.

"Does the guest of honour not merit a glass of something? Champagne is it we're drinking? Good." Someone handed him a glass of champagne. "Where is Charles, Clare?" he asked in a loudish voice, speaking across the room to her. "Odd he hasn't come to welcome me home. I fancy he is grown into a fair-sized rascal by now. He was only a babe in arms when I left. Does he favour you or Papa?"

"You are not Kenelm! Who are you?" she demanded, but hadn't enough strength to stand up, so that her charge lacked conviction.

37

"I am Lord Raiker, madam, at your service, but you may call me darling, Clare, as you used to," he said, looking at her with some dangerous glitter in his eyes. She rang a tongue over her lips and sank back into her chair. The man looked at her a long moment, then turned back to the crowd.

"Do none of my old friends remember me?" he asked, surveying them one by one. "Dear me, I hadn't thought I was such a forgettable fellow as that. I remember you all very well. Really I should renew acquaintances. That's what the party is for." He arose and walked to Lord Dougall and his wife.

"Lord Dougall, and Lady Dougall—charmed to see you again. Did you get that affair of the thieving bailiff settled up? I remember you were worried about it when I left."

He went on passing through the crowd, shaking hands, recalling not only names and faces but taking pains to mention some fact that pertained to the time of his departure. If it was an act, it was a convincing one. Clare said weakly at intervals, "Throw him out," and "He is not Kenelm," but it was rapidly coming to seem that if he was not Kenelm, he was someone wonderfully close to him, not only in appearance but in knowledge. Someone who knew the neighbours and countryside intimately, and who bore a strong resemblance to the Raikers.

While he moved amidst the throng, Aurora turned to her sister. "Is it indeed Kenelm?" she asked.

"I don't know. I just can't be sure."

"Clare says it is not."

"She would. It is like him, but it was so long ago, and I never knew him *well* at all. How could he know so much, if it is not really him?"

Aurora remembered meeting him in the woods a week ago, remembered his questions, knew he had been seeing the servant girl, and possibly other servant girls from other homes, finding out things. "That is the gypsy I told you about seeing in the woods," she said.

"Gypsy? Oh, Aurora, you never mistook this gentleman for a *gypsy*, surely?"

Looking to where he now stood in a very well-cut jacket, smiling politely at a fat matron and occasionally taking a

38

sip of champagne, every inch the debonair gentleman, she was struck with a doubt. Not that he was the same man—he was. But that he could indeed be a gypsy, with such ease of manners and conversation.

The black head suddenly turned toward her. His eyes met hers in a conspiratorial glance. He nodded, took his leave of the matron and advanced toward her, at the same smooth stride that she remembered well.

"Marnie, won't you introduce me to your charming sister?" he asked in a perfectly cultured voice.

"Is another introduction required, sir? She tells me she has had the pleasure of your acquaintance under other circumstances."

"So much for a lady's silence. I should have known better," he said, cocking a playful eyebrow at her and pulling up a chair to include himself in their circle. "But really, you know, ma'am, I was not the only one who behaved badly that day. You told me you were Lady Raiker. Does she often try to pass herself off as you, Marnie?"

"No, sir, passing ourselves off for what we are not is not a thing usually done in the family, prior to the present circumstance."

"At least I have been included in the family circle—inadvertently, I fear. Don't you believe me, Marnie? How can you doubt me? I remember perfectly visiting you and Bernie in London. You wore a *charming* blue striped gown and had your hair done differently—longer. You served us a partridge and some cheese Father had just sent up from the Hall, and we spent an evening listening to you play music—rather badly, as I recall—and Bernard and I sang a duet, also badly. I took you to the Tower next day for a tour. Bernie let on he was too busy to do it, and we had tea at a tearoom where you complained the butter was rancid. There now, I wager I remember more about the occasion than you did."

"I don't remember the rancid butter," she said, her little smile suggesting she was half convinced she was looking at Kenelm.

"Rancid!" he declared firmly.

"But why have you waited so long to come forward?"

"It took a long time to hear of Bernard's death, and a

39

long time to get here after I did hear. I'll tell you all about it later."

"No—I mean it was a week ago Aurora first saw you in the woods."

"Aurora—is that your name? How pretty," he said, turning to look at her. Then he turned back. "Oh—well, I required a new jacket, you see. I have just returned from abroad, and disliked to make my bows in a coat of Indian cut."

"Were you in India?"

"Yes, didn't Papa tell you?"

The Ganges—he had mentioned the Ganges, Aurora remembered. And called his mount Baron—a sort of joke, if he was a baron himself.

"Your father had no idea where you were gone to. That is—Lord Raiker had no idea where Kenelm was," she modified uncertainly.

"The first thing I did upon arriving was to notify him, but it is possible my letter went amiss," he said, with a suspicious look to the sofa, where Clare had collapsed, and was having a feather burned under her nose.

"Where are you staying?" Marnie asked next.

"I have been staying with gypsies while awaiting my jackets, but now plan to stay here, at my own home."

"You can't! *She* is living here."

"Enough to make a grown man tremble, I agree. I have no intention of sharing Mama's roof, but will eject her as soon as possible."

"You can't do that. She has been to London—got everything settled that Charles is you—I mean the baron."

"Only a nisi decree. I looked into it."

"I thought that was the best kind!" Marnie said.

He looked taken aback. "Oh no—it is not a final decree. It will be invalidated when I make my presence known. It was handed down only to facilitate the management of the estate, to free sufficient funds to keep the place running and to keep you and Clare out of the poor house."

"Well! And here she has been shouting 'Nisi decree' at us as though it were something special and irrevocable. I daresay *I* could have been living here all the while as well as she."

"No, actually Charles was the heir presumptive, but I

40

am the heir, and the decree is null and void, or will be as soon as I announce myself."

Lord Dougall, who outranked all other guests in authority, was working his way toward them and soon arrived. "Like a word with you, sir," he said, not brusquely at all but, but quite politely.

The man—gypsy or Kenelm, whoever he was—arose, but did not leave the spot. "Thing to do, I think, come along to Bradhurst Hall with me till you can get this business straightened out," Lord Dougall suggested. "Can't very well stay here at the present time. Have to be an investigation. Daresay it won't take long. Where have you been, eh?"

"In India, working for the East India Company."

"That so? Thought you was looking very brown. Liked it, did you?"

"Very much."

"Good. Good. Well, shall we be pushing off? Party is a bit of a shambles. Pity. Very nice little do Lady Raiker put on."

"I should like to see my brother before I go," the man answered. "Where is he, does anyone know?"

"Charles is outside in the rose garden," Marnie told him. The man nodded and walked out the door.

"Follow him! See if he knows where to go!" Dougall said, with a positively delighted expression on his face.

"What a good idea!" Marnie said, and jumped up, with Rorie and Dougall trailing after her. Without a second's hesitation the man went to the morning parlour.

"Thought so," Dougall said, sniffing in satisfaction. "Picture of his Papa, bar the brown skin. Wonder why Lady Raiker claims not to know him. You must recognize him, my dear?" he asked Marnie.

"He is like Kenelm, but different too."

"He would have changed—eleven years. But you see Bernard in him, don't you?"

"Something of Bernard, yes."

"No doubt in my mind. Very little doubt. Well, he's a young fellow who knows what he's about, and will get it straightened away, I daresay. Missie will be happy I got him to come to us." He walked back to the Blue Saloon,

41

gathered up his wife and daughter and took them to make their adieux to the hostess.

"That sly Alice has got her father to do this!" Marnie said to her sister. "She is up to anything. It will be a match, see if it isn't."

"Dougall will make very sure the young man is who he says he is before allowing it."

"He seems to be convinced already. But I'm not."

"How can you doubt it, when he knew all about the visit to you and Bernard in London?" Rorie asked.

"Oh he is very clever; *that* much is clear. If he isn't Kennie, he certainly knows him, has talked to him at length. He knows the layout of the house and all the neighbours."

"Who else could it possibly be then?"

"Horace Rutley, that's who."

"Who is—" Rorie's question was interrupted by the return into the hall of the man who called himself Kenelm.

"Cute little fellow, Charlie," he said, "but why the deuce does Clare outfit him like a Bartholomew baby, a gaudy doll in blue velvet? And he isn't jumping his pony yet either. Papa wouldn't approve of that, and neither do I."

"His mother keeps him wrapped in cotton wool, in case anything should happen to him," Marnie explained.

"Ah yes, her passport to Raiker Hall, but as the boy can no longer provide that, I hope she'll let him off her apron strings now."

"It is not quite clear Charles is dispossessed," Marnie pointed out, scrutinizing the man closely, as did her sister.

"Marnie, is it *possible* you don't recognize me?" he asked, with a very sincere voice. "Have I changed so much? I recognized you the minute I saw you. Surely I am not so different from what I was. I was sixteen when last we met—already a man nearly."

"Kenelm looked quite different from you. Not so tall, the nose different, less aquiline, and of much lighter complexion."

"Dammit, I've been in India for over ten years! You *must* know me. I counted on you," he said in exasperation.

42

"And Kenelm did not use profane language in front of ladies," she added primly.

"Oh yes I did. You were always jawing at me for it," he answered. She looked swiftly at him when he said this, then looked away, with a quizzical frown on her brow. Rorie couldn't tell whether the remark had been just right or quite wrong, but she thought it had made some sharp impression on her sister.

Lord Dougall and his family came into the hallway. "Well, sir, shall we be off?" Dougall asked, very politely, but not using the man's alleged name or title.

Lady Alice was gazing at him with undisguised admiration, a smile curving her lips. "Do let us go, Lord Raiker," she said, offering her arm.

Regarding them both closely, Rorie saw the little flash of triumph pass over the man's face. What a sly girl Alice was, to be sure! She had most certainly not recognized Kenelm. She was eighteen years old, would have been seven when she left, and could not therefore have been at all close to him. No, she was just allying herself with him to win him over. Kenelm—or whoever he was—took the girl's elbow with the most charming smile ever bestowed on maiden.

"Now why is it I didn't recognize you at once, Sally?" he asked. "Had I seen you coming down the road on your little cream pony you used to ride, I would have done so, I promise you."

"Oh, I outgrew him years ago, Lord Raiker. I am all grown up now."

"I noticed, ma'am, and a very good job you have done of it, too," he returned gallantly. He made his bows to the other ladies present.

"May I do myself the honour of calling on you tomorrow, Marnie?" he asked.

"Yes, we must meet and talk, certainly. In the afternoon, if that is convenient for you?"

"Perfect. I'll call on stepmama in the morning. Good day."

The Dougall party left, and before long the other guests took their lead from Dougall and they too departed, to regroup in smaller bunches at various homes and discuss the exciting turn events had taken. There were two camps set up at once—those who believed the newcomer's claim, and those who did not. The man bore a strong physical resemblance to the Raikers, of course, and he knew a great deal about the family, the neighbours, but wasn't there just a little something of that ne'er-do-well of a Horace Rutley in him? The man more closely resembled Horace than Kenelm, some said. Horace, for instance, had always had that swarthy skin, whereas Kenelm had been paler.

Every family and every neighbourhood has its little scandals, and one of the scandals of this pocket of Kent was that old Lord Raiker occasionally went astray. He was a good man by and large, took care of his property and his people and went to church on Sunday, but he had an eye to a pretty girl. Nel Rutley had been a very pretty girl thirty-odd years ago, the daughter of a fisherman in the village, as near to witless as made no difference, but it didn't affect her looks. The old Lord Raiker had sired a son on her. She had been sent away to some cousin in Hampshire, and later made a match there, but the son was sent back to her parents, who had adopted him. Before he was out of short coats it was patently obvious who the boy's father was. Raiker was writ in every haughty line of his face and the aristocratic set of his head. The boy had been schooled and treated in every way better than a mere fisherman's son could expect to be. Certainly Lord Raiker had taken care of him, but without publicly acknowledging him as a son. It was not too surprising that a child who was neither fish nor fowl, neither an ordinary commoner like his family and friends nor an accepted nobleman or even gentry, should become confused.

He fell in with a fast set of bucks at around eighteen years, and got into trouble, serious trouble, over a horse-trading deal in which one of the participants had been shot to death. It had not been clearly established that Horace had fired the fatal shot. There were three men involved. One ended up dead and the other two vanished, Horace and Elmer Carson. It was believed that they had emigrated to America before they were caught and transported. All this happened some six months after Kenelm's abrupt departure from Raiker Hall, but it was dredged up now and discussed again in full detail.

44

The fellow calling himself Kenelm strongly resembled Horace Rutley. Horace had been more a man when he left than Kenelm had been—perhaps that accounted for it. It was hard to see young Kennie in this fellow that swaggered into town, full of assurance. A lad of sixteen had been less sure of himself, more readily remembered as running through town with a dog at his heels, and likely as not a sugarplum in his hand. It took a certain leap of imagination to picture him all grown up into this fine gent. Horace would know as much about the local folks and their problems as Kenelm. Of course he wouldn't be familiar with all the ins and outs of the family, but he would at least recognize the two baronesses, know what children they had, and might have rehearsed the layout of the house through the courtesy of some of the servant girls. Quite a young lady's man, Rutley, for all he wasn't too bright. Or for that matter he might have fallen in with the real Kenelm any time over the past ten years. It was assumed they knew the relationship in which they stood to each other, although they had never been seen in each other's company. Had they chanced to meet in America, or India for that matter, two expatriots, half brothers—what more natural than that they should have become friends? Rutley, the older and generally credited with being the more wicked of the two, might have learned all he could from the younger man with this very scheme of returning in mind. To return as Kenelm would be to his advantage even if Bernard had lived out his normal span. Bernard was fond of his little brother, and would not be clutch-fisted with him. Another awful and vastly titillating prospect was that Rutley had plain murdered Kenelm when they had heard of Bernard's death. Had already put one man in his grave, so certainly he wouldn't stick at murder. With such a plum as the title and estate to attract him, might not Rutley have killed Kenelm, to come home himself and claim it all? It was conceded that in any case, whoever he was, he'd have some job pulling the wool over Lady Raiker's shrewd eyes.

Clare sat stunned, mute and furious, as her guests took their leave. She detained Marnie and Rorie when they made a move to leave with the others. "We must get together and decide what is to be done about this impostor," she said. The first thing done was to bring Charles in from the rose garden, the implication being that the villain might abduct and kill him.

"What do you think should be done, Clare?" Marnie asked.

"He should be thrown into prison."

"We don't know that he has committed a crime."

"Impersonating another for unlawful gain is a crime."

"Maybe he *is* Kenelm. How can you be so sure he isn't?"

"He doesn't resemble him in the least. He's bigger, darker, wickeder. Kennie was nice, a very sweet boy."

"Eleven years have passed—he would no longer be a boy. I'm not convinced the man isn't Kenelm, though I'm not convinced he is either."

"He is as sly as a fox. You saw him making up to Alice McBain, getting the Dougalls to accept him. Ken was nothing to the Dougalls. They scarcely knew him. You didn't see him saying a word to Hanley, the only one who might possibly have discovered his trick. *I* knew him better than anyone, and *I* say he is not Kenelm. He'll have to prove it."

"I expect so. It cannot be difficult. There are things that no one except the real Kenelm would know. We must put our minds to work and discover what they are, and test him," Marnie agreed.

"It must be done *at once*, before he has time to nose around and find things out."

"He is coming to see you tomorrow, he says," Rorie offered.

"Coming here! I'll not let him in. I'll bar the door."

"That would look very odd, Clare, as though you are *afraid* of him," Marnie suggested, and looked at her hostess with suspicion. She realized that beneath the natural anger, frustration and determination, there was something else that might be fear in Clare's eyes.

"I'm not afraid of him. He can't prove a thing. I shall get my solicitor down from London, and we'll see who's afraid."

"Well, he is coming to see me in the afternoon, and I have agreed to see him," Marnie told her.

"He's using you," Clare said at once. "He'll try to win

46

you over, try to weasel things out of you. Just because he's young and handsome, he thinks he can wind all the girls around his thumb. You owe it to little Charles, Marnie, to refuse to see him."

"If he *is* Kenelm, then I owe something to him too, but I shan't be swayed by his flashing eyes. I'm not a fool."

"You're a woman, and not less susceptible than any other woman to a handsome young man with a fortune and title I must suppose. He'll make up to you, that's certain."

"Credit me with some sense, Clare," Marnie said, becoming angry.

Rorie sat listening silently, her mind in a turmoil. Later she discussed it with Marnie during the drive home, the major part of the trip devoted to Horace Rutley. She did not allow herself to come to a decision, but in the bottom of her heart of hearts, she hoped her gypsy was indeed Kenelm Derwent, Lord Raiker, and she wished as well that it was herself and not Marnie who could help him prove it, but she would be virtually useless. She had never een Kenelm or Horace Rutley, knew less about them han anyone else at the party, with the exception of little Charles and Mimi.

"Who was the nice man that came to see Charles?" Mimi asked. She had been listening to the talk, and making very little sense of it.

"We don't know, dear," her mother told her. "He is a stranger."

"I liked him," Mimi said. "He hugged me."

Marnie bit her lip and considered this for possible significance, but could find nothing in it.

Malone was curious to see them home so soon. She sat out on the lawn pretending to be reviewing Mimi's schoolwork, but in fact she had been drawing pictures in coloured inks in Mimi's tablet, and was pleased too with the results—much better than Mimi's. She realized at once that something unusual had occurred to send her girls back so soon.

"Was it a fizzle then? None of the greats and mighties showed up?" she asked hopefully.

She was told the incredible story, and the shock of it sent her reeling to her chair, to fan her cheeks with her apron tails. "So the profligate son has returned, just like

47

in the Bible," she said. "There'll be no fatted cat killed at Raiker Hall, I warrant."

"I wouldn't be too sure of that," Rorie told her, biting back a smile. "The fat cat was ready to die of anger."

"There will be no rejoicing here either till we discover if he is really Kenelm," Marnie said firmly.

"If he ain't, he's a bolder man than ever before saw the lights of day," Malone opined. "But you never need to fear, my dears, for I'll be by your side when he comes, and no impostor will be gulling us he's our Bernard's brother if he ain't. *I* know things about him, even if I never met him. His lordship told me plenty about Kennie, as he called him. We'll just see if the lad knows about the fenugreek," she said, nodding her head sagely. On this cryptic remark she pushed her charges indoors, where she surprised them all by going to her room without Mimi, to sit silently devising questions to trap the profligate son.

Chapter Five

The ladies of the Dower House were surprised to receive a call from the man who had had himself announced as Lord Raiker in the morning, when they did not expect him till the afternoon. It caught Malone completely off guard. She was out in the back yard setting up traps to catch the gypsies, who had made off during the night with a rooster, and a pretty dull bunch she thought them, to steal that tough old bird, with a dozen tender hens who would have made a tastier meal.

"Good morning, Marnie, Miss Falkner," he said, arising and bowing as they entered the saloon, where he had been put to wait.

Again Rorie was struck by the inconsistency of seeing the gypsy in such elegant attire, at home to a peg in a polite saloon.

"Good morning, Ken—" Marnie stopped in midspeech, her abrupt halt quite obvious.

He quirked a brow at her and laughed. "Your sleep has not brought you wise counsel if you have not yet decided I am me. Shall we settle on some uncompromising name for the interim? The alleged Lord Raiker? Or shall we be less formal, and make it the *soi-distant* Kenelm? Or 'the party of the first part' might be more appropriate, as it seems Mama means to drag me into court."

49

"You have been to the Hall?" Marnie asked.

"Yes and no. I have been as far as the front door, but Wilkins gave me the heave-ho—reluctantly, though. My servants know me. I was refused admittance; and advised to hire myself a solicitor, so I came on over here while I was so close. I hope I don't inconvenience you? I was to come in the afternoon."

"It's no matter. The sooner the better, I suppose."

"The customary phrase when people wish to get an unpleasant ordeal over with, and here I have been looking forward so long to seeing you again." He smiled and looked at Marnie sadly, as though she were breaking his heart. He managed to make his voice sound nostalgic too.

"There will be unpleasantness before it's over," she allowed, determined to steel herself against his insidious charms.

He leaned forward in his chair and regarded her with bright, intense eyes. "I'm going to win, Marnie. Align yourself on the side of the angels. Between the two of us, we can convince them I am who I say I am."

"I want to make it perfectly clear, Kenelm—oh, whoever you are!"

"The party of the first part."

"I am not trying to discredit you, but neither will I be party to any chicanery on *either* side."

"Has she been trying to strike a deal with you already? Marvelous!" he crowed.

"Indeed she has not."

"She will. She's bound to, but if you are quite determined to be impartial I shan't try to cajole you. I am Kenelm Derwent, and it is but a matter of time till I prove it. We never had a great deal to do with each other, Marnie, but I have a good memory, and will undertake to answer any questions you care to put to me on our meetings. I met you first at your wedding. I remember it vividly. Ask me anything."

"Well . . ." She sat back and racked her brains for any little oddity, but he was too impatient to await her questions.

"You wore a white lace gown and carried orange blossoms and lillies of the valley. You looked like an angel, complete with golden halo. I was so jealous of Bernard I nearly wept. We ate lobster patties and drank a great deal of champagne. Bernard let me kiss you once, and when I joined the lineup again, he turned me off. I spent the remainder of the day flirting with the pretty little redhead who was your bridesmaid. Millie something—Kessler, Cotler, something of the sort."

"Cutter," she corrected, but though she was flattered at the tone of his recollections, she realized they were unexceptional—might apply to three spring weddings out of four, and a search of the records would reveal the bridesmaid's name. "Where did we go for a honeymoon?"

"You didn't. You went straight to London."

This was true, and she tried for a more difficult question. Suddenly she laughed and asked, "What happened to the brandy chantilly?"

"Ah—somebody dropped the bowl and it landed in a mess on the floor. Your cat got into it and became roaring drunk." His eyes sparkled brightly; his whole face was beaming. "Don't you remember—it was a particularly ugly tomcat—I never could abide cats anyway—and he took on the hound out in the yard. Bernie and I had a bet for a guinea, and he won, like the tomcat."

Rorie looked from one to the other. She had, of course, missed the wedding, to her deepest regret. She saw Marnie's eyes were shining.

"Oh, are you truly Kenelm?" Marnie asked.

"Ask me more." He waved his hands about in excitement. "Ask me anything."

It became a game. "What did I wear the *second* time you called on us?"

"An *extremely* elegant gown of white crepe. You had your hair done up on top of your head and looked totally ravishing."

"And what did we do after dinner?"

"Bernard stretched himself out on the sofa and snored— dull dog—while I tried to flirt with you, but you made me play chess instead, and beat me. Later you played for me on the pianoforte. You had resumed your lessons, and played better than the first time. Or maybe it was the new hairdress that made me think so. I remember the lamp-light falling on it."

There was a little more of this, and as Rorie sat watching, she realized the man was manipulating her sister as easily as if she were a loaf of dough. Her eyes glowed, and

51

she smiled like a young girl half in love. It occurred to Rorie that he slid in a compliment at every opportunity, implied he had been rapturously in love with his brother's bride, and it went down very well. She doubted Marnie could remember what gown she had worn on each occasion, and how she had dressed her hair, but it was flattering that *he* appeared to do so. If Horace Rutley had systematically questioned Kenelm over a period of time, he might have discovered the rest.

After a longish interval, Marnie sat back with flushed cheeks and declared, "I must say, you have convinced *me* you are Kenelm, and I shall call you so from now on."

The man relaxed with a satisfied expression, then remembered Rorie in the corner and turned to her. "And are you convinced, Miss Falkner?"

"I never knew you before—before I met you in the forest. I am in no position to judge."

"Surely you can rely on your sister's judgement."

She hesitated a moment, for the fact was, she *didn't* rely on it at all. Marnie's judgement had been impaired by the charm of the man. "I suppose so," she said reluctantly.

"Oh what a hard woman you are to convince!" he declared in chagrin. "Did I not meet you at the wedding? Odd I don't remember it."

"Your excellent memory might tell you why I wasn't at the wedding."

He looked at her, frowning. "No, I don't recall. Is it that you were too young?"

"She had the measles, but I doubt you would have heard about it," Marnie said, and had again garnered his attention. "Now, how will you proceed, Ken? With Clare, I mean."

Rorie felt a little twinge of anger, or jealousy, to see how easily Marnie diverted his interest to herself. But she had some suspicion that the interest was spurious, the admiration too assumed to win Marnie's important support. No small point, that Bernard's widow accept his credentials. A few compliments on her "ravishing" appearance, his jealousy of Bernard, and the thing was done. He'd won Alice McBain even more easily. She began to feel that if the man was an impostor, there wasn't a woman in the county who would stand up and say so except Clare.

Her thoughts were interrupted by the arrival of Malone,

who stood in the doorway, arms akimbo, her red hair blowing around her ears, staring hard at the visitor. "Is this the fellow that *says* he's Bernard's brother?" she demanded, subjecting him to penetrating appraisal.

"Yes, that's what he says," Rorie told her.

At the edge in her voice, Kenelm glanced up at her quickly. He was undismayed at the servant's impertinence, but unhappy that the young lady was not convinced.

"Ken, this is Malone. Don't be afraid of her in the least. Her bark is much worse than her bite. She is Mimi's nursemaid. And mine too, I'm afraid," Marnie explained.

Malone strode in with a swagger, planted herself foursquare before him and announced, "We'll soon see who you are. What did they give you when you had the hives at the age of eight, and what happened?"

He blinked his surprise at the question, or the apparition, and thought a moment. "They gave me some ground-up seeds of some sort. I became violently sick—was on my back for two days. I reacted peculiarly to the treatment."

"What seeds?" Malone persisted.

"Greek something I think it was," he said, frowning to try to remember.

Malone waited, but he could not come closer than that. "It was something-Greek," she prodded at last.

"Fenugreek! That's what it was—fenugreek!" he declared. "How the devil did you know that, Mrs. Malone?"

"I know plenty," she warned, narrowing her eyes at him, and having a hard time to resist the "Mrs." and the handsome face. "Now, let's see if *you* know what you should if you're really Bernard's brother, and not an *ulterior ego*."

A little twinkle in the man's eyes was his only overt sign of appreciation of this barbarous Latin phrase. "What kind of apples did you and Bernard used to steal and hide in the schoolroom?" Malone demanded next.

"Pippins," he answered instantly. "And I don't even like them. We used to keep them in the cupboard and throw them out the window at the chickens.

Malone nodded in approval. "Now for number three," she threatened.

"Anything! Ask me anything," the man said, completely confident.

Rorie scrutinized him closely trying to come to a decision. Surely he knew a great lot of detail, but his confidence seemed almost greater than a reliance on fallible memory would warrant. Almost as though he had studied up very well for an important exam, and knew all the answers. The fenugreek—there was nothing in that. Lots of people used it for hives—but then it was unusual to have a violent reaction to it. The pippins—he could easily know they were the most common apple in the Raiker orchard—but the extra detail about throwing them at the chickens seemed unrehearsed. But then, did Malone actually know to what use they were put? If he wasn't really Kenelm, he was a dangerously clever impersonator.

"Who is Cranky Jangler?" Malone asked, and stood with her shoulders back to glare at him.

Kenelm shook his head and laughed. "Mrs. Malone, how the *devil* did you discover Cranky Jangler? I can't believe Bernard would remember him after so many years. Lord, I had forgotten all about him myself."

"Who is he?" Malone repeated.

The man threw up his hands, and for an instant Rorie thought he was beaten. She was aware of a sharp feeling of disappointment, but soon he was talking on. "He isn't anyone, I hope. You might call him myself, or my conscience or my—er, *ulterior ego,* if I may borrow your phrase. He was a figment of my imagination, a little dark fellow I used to imagine followed me around when I was four or five. Sometimes he urged me to behave, and sometimes he suggested the greatest mischief, as on the day he talked me into letting loose the foxes Papa had locked up for the hunt."

"You'll do," Malone decreed, and reached out to shake his hand. "You might have found out somehow about the fenugreek and the pippins, but I can't believe you'd know about a mere pigment of the imagination unless you was really Kenelm."

"Now I think I have convinced everyone here except Miss Falkner," Kenelm said, turning to Aurora. "No questions to put to me, ma'am?"

"How did you come to be travelling with the gypsies?" she asked.

"I only travelled a mile with them. I was uncertain how to proceed when I arrived home. I happened to see the gypsy caravan wending its way toward this area. I knew

54

they made a regular stop in the family forest. It served my purposes well to be close but unknown for a few days to discover what was going forth. I told them I was a scholar from India studying their customs. It is believed now, you know, that they came originally from India, and not Egypt, as the name would indicate. I recognized some Indian idioms in their speech, and their folklore, though they have no written literature, is largely Indo-European. So I joined them."

"Why did you feel it necessary to scout the area, as you might say?" Marnie asked. "Why not just go right to the Hall?"

"I had some little doubts what my stepmama might be up to. A precaution merely," he answered blandly.

"I don't mean to pry, Ken," Marnie went on, "but that sounds a somewhat inadequate reason."

"I left under a little cloud, as you may have heard. I was curious to discover whether it had dissipated, as I hoped, or grown into something more serious. Besides, my hair was too long and I hadn't the proper wardrobe. I *was* curious about the gypsies, too. Anyway, I did it."

This sounded like humbug to Aurora. It sounded like spying. Meeting servants in the woods and asking prying questions, making his grand dramatic entrance at Clare's party—really, that was extremely malicious, and she gave a hint that she thought so.

"It was not at all nice," he agreed readily. "Spite, in fact. It was *you,* Miss Falkner, who gave me the idea to dash to London and discover how things stood legally when you told me Clare had taken control of the estate. But she has got a nisi decree only, so there is no problem there, by the time I returned, the party was only a day away, and it seemed so opportune a time to make my return, at a coming-out party for myself, that I couldn't resist it. My whole time, you see, was not spent spying out things I already knew very well, which is no doubt what I shall be accused of. It was ill-considered of me to have done it. I realize that now, now that it's too late."

"What is the next step in staking your claim?" Marnie asked, satisfied with his explanation.

"I've filed in London. Lord Wiggins is the one who handed down the nisi decree, and he will be trying the case. The next step is up to her. There will be some sort of investigation. I will be required to present witnesses who recognize me, perhaps be posed questions in front of a judge—much the sort of thing we have been through here today, but more formally, and with a variety of questioners, I imagine. Some family members, some old schoolmates or masters. There is no way she can prove I am not me. It is all nonsense, her making such a to-do about it, and unwise of her. If I know Clare, she will be requiring some augmentation of her widow's income. She always spent like a nabob, and her jointure cannot be so very large."

Rorie heard this with suspicion. Was there a veiled hint here that he would be generous to those who supported his claim?

"You're lucky you got back before she spent up your capital." Malone warned him. "A drunken sailor is what the woman spends like."

"But there is enough to go around," Kenelm said with a sardonic smile, "even for two baronesses and a baron. We will do something about fixing this place up for you, Marnie," he promised. And if this was not a bribe, it came close enough to it to thrill one of the ladies, and heighten the suspicions of the other to a new pitch.

"It does seem rather dingy after Raiker Hall," Marnie said at once. She was never one to let a reward slip through her fingers. Much as she loved her sister, Rorie acknowledged this self-interest openly. Her support of this man would be stronger with some hope of material reward. Carrot and stick—he was using both very effectively. Charming flirtation and rewards on the one hand, an implied threat of withholding his protection if she did not fall into line. But Marnie was falling into line nicely. No problem there.

"I heard some mention at Dougall's last night that Rutley has disappeared," Kenelm said. He was called Kenelm by the others, and for lack of any other name, Rorie called him so mentally.

"That happened ages ago," Marnie told him.

"He was never heard of since?"

"Not to my knowledge. The Rutleys may have heard of him, may know where he is."

"I should go and call on them," he said.

"Why would you do that?" Marnie asked, and her sister too listened to hear his reason.

56

"Father always took an interest in him, but more important, there have been insinuations made that I am my half brother, and if I could produce him, or at least discover where he is—America was mentioned—then that possibility could be disposed of. That is the only stumbling block I can see. Who else could I be? And it won't have slipped Mama's notice either."

"Why do you call Clare that?" Marnie asked.

"Because she dislikes it so much," he answered, smiling wickedly. "She is my stepmother, too. As wicked as the worst one ever invented to scare children." He arose and took a look around at the room, as though seeing a friend again after a long absence. "I see the clock still doesn't work," he commented, looking at a head-and-shoulders clock on the mantel piece. "The place hasn't changed much—just got older. I must be going now. We'll meet again soon. I look forward to having a nice long talk with you, Marnie, catching up on old times. And to becoming better acquainted with *you*, Miss Falkner," he added, nodding in her direction. "It isn't every day I have the pleasure of meeting such a pretty family connection. I feel quite cheated to have been deprived of your friendship all these years. We must make up for lost time."

Malone sidled forward to hear a few words on coming to know her better too. "Delighted to have met you, Mrs. Malaprop," he said, with an irrepressible smile.

"Well now if that ain't a caution!" she squealed. "That's *exactly* what your Bernard used to call me, Marnie. Where did you get that name from? It's downright *eerie* is what it is. Malaprop! I haven't heard that name since dear Bernard stuck his spoon in the wall."

"There was a strange link between my brother and myself," he said. "We liked the same names, and people." There was just a barely noticeable peep in Marnie's direction at that point. A slight reminder that they both favoured the elder Miss Falkner?

Marnie read that into it at least, and blushed happily.

He left, and Malone took up a position, standing between the two seated ladies to deliver her opinion of him. "The man's a rascal and a rogue. Got an eye in his head that belongs in a panther. But it seems he's Kenelm right enough."

"He has convinced me," Marnie agreed.

"It's an impalpable story enough, but he knew about the fenugreek and the pippins and Cranky Jangler, and the telepathetic link makes it certain," Malone said. "Malaprop."

"I was just thinking—the gypsy told me a tall, dark man was coming into my life, and she was right," Marnie said.

"She told you he was in trouble too, and that you should help him," Rorie reminded her.

"So she did. They're up to anything, those gypsies."

"They have some occluded powers, in league with the devil likely as not," Malone told them, and left.

Marnie too went off to speak to Cook, but Rorie sat behind, dissatisfied. She thought the gypsy's occult powers might rather be explained by Kenelm's having put the gypsy hag up to reading that particular fortune, to request the lady's help in this romantic, roundabout way. The phrase "golden lady" had been used by her, and Kenelm too had mentioned Marnie's golden halo more than once in the showering of his compliments. She had begun the day hoping he was Kenelm. All the evidence presented indicated that he was, yet she felt a nagging doubt. He was too pat with his answers, too liberal with his compliments, too hasty to hint a reward. And if he could now persuade the Rutleys—who might quite possibly be his own grandparents, surely not difficult to persuade—to say their son was in America, to produce maybe a letter from him, his way was clear.

She did not absolutely accuse him of being an impostor, but she did not close her mind to the possibility. Clare descended on them shortly after lunch to cast a few more doubts, though they fell on no fertile ground as far as Marnie and Malone were concerned.

"He has been *living* with that pack of gypsies for a week," she announced, her fine blue eyes flashing. "Making up to every servant wench in the district. No wonder he knew all about us. Why did he not come to the door as soon as he arrived, if he had nothing to hide? I wouldn't trust him as far as I could throw him."

"Do you think he might be Horace Rutley?" Rorie asked, to a pair of scowls from the others present.

"I wouldn't be in the least surprised, and I shall go to see them this very day. Not that it would do any good. Oh dear—how came we not to think of it? *They* could have been helping him all the while. Giving him any information he didn't already have. It is very odd the way Horace disappeared without a trace."

"Odd the way Kenelm disappeared too, with no reason as far as anyone knows except yourself," Marnie said.

"The *reason*, my dear Marnie, is too awful to be admitted. Even to *you* I am ashamed to tell the truth."

"Has it to do with the missing emerald necklace?"

"Oh, if only that were all! But it is worse than that. Much worse. Half the reason I am convinced it is *not* Kenelm is that Ken would *never* have the nerve to show his face at Raiker Hall again after what he did. It was too low, too disgusting, too utterly shameful. You must know his father would not have turned him off for any paltry reason. It was serious in the extreme."

"You said yesterday he was a sweet boy," Marnie reminded her.

"He *used* to be. I prefer to remember him that way. One tries to think only good of the dead."

"Nobody said he was dead," Rorie said.

"Well, gone—dead to us. Lord Raiker considered him as dead. It grieves me to have to speak of him."

"We must speak of him, all the same," Marnie continued. "He says he wrote to his father from India. Was any letter received?"

Clare considered this a moment. "No, there was no letter to my knowledge. No, there could not have been a letter. It is impossible. My husband was unwell from the night Ken left—no need to go into the cause. I took his mail up to him myself. There was no letter from India. No word from Ken at all."

"The letter could have gone astray. I believe he is telling the truth. He has convinced me he is Kenelm," Marnie told her, with a defiant tilt to her chin.

"He has buttered you up with flattery and offered you money, probably."

"He did nothing of the sort!" Marnie retaliated at once.

But of course he had, ever so subtly, Rorie remembered.

"Do you not mean to stand my friend, then?" Clare demanded.

"I mean to discover the truth. Indeed, I believe I have done so," Marnie replied.

"I never took you for such a gullible fool!" Clare flashed

59

out angrily. "You think to marry him and get yourself installed back at Raiker Hall. That's what it is, and you won't do it. You don't fool me. You mistake your man if you think Horace Rutley will ever *marry* you, my girl. It is Dougall's chit he has in his eye, thirty thousand pounds, and an unexceptional connection in every way. Besides, you are just a little long in the tooth to appeal to him, I think."

"I see no point in continuing this discussion," Marnie said, colouring up angrily at this slur on her youth and beauty.

"What do *you* think?" Clare asked, turning to Rorie.

"I think whoever the man is, he is very sly."

"I pity your sister hadn't a little of our wits. He comes to Raiker Hall tomorrow at ten to meet with my solicitor. His solicitor and mine will discuss the matter; I shan't say a word to him. I was going to ask you to attend, but there is no point in it now."

"I will be there," Marnie said.

"Come if you like, but if you know what's good for you, you won't put all your eggs in one basket. He is *not* Kenelm Derwent, and I can prove it, so don't start packing to remove to my house yet, Lady Raiker."

Her positive statement that he was *not* Kenelm, when put beside the man's equally absolute assertion that he *was*, created just a small seed of doubt, but Clare was not in a mood to expand on the matter.

"You'll see," she said, and swept from the room, leaving her heavy scent behind her. She cast just one look at the firescreen as she went. She would have liked to snap it up and take it back with her, but she had come on horseback, so it was impossible.

"There's a riddle then," Malone said, "A regular Gordian knob it's growing into, but I'll put my money on the prodigious son. He'd never of called me Malaprop or known Cranky Jangler if he wasn't Bernard's brother."

"Certainly he is Kenelm," Marnie stated firmly.

Chapter Six

The meeting the next morning at Raiker Hall had come to a standstill. Both Lady Raiker and the *soi-disant* Lord Raiker came equipped with a solicitor, and to each other they did no more than bow. Mr. Cleary, the gentleman's counsel, said he had filed a bill staking claim to the title, upon which information Mr. Coons, the lady's counsel, said he would protest the bill. An arbitrator would likely be chosen to settle the case, a committee of arbitration possibly. It sounded monstrously expensive, and Lady Raiker mentioned the fact. It was virtually the only comment she made throughout the proceedings. She was stiff, formal and hostile the whole time, while her opponent regarded her with malicious amusement. At the meeting's termination she requested Kenelm to remain behind. Everyone except himself was surprised, most especially the ladies from the Dower House, who were deeply disappointed to be shown out the door with the solicitors.

"What is she up to now?" Marnie wondered.

"Trying to come to terms with the man, I suppose. She is worried about the costs of the case."

"I wish you would call him Lord Raiker, Rorie. Why have you taken this absurd idea not to do so? You don't know him at all. *I* am convinced he is Kenelm, and Malone is convinced he is Kenelm. You never met him in your life

61

till that day in the woods, and it is ridiculous to think you know anything about it."

"You are overly influenced by his charm. He's emptied the butter boat on your gold curls, and you have succumbed to him. I don't say he isn't Lord Raiker. Likely he is, but as Clare says she can *prove* he is not, I withhold my decision."

"He'll drop by and tell me what she is up to," the widow said complacently.

With this probability in mind, Marnie went to her room to freshen her toilette, to pinch her cheeks, as she hadn't yet sunk to painting, and to fluff up her blond curls. She was correct in thinking Kenelm would report to her. In less than an hour he was at the door, and soon seated in her saloon with herself and Rorie, who had no thought of being left out of the meeting.

"What did she say?" Marnie asked at once, in the tone of a supporter.

"She says I am Horace Rutley, as I knew she would do. She beat me to Rutley's place yesterday. She was coming out as I entered, and they told me they hadn't heard from him since he left. They have no idea where he is or what has become of him. At least they didn't call me 'son.'"

"Did she attempt to buy you off?" Marnie enquired.

"Not with cash. I don't think she has much. She made some extremely cryptic remarks about an emerald necklace. The Raiker emeralds I conclude she referred to. Have they vanished?"

Marnie looked at him in a little embarrassment. "They vanished several years ago, Ken. About the same time as *you* vanished, you see. There was a little doubt as to where they had gone."

He frowned in perplexity. "It was said that *I* took them? Is that it?"

"That is the general idea. You or the gypsies who were camped nearby at the time. It was said publicly that the gypsies stole them, but the announcement wasn't actually made till several months later, when her husband died, and as no effort had been made to trace them to the gypsies, the inference—oh, strictly *en famille,* of course—was that you could have run off with them."

"But that doesn't make any sense," he said. "If I as Kenelm am supposed to have stolen them, how can she infer that I as Horace Rutley am to be accused of it? No, she's boggling around, hasn't set on her story yet, but wanted to let me know she'll accuse me—Kenelm, I mean—of theft if I prove I am me. There was never any suggestion that Rutley stole them, was there?"

"I never heard that said," Marnie replied.

"Maybe he did, though," Rorie suggested. "It seems, if I have got the dates straight, that Rutley's disappearance must nearly coincide with your father's death. Possibly Rutley did take them. Their loss was not announced till then."

"When exactly *did* Rutley sheer off, Marnie?" Kenelm asked.

"Very close to that time. Within a week or two of Papa's death, I think. Just before, actually. It was being spoken of as just having happened when we came home to the funeral. In all the confusion, little was made of Horace Rutley's disappearance."

"But Clare implied that *I* had stolen the emeralds? She never even hinted that Rutley had taken them?"

"It was you or the gypsies. This is the first time I have ever heard Rutley's name in connection with them at all."

Kenelm sat thinking, and suddenly spoke. "If she means to claim they were here after *I* left, then that lets the gypsies off the hook. They were here when I left, and *not* anywhere near the place six months later when Horace departed. She's hemming herself in now, whether she realizes it or not. She's got herself stuck with Horace as the thief."

"Oh, no! The gypsies were here then too," Marnie informed him.

"But they come in the spring—every spring, as regular as clockwork. How should they have been here in the autumn?"

"There was a big gypsy fair just outside of Tenterden that fall. Bernard and I passed in on our way home from London, and the band that regularly stops here had been in the woods a little while before, so they were present then too, just to confuse matters."

"Damnation! She thinks of everything. She can still fall back on the gypsies then, if both Horace and myself turn up clean. What she means to do is accuse me of theft if I

63

get myself proclaimed as Lord Raiker. A fine scandal for the family."

"Where is the threat?" Rorie asked. "If you *are* Kenelm, the necklace is yours now. You will hardly prosecute yourself, I suppose."

"It is entailed. The heir, namely little Charles or his guardian, Mama, could institute enquiries. It would be a valid threat, and she must know I am Kenelm, or she would not use it."

"Theft would be a valid threat against Horace Rutley too, would it not?" Aurora asked innocently.

Kenelm looked at her reproachfully. "Why don't you believe me, ma'am?" he asked. "You of all people, who know nothing about me—why should you take into your head to accuse me of such gross wrongdoing?"

"I am not *accusing* you of anything, sir. I am only pointing out a fact that seems to be overlooked."

"Bernard never thought for a moment *you* took them, Ken," Marnie rushed in to calm him. "He thought she had stolen them herself, and I am of the same opinion."

"I had unilaterally come to the same conclusion," he said, turning to Marnie, but with a last dissatisfied glance to Aurora. "And there were veiled hints from Clare of worse exposures to come if I kept up my 'little charade,' as she so kindly called it. As to exposure, she had better look to her own reputation!"

"She said very definitely she could *prove* you are not Kenelm," Marnie told him, hoping to hear his views on this urgent matter.

"I'd give a monkey to know what she's up to," he said, unhelpfully.

"Would it be a matter of a birthmark or scar—something like that?" Aurora asked.

"I doubt she's ready to admit she is that familiar with my anatomy," he answered, and laughed ironically. As he observed that he had inadvertently riled the two of them with this suggestive remark, he rushed on to disclaim any identifying birthmarks or scars. "Help me, Marnie," he finished up. "She's as crooked as a corkscrew. Try to find out what she's up to, will you?"

"I'll do what I can, but we are not on cordial terms at all, as I have told her quite openly I am on your side."

"I wonder if that wasn't a mistake. She'd be more

confiding if she thought you supported her," he said.

Rorie sat back and observed. He was down to outright scheming now. First it was help me, recognize me; now it was spy for me, find out what she's up to.

"What do you want me to do?" she heard her sister ask, and saw that Marnie smiled on him most cordially, even flirtatiously.

"Perhaps it would be best if you tell us exactly why it was you left home, Lord Raiker. Clare intimates it was for conduct too heinous to relate to ladies," Rorie said.

"Ah, you have called me Lord Raiker for the first time, ma'am" he said, turning to her with interest and approval. "May I count on your support to prove it?"

"My support would do you little good. But you haven't answered my question. Why did you leave home?"

"I was invited—no, *tranchons le mot*—commanded to do so. And Clare is right, the crime of which I was accused was much too atrocious to sully feminine ears. I am innocent of the crime, however, and hope it may not come up at all. I shan't mention it unless Clare does." Marnie blushed up prettily and was satisfied with this tribute to her innocence in lieu of an explanation.

Mr. Berrigan arrived in the middle of their visit. He was a local gentleman, one who had had some acquaintance with Kenelm, though he had been closer to Bernard in both age and friendship. He was, of course, well aware of the man's claim, having been at Clare's party, and relished the chance to judge him at first hand.

Rorie sensed some hostility in Berrigan, and was keen to discover its cause, but had soon deduced it was no more than jealousy of a rival for Marnie's affections. She noticed something else of interest too. As soon as Kenelm discovered the hostility, he was onto its cause, and his compliments to Marnie ceased. He then turned to dropping as many references as he possibly could to validate his own claim to being Lord Raiker.

"Do you still ride that big bay stallion, John?" he asked in the tone of an old friend.

"No, I had to get rid of him. Getting on, you know."

"I remember Bernard wanted to buy him from you, some years ago."

"Yes, by Jove, offered me two hundred pounds for him,

65

but I couldn't part with Diablo. Have a mare now. A sweet goer, but she don't have Diablo's fire."

Contemporary matters were of no use to Kenelm. "Did you ever find out who it was that came into your stables that night and set fire to your hayloft? That happened just before I left."

"Never did, no. One of the grooms blowing a cloud, I expect. They never will own up to anything."

After a few more questions of this sort, Berrigan seemed to accept Kenelm for who he said he was, and became civil, enquiring in a polite way about India. This formality done with, Lord Raiker turned his charms on Rorie Falkner, for he was finding her the toughest nut of them all to crack, and it seemed to anger him. He had obviously foreseen no difficulty with the unmarried young ladies. While Berrigan courted the widow, Kenelm arose and took a seat beside Rorie, close enough to allow of some private conversation.

"Do you know, Miss Falkner, I have the unreasonable feeling that you dislike—mistrust me. Now I wonder if it could have anything to do with our meeting in the woods that day. I have racked my brains to try to discover why else you should have taken me in disgust, and can find nothing. I behaved very badly. I admit it openly, but so did you, you know." He smiled a dangerously attractive smile at these words—light, teasing.

"*I* had no choice, if you refer to my having hidden behind the tree. I had no thought of spying on you. It is only that once there, I was afraid to run away, in case you should have chased me."

"You mustn't believe everything you hear about my chasing girls," he answered playfully.

"I haven't heard anything, actually," she told him, and added silently that she had certainly *seen* plenty, however.

"You probably will."

"I'm afraid your philandering will be overshadowed by worse stories."

"Philandering! Upon my word, you are hard on me."

"I was careful to choose a word that didn't exaggerate the offense, sir."

"Oh dear, and the philandering, bad as it is, is but a pale shadow of my worse doings, like running off with the

66

family emeralds. But I didn't do it. I wish I could convince you."

"You have managed to convince my sister; that is of more importance."

"Once I am established as Lord Raiker, we will be connections, neighbours I hope, and I would not like us to be on poor terms. Do you know, I have just been struck by the most *appalling* thought! Poor Marnie will have Clare down on her head once I take over Raiker Hall. There is only the one Dower House. Good God, it is enough to make Marnie turn against me, and pronounce me Horace Rutley. I'll make some other arrangement. I won't condemn her to living with that woman, or you either, Miss Falkner. But then I suppose such a pretty young lady as yourself will not long be living with her sister. You will have more interesting plans. Are you engaged, or only in the process of driving all the local beaux to distraction while you make up your mind?"

The flattering words did not penetrate, left her unmoved, except to anger that he should think her so gullible. "I am not engaged," she answered curtly.

"Indeed! I find that hard to believe," he answered quizzingly, casting a long look into her eyes, then letting his glance descend to her lips and neck. When he got back up to her eyes, she was glaring at him with open hostility.

For a moment he was obviously taken aback at her totally wrong response to his maneuver. He must have found this trick to be very effective in the past. He straightened his shoulders and tried a new tack.

"Tell me, is your sister interested in John Berrigan? Romantically interested, I mean. I begin to understand you like plain speaking."

She regarded him haughtily. "I have thought so. I may be mistaken. It is a little early yet for that." She meant to tell him nothing.

"Yes, Bernie only dead a year, it *is* early, but Marnie always struck me as the sort of a woman who is happier with a man—married, I mean. Some women are like that. You know what I mean?"

"Yes," she answered, and found that she did know exactly what he meant, though it had been a vague, generalized sort of a statement. Marnie was not a good

67

widow at all. She wanted a husband to mother and fuss over, and a man to take care of her.

"I think she must have made Bernard a wonderful wife. They seemed happy together."

"They were."

"You're not much like her, I think. Not the mothering kind. I am not like Bernie either. A clinging vine would drive me crazy. Odd, isn't it, how brothers and sisters can be so different?"

"I suppose it is. Tell me, Lord Raiker . . ." she began, thinking it time to learn something useful, but not quite knowing how to phrase it.

"Yes?"

"What did Clare mean, she could *prove* you are not Kenelm?"

He rubbed his chin and thought. "I haven't the faintest idea. She got to Rutley's before me. She may have learned something there that she feels she can put to use. I don't know what it could be."

"If she means to bring Horace into it—to say *you* are Horace, get the Rutleys to substantiate it—then what about the real Kenelm? She would still have him to worry about, wouldn't she?"

"*I* am the real Kenelm, ma'am, though you cannot bring yourself to accept it. If she means to insist I'm Horace Rutley, then she would have to know the real Rutley is either dead or far enough away that he has not heard of her scheme. There would be no advantage to claiming I am Rutley, and he me. It would put Charles out of the running either way."

"Unless she struck a deal with Horace, some financial arrangement to his advantage."

"She wouldn't be so foolish. She'd have no pressure to make him keep to his bargain. Once he was declared the baron, he could cast her aside—she'd be at his mercy. He's worse than I am," he added with a little smile. "You don't believe it? It's true. A deep-dyed villain, brother Horace, according to legend at least. I scarcely knew him to nod to, myself. We were not allowed to associate with him for fear of contamination. No, it can't be that. She knows she's safe from Horace—must know it, or she's taking a devil of a risk. A pity. It would solve my problem nicely if I could find him."

"It is generally said he went to America."

"That will take time, to track him down. I hadn't looked for so much trouble. In my innocence, I thought I would have only to come walking in, and everyone would recognize me. Funny they don't. I recognize everyone else."

"You were only sixteen when you left. You've changed, whereas the others—Lord Dougall and John Berrigan—they were grown up at the time, haven't changed so much. That accounts for it I suppose."

"Yes, and the doubt Clare has managed to add hasn't helped either. I wonder if I'll recognize my schoolmates, Jimmy Vickers and Larry Styles. *They'll* recognize me, surely."

"I expect they will," she said, and found to her dismay that she believed it. No more than Marnie had she withstood five minutes of his presence. He had won her over too, and he hadn't even bothered flirting with her, or complimenting her.

"They must. We'll have a thousand shared memories—four years of Eton together."

"They'll know you. I'd know *my* schoolmates after twenty years, I am convinced."

"You believe me then?" he asked, with no smiles and no charm, just a direct question.

"I am inclined to. Yes."

"Good. I'm very glad." He looked as if he meant it, too. "I should leave now. I am to lunch with Sally McBain in town."

"Lady Alice had no trouble recognizing you."

"She couldn't have recognized me. Just wanted a new beau to play with, I expect." He laughed. "But beggars can't be choosers."

He turned to direct some comment to Marnie, and Rorie said a few words to John. The two gentlemen soon arose to leave together. As soon as they were gone, Marnie said. "Kennie is going to get a place for us when Clare moves here. Some other house, so we won't have to live with her. I'm very relieved he mentioned it. Truth to tell, I was not looking forward to living with her."

"You might have managed to steal back your engagement ring," her sister suggested.

"More likely she would have got my gold band from me too! John is convinced our newcomer is Kenelm."

Rorie was convinced too, without quite knowing how it had happened. He hadn't proved a thing, and she had been charmed into it, which was not right. She must keep a corner of her mind open to doubt.

The corner was still open for something to occupy it when Clare called in the afternoon, asking specifically to see herself, and not Marnie, although Marnie as well went along to the saloon.

"My solicitor is gone off to London to make arrangements for the formal questioning," Clare informed them. "I mean to get it done as quickly as possible so that that man has no opportunity to make mischief, to wangle his way into everyone's confidence and discover what Kenelm would know. Mr. Coons says the questioning board must be composed of family, old friends and scholastic associates of Kenelm. Some schoolmates will be selected without the man's knowing who they are, to prevent his getting to them. The interview will take place at Raiker Hall a week from today. I wish it could be sooner. That gives him too much time. In the interim, I refuse to see him at all, and I do feel, girls, that you ought to refuse him admission here too. You will look perfect fools when he is exposed as an impostor in a week's time if you have let him run tame here."

"We will look no more foolish than Lord Dougall," Marnie pointed out.

"That was a clever stroke on his part, having the wits to strike up a flirtation with Sally McBain to get himself invited to Bradhurst Hall. And he managed to get to Rutley's before me too, to inform his grandparents they were not to recognize him."

"He said he met you coming out as he went in," Marnie told her.

"Did he say so? Well, that proves he is a liar, not that it needed proving in my opinion."

It was impossible to know which was lying, but in any case if the man was Horace Rutley, he would presumably have been in touch with his grandparents long since, and not have left it to this late date. "What did the Rutleys say about Horace?" Rorie asked.

"They haven't heard from him since he left, they *say*. I took a sharp look about to see if they had had the place done up lavishly—a dead giveaway Horace had been send-

70

ing them money—but there was nothing of the sort. A shabby little hole, and filthy to boot."

"From what one hears of Horace Rutley, he wouldn't be the kind of son to send his grandparents money," Marnie mentioned.

"No, not in the ordinary way. He was fonder of his mother, actually. Perhaps because he didn't know her very well and could keep his illusions, but then this fellow who is calling himself Raiker has money to throw about."

"I wasn't aware you were acquainted with Horace at all," Rorie said, her interest sharpened to hear Clare knew more than she had ever said before.

Marnie latched onto a quite different part of the speech. She knew the man wore a well-cut coat and rode a fine mount, but "money to burn" was an unknown piece of intelligence and required explaining.

"Indeed yes," Clare told her. "He has bought himself a dashing curricle and team of grays, has set himself up with a groom and valet from London and all the rest of it. I heard he has taken over the largest suite at Lord Dougall's, and has the stables filled with boxes and cartons of *objets d'art* from India."

"Then he was in India!" Rorie said.

"Yes, apparently that story about America was a mistake, but no one ever *knew* Horace went there. He left here, that was all we actually knew. There is a rumour running around the village about the man's having opened a very considerable account at the banker's as well, but it is only rumour. Everything gets exaggerated out of all proportion. As far as that goes, there is no saying what schemes he has been up to all these years. He might have managed to come into money, one way or the other. The emerald necklace would have been a good start."

"You think now it was *Rutley* who stole it, and not Kenelm as you used to say?" Marnie asked, pleased to catch her relative up in this little inaccuracy.

Clare was far ahead of her, and had her answer ready. "It becomes clear to anyone whose head is not turned by the man that the two of them have been together. How else should Rutley know so much about us? It is perfectly obvious to *me*, who knew Kenelm so much better than everyone else, that Kennie stuck at owning up to some

71

things, and they will be the man's undoing. Well, I'm off, ladies. Will you see me to my carriage, Rorie?"

This was a departure from the usual routine, but Rorie was interested enough to discover what Clare wanted with her that she went along happily enough. "Your poor sister is besotted with the man," Clare said sadly. "It will be for us to prevent her making a dreadful fool of herself. I wish you to keep me informed what she is up to."

This was of course understood by both ladies to mean what *he* was up to. "I have not taken sides, Clare."

"You are on the side of right and truth, I trust?"

"Certainly I am, and so is Marnie."

"Well then, where is the problem? You *must* help me, Rorie. The family must stick together and balk this fellow's schemes. If he succeeds, it will mean you have me on your hands here at the Dower House, you know. Think about it!" she said, and left with an ironic laugh.

It was a terrible enough thought to consider, but the man was a step ahead of her—had already removed that little impediment in Marnie's way by promising a different arrangement. It was hard to say which of the two was the wilier schemer. They seemed a pretty even match.

Chapter Seven

Nothing of staggering interest occurred during the next week. Kenelm was busy ingratiating himself with the neighbourhood. He was seen in the village every day with Lady Alice, who paraded him amongst her friends as though he were a prize of war. Her set accepted him wholeheartedly, and under the protection of Lord Dougall he was being invited to the best homes. There was no communication between Kenelm and Raiker Hall except as took place indirectly through the Dower House. He twice came to visit Marnie and Aurora, bringing on the second occasion a pretty silk scarf from India for each of them and a set of ivory carved elephants for Mimi. Nor did he forget Malone. He rifled his treasure chests for some artifact to get a rise out of her, and with an unerring eye, chose a reproduction of a voluptuous goddess, Parvati, wife of Siva.

"Goddess, is it?" she asked, her eyes bulging at the scantily clad lady before her. "Looks like a belly dancer to me. And what has she got a beehive on her head for?"

"That is a sort of crown, I expect," Marnie told her.

"I'll not be genuflecting to this one," Malone decreed. "St. Anne and St. Anthony are good enough for me. I'll just stick this away in a drawer so my Mimi don't see it and go

73

getting ideas. Is this the way the Hindu gods carry on then?" she asked Kenelm.

"Oh yes. They have raised the fine art of love to a religion," he assured her.

"No better than I expected of them. They've made the sins into virtues. I suppose it's a mo   sin in that place to be doing your neighbour a good turn."

"It's viewed askance," he assured her readily.

Clare came three times to them, bringing nothing but questions. Marnie mentioned inviting Kenelm to dinner, but with Clare's constant reminders that she could prove him an impostor, the invitation was delayed, just in case. She did behave with perfect civility, however, when she met him at dinner at the Spencers'. Under the circumstances, Lady Spencer thought the dowager Lady Raiker would not care to attend, so saved her the embarrassment of having to refuse by not inviting her. This was a cruel blow for Clare, after the promise at the party of an invitation, but she hardened her heart to all such slights, merely storing up the memory for retribution after the man was got rid of.

The day of the interview came at last. School friends from Eton had been contacted and brought to Kent for the occasion. An aunt and uncle with whom the alleged Lord Raiker had not been in contact since his return, but who had been familiar with him before his running away, were chosen to represent the family. A schoolmaster and an old tutor were also there, as was a retired footman who had been in service during Kenelm's residency at Raiker Hall, since retired. A battery of miscellaneous questions was hurled at the claimant's head, and he acquitted himself well enough that the verdict was in his favour. In the opinion of the committee, the man was Kenelm Derwent, Lord Raiker, and so they would inform Lord Wiggins, the judge handling the case.

The dowager Lady Raiker squared her shoulders and set her jaw to do her unpleasant duty. "You leave me no option, sir," she said to Raiker, "but to tell the truth. You are not Kenelm Derwent. He is dead, and I can prove it."

There was a hushed, awful silence in the Blue Saloon. The questioners looked at the man they had just decided was Kenelm, they looked at Lady Raiker, they looked at each other, and said not a word. There was dead silence for forty-five seconds, when the claimant recovered his wits and broke into unholy laughter. "Clare, you witch!" he said. "Who the devil have you murdered and chucked into a grave to have a body ready against my return?"

"I shall overlook that slanderous remark, sir. Mr. Coons, you will proceed with the exhumation order we have had made up to cover this contingency. I think there will be no doubt as to the identity of the corpse. It will be long decayed, of course, but no doubt the clothing and some personal effects will bear me out."

"What? Did you actually dress your victim up in one of my outfits?" Raiker asked. "You are up to anything. I always knew you were as devious as a nawab, but I never began to appreciate your foresight till now."

"There is no point in continuing this discussion," Clare said to her solicitor, then turned a disdainful eye to Raiker. "You will be notified of the hour of exhumation, sir, that you may have your counsel there, and yourself, if you have the stomach for it."

"I wouldn't miss it for the world. I want to see what outfit I chose for my interment. Where am I buried, Mama?"

"Kenelm is buried in the family plot, naturally, as any member of this family would know."

Kenelm turned to the committee members. "Am I to assume the verdict in my favour still stands? I am the living Kenelm Derwent, while simultaneously mouldering in my grave?" he asked with relish.

His old schoolmates were eager to support him. How the deuce could anyone but Kennie know about putting the frog in Chuck Dalmy's milk, or sousing that old mugger of a tutor with a bucket of water when he was slipping out the back door to meet his doxy, or the series of anonymous letters perpetrated during their last term at Eton, threatening the headmaster with revelations of his scarlet past, and the man a dead bore who never did a thing wrong, but still went into a quake every time a letter was received? Such were their questions to the claimant, who entered into the memories with delight and a plethora of details that led some to believe he had been the instigator of all the mischief. The school friends were convinced, but agreed to go along with the others and withhold judgment, as their number did not constitute a majority in any class.

There were, of course, questions posed to Clare to expand on her announcement, but she sat like a sphinx, giving away nothing. The meeting broke up, and Lord Raiker turned his mount immediately down the road to inform the ladies at the Dower House of the latest development, and to try to discover of them who the corpse might be, though he had a fair idea. They had been waiting on pins and needles for his arrival, as he had arranged to come to them at once, whatever the verdict. Malone too was on hand. She had become a firm supporter of Raiker—admitted quite bluntly she had become "abscessed" with the whole affair, and rarely thought of anything else. The butler announced him, and he entered smiling broadly.

"He used the wrong name," he said. "He ought to have called me the late Lord Raiker."

"You got here sooner than we expected you," Malone assured him.

"Late as in dear departed. Mama's got me killed and buried in the family plot. Well along in decay by now, as it seems I have been there ever since I ran away."

Three shocked faces tacitly demanded an explanation. "Yes, quite a shocker she has been saving up. I am no more. Gone to my just deserts long ago. I'm dying to hear how I met my end—no pun intended. She wouldn't tell us a thing, not a single detail. I wonder how the devil she means to account for my untimely demise. Some terrible accident, I suppose. Dead drunk and walked into a pond."

"No, it can't be that," Rorie pointed out. "You must have met a more disgraceful end, or you would have been buried properly, with an announcement and funeral service and so on."

"How quick you are, Miss Falkner. And perfectly right, of course. I met with some disgracefully fitting end."

"She has dropped dark hints from the beginning that you performed acts too atrocious for us to hear about," Marnie reminded him.

"Suicide! She's had you killing yourself," Malone decided at once.

"I wonder if that's it. No—that isn't bad enough for me. It was more likely justifiable killing. I was caught out in some beastly crime and it was necessary for one of them to do me in."

76

"A duel?" Rorie mentioned.

"We'll just have to wait and see what the carcass tells us," Raiker said. "Do any of you happen to know where I am buried? I would like to pay my last respects to whatever remains of my mortal remains. I am in the family plot, Clare says."

"Oh, in that case, I think I know," Marnie said. "There is an unmarked grave just at the very edge of the family plot. It has been there ever since I came to Kent with Bernard—a recent grave when first we came. We asked Clare about it, and she *implied*, though she didn't actually say, that it was a stillborn child of one of the unmarried servant girls. The inference was that it was done up quietly to save the girl from public disgrace. It is rather a smallish grave, but would hold an adult I suppose. The corpse must be in a small box."

"I wonder if I got a coffin at all. A simple shroud to hasten my decay is more like it. Can you show me the spot, Marnie?"

"I can't leave at the moment. I am expecting Mr. Berrigan," she explained with a becoming blush." On *business*. He is helping me look about for a cottage, as you were kind enough to say, Kenelm, that you would help me a little in that respect, and I would not like to continue on here with Clare."

"I have been looking into a place for you myself, and thought you might be happy at Gypperfield's place. It is up for sale, you know, and Dougall tells me it is quite a bargain."

"Gypperfield's place! Oh, I could never afford it; it is much too grand."

"I told you I would look after you, my dear, and I don't wish to see Bernard's family in a cottage. Have Berrigan take you to Gypperfield's. The agent—Hudson is his name—has the keys. He will be happy to take you through it. I told him we would probably be around to look it over."

"Oh, Kenelm! I hardly know what to say. It is finer than here. Ever so lovely. I would adore to have it." Her eyes shone. "But are you sure you can afford it?"

"Certainly. I didn't quite sit on my thumbs while I was away, you know. Full of juice. There is plenty of money to be made in the east. Can you tell me exactly where the grave is? And I'll go have a look by myself."

"Rorie—you know where it is. Why don't you take Kenelm?" Marnie suggested.

"Would you?" he asked, turning to her.

"I would be happy to." She was happier, more excited than a trip to a graveyard warranted, for this excuse to be walking with Raiker alone. Many times she had seen Lady Alice swaggering through the village on his arm, and had always felt a twinge of anger, jealousy, to see it. She felt in some unreasonable way that as she had seen him first, as a gypsy in the forest, she had a claim on him. She was nearly totally convinced now he was Kenelm, and indeed the neighbourhood at large no longer admitted of such question in the matter. In the interest of justice she did not completely close her mind, but if her mind still held a doubt, her heart had long since decided on his innocence.

But as they went together, their talk was of a business nature. "Other than Clare's little surprise, how did the questioning go?" she asked.

"It was ridiculously easy. I had them all convinced. They decided I am me before Clare exploded her shell. Well, my old schoolmates and Smidgins, a footman who had made a pet of me in my youth—there could be no question. Aunt Hennie and Uncle Alfred too—I spent two summers with them when I was ten and twelve. They knew me at once. Little things, you know, about what kind of cookies Hennie used to have baked for me. That sort of thing. Truth to tell, I would have had a little trouble recognizing them. How old-looking Hennie is become."

"Why is she called Hennie?"

"Short for Henrietta. Named after Grandmama."

All the little details came so easily, so readily, that even her mind was convinced. If his school friends accepted him, how could not she? "I suppose you are thinking the same as I am myself, about this mysterious body that is supposed to be you. It must be Horace Rutley," Rorie said.

"I am convinced of it, and my only question is what she has planted with the body to convince the world it is me. She mentioneed clothing and personal effects. God, to think she must have been laying her plans for ten years!"

"It's rather worse than that, actually," Rorie ventured uncertainly.

"Yes, she knew Rutley was dead all this time, and let

78

his family go on wondering. There's so much to consider my mind is awhirl. How did he die? In what manner did it fall out that *she* know of his death and others did not? Why did she arrange a secret grave for him? She is working herself into a devilish tight corner. What a lot of explaining she is going to have to do when we prove it is Horace Rutley in that grave, and not me."

"If you prove it."

"I'll prove it. There is no question of that. I went to India directly from home. My time is quite well accounted for. She may think I wandered around at loose ends for some time, long enough to cause some doubts as to just who boarded a ship for India, but if she counts on that, she'll come a cropper. I met one chap on the boat going out whom I knew fairly well in England, and bumped into him a dozen times over the past ten years. It can all be proved, but it will take time. In the worst case, I can send to India and have Welbridge come to England and testify. An outrageous imposition, but he might not consider a free trip home in that light. I really don't know what Clare is about, to make such an unholy fuss, to make an implacable enemy of me. I could ruin her."

"She must have some final trick up her sleeve. She is no fool, and wouldn't go out on a limb without an escape."

"She has, though, whether she knows it or not." He stopped halfway through the graveyard and looked around at the tombstones, with a sober expression on his mobile features. "I hate graveyards," he said simply. "Chill my blood, all these reminders of mortality. I'd like to live forever. The Hindus believe in reincarnation, you know. Not a bad idea. How would *you* like to come back next time, Miss Falkner?"

"Do they really believe that?"

"Oh yes, but you'd better not tell Malaprop. She's a treasure, isn't she?" He didn't wait for an answer, but went on, "I'd like to see Papa's grave before I see Rutley's. Bernie's too. Imagine, my father and brother buried since I left! I can hardly believe it. They are buried beside Mama, I suppose." He turned without hesitation to his mother's corner, and stood looking silently at the family tombstones, his father's a white marble slab with a cross on top, Bernie's a little smaller but similar. For a few

79

moments he stood with his head bent, thinking, praying, she didn't know what.

His face changed from sober to sad, and finally flushed with anger. "By God, I hate that woman," he surprised her by saying when he looked up, and there was a truly murderous expression in his obsidian eyes. From his words and tone it almost seemed he held Clare accountable for the two deaths, but this of course was absurd. The elder Lord Raiker had met a peaceful end, and Bernard had died of an ear infection. There was no possibility of foul play in either case.

"I suppose you think I've run mad. But I hate to think of Papa lying there, dead, and I never had a chance to make my peace with him. He was always a good father to me, and for him to think . . . She might at least have showed him my letter. I wrote from India, and the letter certainly got home. Why should it not? She took it, hid it from him. She has been planning to get Raiker Hall for herself from the day she married him."

"No, you are upset, Lord Raiker. She had nothing to do with your father's death, nor Bernard's either. It was mere chance that events fell out as they did. She couldn't have been planning this for so long. She is up to something by saying you are buried in the grave, but the rest of it cannot be her doing."

He regarded her pensively, simmering down slowly. "What a sane little creature you are," he said with a rueful smile. "You bring me down to earth, and I need such bringing down, too. I am liable to let my wrath run away with me. No, she would stick at murder, but not much short of it. So, where is the other grave, Rutley's?"

"This way." She led him to the fence which cut the meadow from the family burial ground. They stood together staring at a slight hump in the earth, with grass and weeds growing over it, and no marker of any sort.

"It is fitting that Horace have a corner of the family plot. Poor devil. He was a wrong one, but who can blame him under the circumstances? I wish I had known him better. I was too young to appreciate his plight before I left. It must have been hard for him, knowing he was one of us, and being treated as an outsider. What an awful thing to do to a boy."

80

"His mother should be notified. The girl—Nel Rutley was her name—she ought to be told."

"Presumably the Rutleys will tell her when we have positively established that this is indeed Horace. What ever happened to Nel? She was packed off to some relatives at the time of her disgrace—got married to some-one."

"Marnie might know, or Clare."

He continued on, staring at the grave. "I'll have a stone erected," he said, and turned away. They began walking back toward the park.

"Do you know, Lord Raiker," Rorie began, "I have just thought of something.

"So have I. I have noticed that you now call me Lord Raiker without balking. Why don't you call me Ken? We are connections, and friends, I hope? Of course I am really angling for permission to call you Aurora."

"My friends call me Rorie."

"They shouldn't. It is too raucous a name for such a quiet little soul, and Aurora—Dawn—is a lovely name. I shall call you so, if I may?"

"I would be pleased. Now may I continue?"

"Sorry. I was a commoner in my last incarnation, and common traces linger yet."

"Clare said at one point, a week or so ago, that you, meaning Horace Rutley, must have fallen in with Kenelm. That was held to account for your knowing about events here, the people and family doings and so on. But if she knows that is Horace buried back there—well, she was lying the whole time. She knew perfectly well Kenelm and Horace never got together."

"She didn't think she'd have to reveal the contents of the grave at the time. Thought I'd dart off like a frightened rabbit when she threatened to accuse me of stealing the emeralds. This was a last resort. Her hand was forced when the committee accepted my *bona fides*. And it means Rutley didn't steal the emeralds, too, unless we find them in the corpse's pockets. What a rare pickle she's landed herself in with all this scheming. I'm tempted to go to her and try to smooth the thing over before she's hauled into court for murder. She *is* family, much as one dreads to acknowledge it. And there is little Charles to consider, poor devil. I wish I could get my hands on him. Don't *stare*,

81

Aurora. I don't mean to wreak revenge on the poor innocent, but to save him from that terrible woman. She'll poison his mind against us—me—and he is my half brother. Will be my heir till I have a son of my own. Rather a pity Marnie hadn't given Bernie one, and all this would never have happened."

"It had already *happened*; it just wouldn't have been revealed."

"There you go, dragging me down to earth again, dead weight, confusing me with facts." He smiled at this speech, and as she returned the smile, he took her arm. "I am certainly sorry events have fallen out as they have. I looked forward to coming home and stepping into Bernard's shoes and taking up a normal life. Meeting some nice English girl—someone like you, but I never thought our promenade would be through a graveyard, and with a messy court case staring us in the face. Things will get worse before they get better, as the old wives say about pregnancy. But we'll get down to some serious merrymaking after it's all over. You plan to stay on with Marnie, I hope?"

"Yes, for the time being at least," she answered, with an uncontrollable burst of pleasure at the question, and the interested look that accompanied it.

"You won't want to stay here after she marries John, but that won't be for a good while yet."

"It is not at all settled she will marry Mr. Berrigan," Rorie pointed out, but her mind had focused on quite a different aspect of the speech. Kenelm was not looking in Marnie's direction himself. She had early on taken the notion he was. Of course there was Lady Alice, who had staked him out for her own. That he didn't mean to have Marnie meant nothing.

"I think it is pretty well settled in John's mind, and she isn't indifferent. I have no objection to Berrigan as a connection, if he has none to me. The family name must be smudged a little, with all this business. Do you think it is enough to turn the young ladies off from me, Aurora?"

"Not the more venturesome ones, and I don't imagine you are interested in the other sort."

"Those with their feet firmly on the ground, you mean? Oh, but that is exactly the sort I favour. I am ramshackle enough for two, and mean to ally myself with a perfectly respectable little lady. I have no objection even to a prude."

"I believe Lady Alice is perfectly respectable," she replied, looking at him questioningly.

"But no prude," he rallied, with a look that set her to wondering just what was passing between the two of them.

Marnie and Berrigan were leaving when they arrived back at the house, and Kenelm left too, as he had arranged to meet his old school friends in the village. When it was learned that Aunt Hennie and Uncle Alfred were put up at an inn, a message was sent to them to come to the Dower House. Before they arrived, and before Marnie returned from her outing, Rorie received a note asking her to go to Raiker Hall. She was curious enough that she did not resent this in the least. She went with the greatest curiosity to discover what she could from Lady Raiker.

Clare made no pretense that the visit had any other end than gathering news. "What does he say? What does the man mean to do?" she asked eagerly.

"He says you are wrong, Clare, but he can do nothing till the body is exhumed. He also says that his aunt and uncle recognized him, as did his schoolmates and the footman."

"What a farce it was, from beginning to end! The Gowers never could stand me. They'd have claimed it was Kenelm if it had been a monkey or a baboon standing before them. They didn't recognize him, I swear, but only nodded and shook their heads up and down at every word he said. As to the footman, I turned him off for thievery, and it wouldn't surprise me if the man arranged in some way that *he* was the servant called. Anything can be done with money."

Rorie heard this without putting much faith in it. "Schoolmates would be hard to fool in any case, and Raiker had no say in choosing them."

"That was easily enough arranged, my dear. The fellows were both friends of Hanley McBain; they must be—they were all at Eton together. Lady Alice is determined to see this fellow made Lord Raiker so that she may have a husband worthy of her. Lord knows she is having enough trouble landing a man. You don't suppose she's been doing nothing but making up to the impostor all week? She has been busy quizzing her brother to find out what she could

83

of the school business and feeding it to Horace Rutley, so that he might pass himself off as Kenelm. They didn't ask enough questions. The whole crew of them were determined to find in the man's favour. I never saw a more prejudiced body in my life. And even with all his help and prompting it is not as though he could answer every question by any means. There was something about ginger cakes Aunt Hennie used to make for Kenelm, and Rutley said seed buns, but the woman just nodded and said, 'So I did put seeds on them. What a memory the boy has. I had forgotten it myself.' It was all like that, for the answers were written out in advance, you know. The magistrate insisted on it to avoid tampering with the truth, but it was a wasted effort. They each took Rutley by the hand and led him to the answers. *I* was not allowed a single question, and I knew him better than any of them. But *I* am not a disinterested party, you see. That is how they kept me out of it."

All this was heard with a sinking heart. Having come at last to the conclusion that the man was Kenelm, she disliked being thrown into uncertainty again, but there was enough of possibility in Clare's remarks, especially with regard to the school friends and Lady Alice, that it could not be discarded entirely. No reply was necessary. Clare was so incensed she was soon off on another tirade.

"It is said in the village that he means to give Marnie the Gypperfield mansion for her part in pretending to believe him."

"She does believe him."

"I come to think I should let on he is Kenelm myself, if he has that sort of money to throw around. I wonder what sum he wouldn't give to shut me up."

"You say it is Kenelm in the unmarked grave, Clare. How did he die?"

"Don't ask, child. I made a vow of secrecy to my husband, and would not tell it to a soul if it were not for this man's trying to take over little Charles's inheritance. I mean to persuade the magistrate to make a vow of secrecy on those few who must hear it. It is the least I can do for . . . Ah, but I can't speak of it. It is too painful." she raised a hand to her brow and looked away, but there were no tears in her eyes.

She was able to bring herself to speak of other things

after a moment, however, and in a surprisingly calm voice. "So he has said nothing about what he means to do? Has given no idea at all?"

"None. He can do nothing till the body is exhumed and identified."

"How sly he is. Getting Marnie to tell him everything, and he says nothing but how pretty she is, and what he will give her for supporting him. He had better hold onto his cash. He will have to repay the estate for the emerald necklace he stole—" She stopped suddenly.

"Or Kenelm stole."

"They are half brothers, Aurora. Blood runs thick. Kenelm *did* steal it, but I doubt he was alone in the matter. Where did this fellow, Rutley, get so much money? There is more to this than I ever suspected before."

There was such a plentitude of possibilities that Rorie's head was reeling, but as she rode home, only one of them was subjected to much scrutiny. Was Clare right, and did all those people questioning him help him along with the answers? The fact was, no one liked Clare in the least. No secret she had had a falling out with Aunt Hennie and Uncle Alfred. Quite possibly the old footman as well, and the testimony of the schoolmates she had managed to cast a doubt on. Really, one was no closer to the truth than ever. The man *had* held out a very enticing bribe to Marnie in the Gypperfield mansion. It might be the impulse of a generous nature, or it might be bribery. Who could say?

Chapter Eight

Marnie had returned from viewing the mansion while her sister was at the Hall, and a rare mood she was in. Not a *good* mood, considering her most recent occupation and her companion. Either one should have been enough to put a smile on her lips, but she was clearly in the boughs about something.

"Did you not like the house?" Rorie asked.

"It was gorgeous," Marnie said, still scowling.

"Too expensive?"

"No. I don't know. It is very dear, but Kenelm didn't specify a price, and I imagine he knows the price, as he suggested it, and had spoken to Hudson."

"Berrigan," Malone informed Aurora from behind the sofa, where she had taken up her position of vigilance.

"What has Mr. Berrigan to say about it?" Aurora asked.

"Mr. Berrigan, if you please, has seen fit to *forbid* me to accept a house from my brother-in-law," Marnie informed her.

"Isn't that nice of him," Rorie responded in the proper spirit of irony.

"He's right," Malone decreed.

"Hush up, you foolish woman," Marnie chided. In an emergency, she occasionally tried to take control of her household.

86

"Dead right," Malone added mulishly. "Ain't fitting. Why should he be giving you such a grand house for? Doesn't look well."

"He is the head of the family, and as rich as Croesus," Marnie pointed out.

"I wonder—is it because we aren't quite sure he *is* Kenelm?" Aurora asked.

"Certainly not. We *are* sure. It isn't that."

"What is it, then?"

"He says it is too much—indicates too close an alliance between us. If it were old Lord Raiker he would not object, he says. Don't stare, Rorie. He means Kenelm is in love with me."

"Oh."

"And of course it is no such a thing. He *likes* me—flirts a little, of course—but he does that with all the young ladies. It is his way."

"Berrigan is in no position to forbid anything, so far as I can see," Rorie mentioned, surprised Marnie hadn't raised this rather obvious point herself.

"He will not continue my friend if I accept the house. Oh, it is so mean of him I could . . ." She threw up her white hands to indicate the crime was too bad to be put into words.

"Widgeon," Malone erupted. "He wants to marry you. How would it look, Kenelm giving you a fancy house, then *he* moves into it?"

"Why didn't he say so, then?" Marnie asked angrily.

There was more futile bickering of the same sort, but the mystery was cleared up. Lady Raiker's pique was rooted in the fact that Berrigan hadn't come out and made the offer in form. He was taking to himself the fiancé's privileges without a declaration, and it was not to be borne. Not in silence, at any rate. Marnie flounced from the room.

"That one could manage to make a sow's ear out of a silk purse," Malone declared. "What did Clare want with you?"

"Just snooping. She is not happy with the outcome of the questioning, of course. She suspects deceit and collusion."

"She's the number would know about deceit, and as to collision, I wouldn't put that a rung beneath her either. She'd try her luck banging up against anybody."

The Gowers, Hennie and Alfred, arrived at the Dower

House in the late afternoon, and were very excited about the return of Kenelm, even more excited about Clare's plans to install Charles.

"That woman is up to anything," Hennie announced at once. She was tall, thin, pale-faced and gray-haired, but gave no impression of grayness or dullness. She was alive with curiosity and spirits. Her husband, on the other hand, had jet-black hair and red cheeks, but was silent and colourless in personality.

"What old Charles meant by marrying a mischief-making chit as common as dirt is beyond me. A Miss Marlowe from Somerset—no one ever heard of them. Oh, she appears well enough—has learned the right accent and speaks like a lady. I refer to her pronunciation only, and as to the content of her speech, it is best forgotten. Always after the men, too—always had an eye to them. We came to meet her right after the wedding. You weren't married to Bernie yet, Marnie, and I don't scruple to say the woman was rolling her eyes at him shamelessly, right under Charles's nose. Well, at Kennie too if it comes to that, and he no more than a schoolboy, though he was always a handsome rascal. She'd have been happy enough to have a go at my Alfred as well, if he'd had the gumption to raise his eyes from his boots. Look up, Alfred."

Alfred looked up shyly, but made no oral contribution. Marnie said, "I am aware of her behaviour. Bernard mentioned it to me."

"Bernie behaved very well, my dear. There is no cause to poker up. He was aghast at her carrying on. He never made up to her in the least, but certainly Kenelm had an eye to her, the rogue."

Rorie became alert at this. She found it not in the least difficult to believe, and was strongly inclined to hear more.

"Tell me, Marnie," Hennie ran on, her faded eyes flashing, "for you were here at the time. Did she have any fellows on the string when old Charles died?"

"I was not here till immediately after the death. She had no one then, I am convinced. She never left the house. Later, when Bernard and I were living at the Hall, we had little enough to do with her. We maintained cordial relations, but were not bosom bows. She had her own set of

88

friends whom she met here at the Dower House. I don't know that one of them was any special beau."

"She'd be happier keeping court," Hennie decided.

"A handsome gel," was Alfred's only contribution to the talk. He was rewarded with a pair of scowls.

"Who does she have her eye on since she's been working at getting little Charles made baron?" Hennie asked next.

"She has dropped the old crowd. I never see any of them at the Hall. She has very few callers, to tell the truth. I think she must be lonesome. She is not much taken up by the respectable people and no longer favours the other sort. I suppose *we* are the closest she has to a friend."

"Lord, and not a man in the house save the servants. She'll be setting up a flirtation with the butler if we ain't careful. Wouldn't put it past her," Hennie said, slapping her knee in delight. "Wilkins, isn't it? She won't get far with that old stick. He never had any use for her."

The Gowers were to remain a few days. Hennie said bluntly she wouldn't miss the exhumation for a thousand pounds. She was too curious to see who Clare had murdered, and how she had done the deed.

She didn't actually get to see the corpse. Rumours of the digging up had leaked out, and to avoid a crowd, the thing was done at seven-thirty in the morning, in the middle of a cold, drizzling rain. The dowager Lady Raiker was there with Coons, the man who called himself Lord Raiker was there with Cleary, and the officials appointed by the court were there. There were as well two gravediggers, but this was the complete audience for the grizzly show. With so much animosity existing between those present, there was not a word spoken as the shovels dug into the firm earth. In the ten or so years the ground had been allowed to settle, it had baked into something resembling black clay, and was not easy to disturb. But eventually the shovels hit wood, and as the top layer of dust was scratched away hearts beat faster, breathing was quick and light. After an eternity, a raw wooden box was lifted out, rougher even than the coffin of a parish pauper. The lid had been nailed shut, but the wood had begun to decay, and no hammer was required to pry it off. The two gravediggers did it with their bare hands.

There was a gasp of surprise. Lady Raiker reeled back into the arms of her solicitor, but Lord Raiker stood staring in fascination. Ten years had been sufficient to remove any human features from the corpse. There was black hair, teeth, bones, with some congealed matter adhering to them in patches, but gruesome as this sight was, it received scant attention. The remainder of the box's contents were too bizarre. A mildewed, spotted uniform covered the remains of the person. It had once been scarlet, was now mottled with purple and blue. The brass buttons and gold lace too had lost their lustre, as had the medals on the chest, but the skeletal hands crossed over the chest bore two magnificent untarnished rings. One was a heavily chased gold affair with a large ruby glowing in the hazy light of dawn. The other was a signet ring, also gold, with a diamond in the lower left corner of the ring's crown.

They were both familiar to anyone connected with the Raikers. The signet ring was a sixteenth birthday present to Kenelm, a replica of that given to Bernard at the same time, and the other family heirloom also given on his sixteenth birthday, by tradition, to the younger son. What they were doing in the coffin, and even more curiously what the body was doing in such a handsome uniform, was a matter of great interest. The uniform too was familiar to the Raikers and their associates, though it had never before been worn by anyone.

Lord Raiker, old Charles, like all the nobility in the area, had established a volunteer brigade to protect the coastal area in case of attack by Napoleon. It had been set up some years prior to Kenelm's departure, but still existed at that time, and Kenelm had been made one of its captains on his return from school that spring. To please an adolescent son, Lord Raiker had had a gaudy uniform designed and made up, and this was what remained of it. It had never even been tried on. At the time of the family quarrel, in fact, the sleeves were only basted in, and the thing had not been finally fitted. What it was doing on this or any other body passed imagining.

The dowager recovered sufficiently to recognize the rings and uniform. Lord Raiker stood staring, his face blank with astonishment. For a long moment he looked, taking in every detail of the spectacle before him, then he raised his eyes slowly to Lady Raiker's white face. It was impassive. Not triumphant, not frightened, certainly not

90

surprised—it was cold. Satisfied, perhaps, was the closest he could come to reading that white mask. He went on regarding her closely for some time, then turned to his solicitor.

"It is time we heard Lady Raiker give us her explanation of this matter," he said.

Clare nodded her head in acquiescence, and they all walked, carriages being ineligible in the graveyard, to Raiker Hall, which had been chosen as the scene of her deposition. They said not a word as they walked through the rain, but their separate minds were seething with conjecture. Within a quarter of an hour the principals in the drama were installed in the study. The gravediggers hauled the coffin onto a wagon and took it to the local doctor for examination.

The magistrate asked Clare in a polite tone for an account of the proceedings that had led to this death and her knowledge of it, along with her reasons for withholding her evidence for so many years.

She composed her face to gravity, only her breast heaving up and down revealing that she was at all ruffled. "It all happened eleven years ago," she began in a low voice, "when Kenelm came home from school. He was—attracted to me," she said simply.

Kenelm sat with his jaws and fists clenched, but uttered not a word of contradiction.

"He used to follow me around, pester me—try to make love to me," she said, her voice falling lower on the last phrase, while a blush suffused her cheeks. "I made a joke of it at first—did not want to be rude to him because of my husband, but told him firmly he must not be so foolish. One night my husband retired early and I went to my own study to read. Kenelm came in—he had been drinking. Drinking a great deal, which he did not normally do, of course. He began making advances, very improper advances. I hesitated to call for help because of making a scene before the servants—it would be bound to get around the neighbourhood. I fought him off as best I could, but he forced me to the sofa, a chaise longue I used to sit and read on. When I saw he was going to overpower me, I called for help. Unfortunately, it was my husband who came in and saw what Kenelm was about. He ordered him from the house on the spot. Told him never again to darken the

91

door. I left then. That is all I know firsthand, but I learned the rest later."

She took a sustaining sip of wine, cleared her throat, and went on. She had an attentive audience. There wasn't a sound but the scratching of a pen moving rapidly over a page, the scribe taking notes for her to sign. She lowered her eyes modestly, as though ashamed to have to relate such a tale. "I knew nothing more for six months. Kenelm left. I never saw him again from that day, but assumed he had gone abroad. My husband refused to discuss it, or allow me to. 'He is no longer my son' was all he would say. As you perhaps know, some six months later my husband was standing at death's door—it was all too much for him. He was never realy well again. His conscience bothered him at the last, and he told me the rest of it, just so I would know, but it is hearsay evidence, you understand. He told me Kenelm demanded money, said he would not leave the house without money, and my husband agreed to give him a certain sum, a thousand pounds he always kept in the family vault. Kenelm demanded more, demanded some other things, jewelry, a note, I don't know what. My husband refused, and Kenelm, his own son, struck him. Began beating him repeatedly till he feared for his very life. Kenelm was drunk, of course—he would never have done it otherwise. He was not really a *vicious* boy, except when he drank," she assured her auditors, with a forgiving eye.

"My husband kept a pistol in the safe, a loaded pistol. He managed to get hold of it and shot Kenelm, to protect his own life. It was self-defense. Joe Miller, my husband's groom and faithful old retainer, took care of the—the burial. I can't imagine why he chose the uniform. I expect the outfit Kenelm wore was—bloodied," she said with distaste. "Out of respect for the dead, I suppose, he chose the uniform. Charles, my husband, wanted his son buried in the family plot, but could not reveal what had happened to him. He was afraid of the scandal—a trial and all the rest of it, and Kenelm disgraced. There was little Charles and the rest of the family to think of. A simple burial seemed to him the best way. One of our servant girls had just given birth to a stillborn child. She was not married, and we said it was the child's grave. Actually the child was buried in another parish by my husband. He didn't tell

92

me where, unfortunately, so I cannot tell you that. He was weak at the end, you know, and had trouble telling me even this much. But in this manner my husband managed the last rites of his son with some decency. He was buried with the minister in attendance and so on. Charles told me all this on the night he died, and told me never to tell a soul. I never have, nor intended to. His way of handling the matter was irregular, of course—he may even have broken a law—but he did the charitable thing, what he felt was best for the innocent survivors in the family. This man—" she glared at Kenelm with loathing "—has made it necessary for me to break my word to my husband, and reveal the truth about Kenelm."

Raiker rose to his feet, his face set in rigid lines of anger. "Hypocrite!" he said to Clare. "I might have forgiven the rest, Clare, but not this. I was only amused at your attempt to cut me out of my rightful inheritance—it was no more than I expected of you—but now you've gone too far, to accuse my father of murder, and myself of having the poor taste to want you. I should have told him the truth." He pushed aside his chair and strode from the room. No one made a move to stop him, nor did his counsel follow him.

"We'll be wanting a few details," Cleary said to her in a businesslike tone. "The exact date, name of that feller did the burying, name of the minister who officiated, name of the servant girl who had the . . ."

She obliged him by repeating the name Joe Miller, since dead, and the minister retired to Cornwall, but was unsure of the servant girl's name. Smith, she thought, or possibly Jones or Brown.

"I'll speak to the doctor then, and see if we can find out who this corpse *really* is. Horace Rutley, I expect," he said, and he too took his leave.

Lady Raiker went to her room and locked the door, but within an hour had called for food, so her household concluded when the empty tray was returned to them that she would recover from her ordeal.

Chapter Nine

At the Dower House, Kenelm's arrival was most eagerly awaited, but all the day long he didn't come. Mr. Berrigan came and had not relented a whit regarding allowing Lady Raiker to accept a house from her brother-in-law. Nor did he quite screw himself up to an offer, but told Marnie in a backward way that he had no notion of making her stay in the same house as that "dashed dowager," if that was what she thought. Every half hour Aunt Hennie pulled out her hunter's watch and demanded to know what was keeping Kennie, and at three-twenty even went so far as to suggest a run over to the Hall to see what was going on, but no one arose to accompany her, and she sat down again to her impatient vigil. At dinnertime they were no better informed about the exhumation than the lowliest villager. They had heard from the dairymaid that the body wore a grand uniform and had his hands stuffed with fabulous jools, but they treated this rumour with the contempt they thought it deserved, just wondering ten or twenty times if it was the emerald necklace that was meant. Malone declared that she hoped she knew truth from faction, and waited as eagerly as the others for the bearer of hard news to arrive.

Not till eight p.m. did he present himself at the door, and he was in such a pelter still that they had every hope

94

for a good story from him. Malone might have stayed away, considering the presence of the Gowers, but with such "unpresidented" goings-on to hear, she took up an inconspicuous stand behind Marnie's chair with her ears flapping, and refused to budge.

"Kenelm, do come in and tell us what happened!" Marnie pleaded. "We have been hearing such strange tales of buried jewels and uniforms that there is no making any sense of it."

"True—all true!" he said, striding in. He was so angry, so upset, he could not remain seated, but like Malone stood leaning on the back of the chair, Aurora's chair, from which he took several turns about the room. "There was the corpse—skeleton, really—of a man in a box, and he wore a uniform. It wasn't even a proper pauper's coffin, but an old gun box that Papa had received rifles in for the volunteer brigade. They didn't even give the poor devil a proper wooden box. And he wore *my* uniform."

"You were never a soldier," Marnie pointed out.

"I nearly was a volunteer one. I was to be captain of one of the groups of Papa's volunteers. I had a swanky scarlet tunic and black trousers— unfinished, incidentally. The corpse wore a jacket with the sleeves basted in, and it also wore my rings. You remember, Marnie, my signet ring with the diamond, like Bernard's, and my ruby. A family heirloom. Now why the deuce did she bury those valuable rings? That doesn't bear the stamp of Clare. That is unlike her, to allow those two valuable rings to be buried."

"Was it Rutley, the body?" Malone demanded.

"The height and size seem right. Dr. Ashton figures the man must have been close to six feet. I rode down to talk to him this afternoon, after he'd done his work. What a job! I was under six feet at the time actually, about five feet ten in those days. The teeth are sound and in good repair except for a few small cavities. There's a wisdom tooth missing on the bottom. I have all mine still."

"How did she kill him?" Hennie asked, smiling in glee.

"He was killed by a bullet in the back. Nice touch, don't you think? Can't you just see Papa shooting me in the back?"

"She never said Charles did it!" Hennie gasped.

"Oh, yes, for conduct on my part too reprehensible to repeat. Beating him up. But there were extenuating cir-

95

cumstances. I was drunk at the time. I was always a little vicious when drunk, it seems."

"Oh Ken, she didn't say that!" Marnie asked, her eyes round with disbelief. "You used to be so *silly* when you drank a little too much. You used quite dreadful language, but were not *vicious*."

"It was after I had much too much that I became vicious. And beating Papa is but the tail end of my conduct on that infamous night. Had I done a half or a quarter of what she accused me of, I would have deserved the bullet. By God, I won't stand still for this."

"You was raping her, I suppose?" Hennie asked greedily.

Kenelm glanced at her and scowled, in a repressive way. "There's more. I demanded a reward for my performance. A thousand pounds was not enough—I wanted jewels and a note as well. She said I struck him and was beating him to a pulp so that he had to kill me in self-defence. The foolishness of it, saying he kept a loaded pistol in the safe. As though anyone would. And how did he get hold of the gun, with me busily taking him apart? It makes no sense. No one could believe such a story."

"*Did* they believe it?" Rorie asked him.

"I don't know. No one tried to stop me when I left, and I haven't had a constable at my heels all day."

"What accounts for the uniform?" Malone asked.

"Just to add a touch of respectability. Papa—no, it was Joe Miller, since conveniently dead, you know. I knew it must be a dead man who performed the act—disliked to bury me in a bloody jacket, and chose for my shroud an uncompleted uniform. I don't know why Joe should have decided to rifle my jewelry box and stick those two rings on my fingers. That will always remain a mystery, I fear."

"What did Clare say about that?" Marnie asked.

"She says it is all hearsay, a deathbed confession from Papa, and she knows only what he told her with his last gasp. That leaves her free to be ignorant of any details she hasn't figured out an explanation for. Oh, and there is more. Not a stitch under the uniform. Naked as a needle but for the jacket and trousers, Ashton says. And boots. I was buried in my boots. Corpses never are, you know. I don't understand. I just can't make any sense of it. I've been cudgelling my brains all day. I thought at first someone was wearing the outfit for a masquerade party, but then the jacket would have a bullet hole, and it doesn't. It is in good condition except for the mildew and a little rot, and of course the basted sleeves. It wouldn't have been worn unfinished. Besides, something would have been worn under it. It was put on after the death—call it murder, a shot in the back."

"Swimming!" Malone suggested. "The man could have been swimming and been shot when he was naked. Maybe they didn't have the clothes when it was time to bury him, and just grabbed up the uniform as the handiest outfit in a hurry."

Raiker considered this with interest. "Yes, but why would they also grab up those two valuable rings?" he asked. There was no answer.

After a moment, Rorie got an idea. "Did you wear the rings every day?"

"No, I had done no more than try them on. They were in my jewelry box."

"Maybe it was to be said you had taken them with you. Family heirlooms, items of sentimental value—you might have taken them away," Rorie said.

"I might have, but I didn't, and that doesn't explain why they're buried. I can see Clare taking them and selling them and telling Papa I had taken them away. That I would believe with no trouble, but not burying them. Not without a damned good reason."

"The best reason in the world," Hennie advised him. "The fact that they're buried makes us all doubt Clare was the one who had the overseeing of the burial. What they call a red herring, isn't it?"

"That would only make sense if she thought the body would ever be dug up. *Did* she think so, I wonder?"

"I begin to wonder if poor Clare had a thing to do with it," Alfred was obtuse enough to say aloud.

"Be quiet, Alfred," his wife ordered. "If you have nothing sensible to say, keep still." He obediently fell silent, which allowed her to proceed to the next item.

"Why were you really sent off, Kennie? You've been mute as an oyster on that score, and we mean to hear it, so brace yourself to tell us."

"Leave me some privacy. It was a misunderstanding.

You may be sure I was neither drunk nor beating my father, nor demanding money from him."

"Very cool, but what the deuce *was* you doing that he ordered you from the house? Caught with your hands on your stepmama I warrant," she answered herself when he remained stubbornly silent.

Raiker, pacing from fireplace to chair at the time, glanced at Aurora and frowned. She looked swiftly away, and felt herself blush. Now why should *she* blush because *he* had been caught with his father's wife? She was angry with herself and with him, him because she believed this was the act that had caused him to be turned off.

"If my hands had been on her, it would have been in anger," he replied fiercely, which sent Rorie wondering if he had been striking her. This, bad as it was, was more acceptable than making love to her.

"In self-defence more likely," Hennie added. "*I* know what she was like with Bernard."

"That has really nothing to do with it," Kenelm said, turning the conversation firmly aside from his reason for leaving home. "If the corpse is Rutley—well, it must be, who else could it be?—if it *is*, how did he come to die? Who shot him in the back, and why? And why was he buried in my jacket and rings?"

"*She* killed him. No doubt in my mind," Hennie answered at once. "And if he wasn't her lover, it's more than I know. You said she hadn't any men hanging around at the time, Marnie. That's why. She'd just murdered Rutley, and hadn't gotten around to finding a replacement yet."

"You said the grave was fresh when you came down to my father's funeral, Marnie?" Kenelm asked. "And Horace Rutley had just disappeared, so it must be him. It is too much concidence."

Marnie frowned, trying to remember exactly. "It was newish—the hump was still visible."

"There's something wrong here. I remember the Jenkins girl was well along in pregnancy when I left. That I assumed was the unmarried mother whose stillborn child was supposed to have been buried there all these years."

"Yes, it was new," Marnie decided. "I remember Clare saying the girl was going to plant flowers. There was nothing there—just freshly turned earth. The time is

98

exactly right for it to be Horace's grave if he was killed, and didn't run off at all."

"Well, the time is about five months wrong for it to be the Jenkins baby."

"Easily enough done," Hennie explained. "They dug the poor bastard child up and shipped it off somewhere else. Or tied a rock around its neck and threw it into the sea. I never heard of anything so disgusting in my life," she finished up, with the greatest relish.

"It's downright wicked," Malone agreed, equally thrilled.

"Shocking thing," Alfred added, shaking his head.

"What happened to the Jenkins girl?" Kenelm asked. "We could learn from her exactly where her child was buried."

"She left as soon as she recovered from her lying-in," Marnie informed him sadly. "I doubt she could be traced."

"Rutley supposedly gone to America, Joe Miller dead, Miss Jenkins gone God only knows where. How can I get ahold of any solid evidence?" Kenelm asked of the room at large.

"The corpse is solid enough," Hennie reminded him. "What we must discover is why she killed her lover, and who buried him. I don't suppose she did it herself."

"The new lover would have got that job, I fancy," Malone suggested. "But who was he? If she still has him on the string, he won't say boo either."

"Did Clare ever have an affair with Rutley?" Raiker asked Marnie.

"Not that I heard about. It was carried on in the greatest secrecy if she did."

"She'd hardly broadcast it," Hennie pointed out.

"We are *assuming* the corpse is Rutley. That may be leading us astray," Raiker said, trying to make sense of the senseless.

"Pooh! Who else could it be?" Hennie demanded. "A tall, strapping fellow with black hair and goodish teeth. They don't grow on trees, and don't up and disappear without leaving a trace every day either. Rutley's gone, and the body is found on his doorstep—the time of the grave just right. Got to be him. She had the little bastard child moved, just as we said, and shipped the mother out so she couldn't be questioned."

"I have just thought of something!" Marnie said, but

99

when she got down to explaining, it was no very helpful memory. "She accuses Rutley of taking the emeralds. If we prove the corpse is Rutley . . ."

"Then the thief reverts to being Kenelm—or the gypsies," Raiker pointed out.

"Or Kenelm and Rutley in league," Rorie stated. "Actually, that is another little knot in her story, saying that, when she must know Rutley never left at all."

"Oh, have I been in league with Rutley now?" Raiker asked with interest. "That's a new one on me. The emeralds, though, they are another concrete item, along with the corpse. A missing item, but still useful. I didn't take them, and Rutley didn't take them as he's stone cold in his box, and I'd be mighty surprised if the gypsies took them. I never heard of their being as daring as that. A chicken occasionally, but never anything as valuable as that necklace, especially from a nobleman. They'd be afraid to do it. No, she has the emeralds herself, and if we could find them on her . . . Well, I don't know what it would prove actually, but it would prove she's a liar and a thief at least, and that would be a step in the right direction."

"We *know* she's a liar," Marnie assured him. "She's had the necklace stolen by three different parties the past week."

"I've got it!" Malone said, and in her excitement she came forth from behind her chair to take up a position in the centre of the floor. "I've been racking my poor old brain, and I think I've got it figured out. She stole them emeralds just like you think, Ken. But what can she do with them? Can't wear them, and can't sell them herself. So she gives them to Rutley to disclose of for her, and he tricks her. Comes back and says he lost them, or only gives her a bit of what they're worth, or what have you, and she ups and shoots him in the back in a fit of revenge. I think we know how to account for the man being stark naked when he was shot too," she added, with a sapient eye. "We know he was her lover."

"We assume it," Raiker parried. "Damme, I hope that isn't how it was. I was counting on her still having them, so that I might find them on her, and prove her a thief."

"It still wouldn't explain the uniform and rings," Hennie said.

"Nor the boots and lack of underclothing," Marnie added.

100

"Don't explain nothing," Alfred said dampingly. "Don't explain who buried him or what happened to the Jenkins baby."

"It explains why he's dead anyway," Malone maintained stubbornly. "Something must account for it."

"We don't even know for *sure* the body in the grave is Rutley," Rorie mentioned.

For another hour the same facts were gone over again and again, and at the end of it all no unanimous conclusion was reached, except to wish to be told what Raiker was going to do about it.

"I'm going to catch her. I don't know how, but I'm going to do it," he said firmly. "This body doesn't change the verdict taken yesterday morning. There is an excellent chance the body is Rutley, and with that fact proved, I can still get myself proclaimed Lord Raiker. Once I get into Raiker Hall I'll question the servants till their teeth ache, and tear every stone apart with my bare hands if I have to, to find the emeralds."

"She'd never leave them behind," Marnie told him.

"The emeralds are long gone. Rutley sold them," Malone decreed.

"It's checkmate," Alfred decided after some considering. "She can't keep you from getting your inheritance. Her story is all hearsay and won't hold up in a court of law. You can't prove she's lying, as she's dragged in your dead father and a dead groom—no witnesses. And she's had ten years to do something with the emeralds, so you'll never lay your hands on them. You'll get your title and estates, and she'll get off scot free from murdering Rutley and selling the emeralds. Might be best to leave it at that."

"The hell I will," Kenelm said, with a rigid face and a murderous light in his eye. Then he got up and left the house abruptly, forgetting to say goodbye to anyone in his abstraction.

When Rorie lay in her bed that night, her mind was made up again in favour of the gypsy who seemed to be Kenelm. Everyone—his aunt and uncle and Marnie—accepted him. He spoke without doubt or hesitation about the past, knew everyone and everything he should. His fury at Clare's charges against Kenelm and his father seemed too authentic to be assumed. Surely he wouldn't be so angry if he were not Kenelm Derwent. And what the

101

devil had he been doing with Clare that his father had turned him off into the night, and never spoken of him again? More than drinking a little too much, and using bad language. *That's* why Marnie had given him that strange look, the first day she saw him, when he told her she used to jaw at him for profanity. If only she could believe that profanity was his worst crime!

Chapter Ten

Lord and Lady Dougall called at the Dower House in the morning to pay their respects to the Gowerses. They brought with them their daughter Alice, who made it her business to sit with Lady Raiker and inform her she must not worry in the least about Kenelm, for he most certainly was Lord Raiker, and no impostor.

"I know it well," Marnie told her. "You must know I was acquainted with him before he left."

"You had *met* him a few times, I understand, but *you* did not live here. I knew him very well—an old family friend." She smiled a confident, serene, smug smile, which did little to endear her to either sister.

"Has he finally convinced *you*, Miss Falkner?" Lady Alice asked. "He said *you* had taken the notion he was an impostor."

"I had not met him before. There was some doubt in my mind, but my family has convinced me the man is indeed Kenelm Derwent."

"Of course he is. Hanley remembers him vividly, and so do I if it comes to that. He didn't recognize me at once, but he remembered that I used to ride my little cream pony and later we recalled a dozen memories that quite settled it in my mind."

"I had the impression your mind was made up from the

beginning," Marnie remarked, not at all spitefully, but she could deliver a touch of acid with honey very well. The girl understood her.

"I hadn't a notion who he was that first day at the party. I only knew I wanted to become better acquainted with him, for I never saw anyone so handsome and dashing."

After a little general discussion, it was asked where Kenelm was that morning, and what he was doing to confute Clare.

"He's gone off to find the men Horace Rutley used to chum around with, to see if any of them have heard of him," Lady Alice answered. "He and I decided that was his best move."

The sisters exchanged a speaking glance, saying silently that the girl clearly thought she owned him. Marnie was the real object of her various claim-stakings. She had heard about the Gypperfield-mansion scheme, and feared Lady Raiker's brother-in-law was fonder of her than was right.

The Dougall party stayed for over an hour, and before they left, Kenelm came as he had promised Lady Alice. He took up a seat beside Miss Falkner, however, and before joining in the general discussion he said to her, "Are you busy this afternoon? I hope not. I want to show off my new curricle and team to you. Sixteen miles an hour, but I won't go above fifteen and a half if you dislike fast driving."

"I don't dislike it. I would like to go," she answered, and felt guilty. Was it because Lady Alice was straining her ears on Kenelm's other side, or was it because some little trace of doubt still hung about him? Or was it possibly that, even if he was Kenelm, he was no proper friend for her, a man who had either beaten his stepmother or made love to her?

"Good. Is half past two suitable?"

"Yes."

"Kennie, I think we ought to be going," Alice said, tugging his arm to get his attention. "Your schoolmates are still at the inn, and we said we would see them off, you recall."

He waited a moment before acknowledging Alice's words and tuggings. Rorie took the idea he did it on purpose to make Alice angry. He turned at last to Alice. "I saw them off before I came here, as it was getting late," he told her.

104

"Ah, then we will go home and get into those cartons from India, and you can show me—"

"I have already made plans for this afternoon, Sal." Alice glanced jealously to Aurora. "Miss Falkner has recklessly agreed to ride out with me and let me show off my new team."

"Oh—Hanley said something about calling on you," Alice said at once to Aurora. This was merely a tactic. He had said nothing of the sort, nor did Aurora believe he had. Any romance in that direction existed solely in Malone's head.

"He didn't mention it to me," Rorie answered.

Kenelm's quickened interest told Lady Alice that inciting jealousy was a poor strategy, and she let the matter drop. "You will be sorry you accepted, Miss Falkner. Kennie's team go like the wind. Ken always has to hold me on when we ride in the curricle."

"You see the wisdom of a fast team. Gives me an excuse to get an arm around the girls," he said, laughing to Rorie.

While they still sat talking, a note arrived for Miss Falkner from Raiker Hall, asking if she would spare Lady Raiker a few moments at her earliest convenience. With her afternoon so pleasantly planned, she decided to dash over at once, before luncheon, and excused herself. She made no explanation to the group regarding her errand, knowing it would cause an uproar, and she wished to get it over with quickly. She was, of course, curious to hear what Clare wanted. She had her mount saddled up and rode through the meadow, keeping an eye out for gypsies, but she saw none.

She first thought Clare wanted only information. Formally estranged from the rest of the family, she wished to maintain one link, and Rorie as the least involved was the likeliest one.

"What is going on?" Clare asked. "I was in the garden doing a water colour of the roses—so lovely this time of the year—and saw the Dougalls' carriage go down the road. Rutley is there too I believe?" She tried to sound only moderately interested, but there were telltale traces of anxiety in her eyes.

"Nothing is going on. They are just visiting the Gowerses, who have come to stay with us awhile."

105

"They are all against me. All want to see little Charles deprived of his inheritance, but I depend on *you*, Aurora, to let me know what they are up to."

"They aren't up to anything. Naturally they are talking about the body and all that. The oddness of the uniform and rings."

"I explained about the uniform, and have been thinking about those rings. What a shock to see them on Kenelm's fingers. He didn't usually wear them, but he was leaving, you see, and would naturally have picked up anything of value belonging to him. He wouldn't leave home forever without his jewelry. That explains it, I think, and in the haste of the burial, Joe Miller hadn't the wits to pull them off his fingers. But in a way, I am glad, as it proves beyond a doubt that the body is indeed Kenelm's, and not Rutley's, as they are trying to say."

"Funny he didn't have a watch."

"Oh, but the clothing was changed! The watch would have been in his jacket pocket. Very likely Joe Miller buried it, or burned it, or stole it for all we know."

"It would be interesting if Kenelm—the man who says he is Kenelm—could produce it," Rorie said, and looked to Clare for a reaction. There was none.

"The watch Rutley uses is not Kenelm's. It is an odd-looking thing—from India very likely."

"Still, he might *have* it. If it broke in India, he might have put it away, kept it, to be repaired here in England."

Clare looked a little nervous at this, she thought, and she determined to ask Raiker about his watch. "The man who is buried seems to be a little taller than Kenelm was. Some two inches difference."

"There wasn't an inch difference between the two of them, and with the state that corpse was in, no very accurate measurement could have been made. Not that accurate. I came to Kenelm's chin, and not more than an inch lower on Rutley."

"I didn't realize you had had the opportunity of measuring yourself so closely on *Rutley*," Rorie took it up at once.

"He was here several times. My husband gave him money—a regular allowance—and usually the fellow came begging for more between quarters. It is why I am so sure that man is Rutley. The others knew Kenelm, but they didn't know Rutley; *I* did, and I recognize him in that man.

106

But Lady Alice has decided to marry him, and Marnie wants the Gypperfield mansion, and the Gowerses hate me, so little Charles is to be done out of his inheritance."

"Why didn't you say you knew Rutley? I never heard you say so before, Clare?"

"My, you are becoming a regular little inquistor! What wouldn't they have made of my knowing Rutley? Say he was my lover, or any other slanderous thing they could think of. But I have a favour to ask of you, Rorie. I didn't ask you here to discuss Horace Rutley. I have to go up to London for a few days, on business connected with this case. I don't like to leave little Charles alone with only the servants. There are the gypsies hanging about for one thing, and Rutley—I wouldn't put it a bit past him to do the boy a mischief. Then too, Rutley might break into the hall and do some snooping around. I wouldn't put it past him to secrete the emeralds, and make it look as though *I* had them the whole time. I can't even trust my own servants. Your sister's accepting Rutley has turned them against me. Wilkins, my butler, looks at me as though he'd like to spit in my eye. I'll turn that man off as soon as this case is over. So the favour is this: will you stay here for two days while I am gone?"

"Oh dear!" Rorie was appalled at the idea. It would be dull and lonely, and it would publicly put her in Clare's camp, where she had not the least desire to be. But then, what if she was telling the truth? Everyone was convinced she was a scheming liar. She had lied about some things, but not necessarily about the man's identity. What if Clare was right after all, and the man Horace Rutley was making a May game of them all?

"Of course I'll pay you," Clare said, sensing the girl's indecision.

"I don't want pay! I'll stay," Rorie said, but was very unhappy to feel obliged to do it.

"You won't be sorry," Clare told her. "Rutley isn't the only one who can buy allegiance. There will be money to spare once I get the whole of the Raiker income—for *Charles*, I mean. Naturally I will only administer it for him till he grows up. I'll remember you did this for me, Rorie."

"No, you're not buying me, Clare, I will come because I feel it the proper thing to do. Until the matter is settled

107

one way or the other, I don't feel it fair to assume you are wrong, but I am not at all sure you are right either. It is close to eleven years since those two men left. They would both have changed a good deal. Marnie and the others might be wrong, or you might be. Time will tell."

"Fair enough. An open mind is all I ask. That's more than the others have granted me. I wonder Kenelm hasn't favoured *you* with a flirtation, to turn your head like the others."

"I'll leave now, if there's nothing else. What time would you like me to come tomorrow?"

"Early. Stay here tonight if you wish. I hope to get away by half past eight."

"So early? London is only half a day with your team."

"I don't want to waste any time. Even my beauty sleep must go by the boards at such a time. Why don't you come tonight?"

"No, I'll be here at half past eight tomorrow. Goodbye, Clare."

As Rorie rode home, she considered what she had got herself in for. Marnie would be furious. The Gowerses and Malone would think she had run mad, and she began to think so herself, too. As to what Kenelm would think, she had no idea. Clare was not to be trusted. To try to *buy* her support! "I'll pay you." That was an unforgivable insult. That she was so familiar with Rutley that she knew exactly how high she reached against him—that sounded like a closer intimacy than watching her husband give him money. How could her husband have permitted her to be present when he gave his illegitimate son money? Clare could say anything now that Charles was dead, and who was there to contradict her?

She had been a fool to say she would go, but at least her conscience was clear that she did it out of pique because Kenelm had not honoured her with a flirtation. She was driving out with him that very afternoon, and the anticipation of it took the edge off her gloomy thoughts to no little extent. If he had made up to Marnie and Lady Alice because their support was helpful to him, the same was not true of herself. She could add no proof that he was Lord Raiker. She was as close to an objective party as existed. She hadn't known him before, had nothing to gain, but still Kenelm was favouring her with his attentions. She

108

suddenly sat up straighter in her saddle: "I wonder Kenelm hasn't favoured *you* with a flirtation." Clare had called him Kenelm! She made it a point always to say Rutley when she spoke of him, but that once the Kenelm had slipped out. If Clare thought of him in her secret heart as Rutley, she would not have made the slip. Did she know perfectly well he was Kenelm then, or was she only uncertain? She must at least be unsure, or the name would not have been used.

The Dougalls had left when Rorie got home, and had taken the Gowerses with them for a few days. The house was crowded with the extra guests, and this arrangement would allow them a better visit with Kenelm.

"What did the she-devil want with you?" Malone asked, having apprised herself from the butler where Rorie's errand had taken her.

The visit was explained, and Rorie confessed that she had agreed to the request, not without fear of a scolding.

"Perfect!" Malone surprised her by saying. "It will give you a grand chance to poke around to see what you can find."

"That's not why I agreed to it."

"Rorie, it is your *duty* to help Kenelm in any way you can," Marnie charged her. "Not that Clare would be slow enough to leave any clues sitting around. I'll give you the combination of the safe and you look to see if the emeralds are there."

"Rutley sold the emeralds," Malone pointed out, this opinion having been established as a fact in Malone's theory regarding the body in the coffin. "No, you won't find the emeralds, but you may find a receipt or a fat deposit in her bankbook at the right time."

"I have no intention of going through her private papers."

"We'll never have another such chance. It is your *duty*," Marnie repeated.

"It's not my duty to help you to the Gypperfield place, Marnie," Rorie was goaded into saying, after which Marnie maintained a rigid silence.

"The she-devil chose well," Malone said, eying Miss Falkner askance. "She knows a flat when she sees one. It's an enema to me how you are so taken in by the woman. If you were wide-awake as young Lady Alice you'd be making up a bit to Kennie, instead of letting that chit waltz off with him while you sit with your face as stiff as set plaster every time he comes around. You never were half as sly as your sister."

Malone as well as Rorie was now in Marnie's black books, and she left them to each other's company. "It happens I am driving out with Kenelm this afternoon," Rorie said.

"Fine. No doubt he'll leave you sitting on the doorstep when he finds out what you're up to, supporting the she-devil. If you're wise you won't tell him."

"I'll tell him."

"Be sure to tell him you have a particular inversion to tall, handsome, edible lords as well. We don't want to leave any stone unturned in setting him against you." Malone strode off, in high dudgeon.

It was Miss Falkner's intention to tell Kenelm at the first opportunity that she was to go to Raiker Hall. Before they left the house, she asked him the time, and he pulled out his watch, a bizarre affair from India, with enamelled work on the outer case. She commented on it, in order to discover if he still had the one he had worn when he left.

"It's only a cheap thing really. Rather garish, but it chimes the hour at six and twelve. It appealed to me when I was a green youth, and has continued working well, so I never bothered to replace it. I bet Charlie would love to have it." Then he stuck it back in his pocket and held the door for her.

"Did you not have a watch when you got to India?" she asked.

"Yes, but I pawned it the day I arrived to raise the wind. The trip left me pretty short. I didn't *really* beat a thousand pounds out of Papa, you see. I had only my allowance, which was barely enough to get me there."

"You never redeemed it from the pawn shop?"

"No, it had no particular value, either sentimental or monetary. Just an ordinary watch Bernie gave me when I was fourteen. Why the interest in my timepieces?"

"I was justing thinking that no watch was found on the corpse that is supposed to be you. If you had your watch it might be some sort of substantiation that you are Kenelm."

"Or on the other hand, it might prove that Horace Rutley had stolen it from me, somewhere along the way.

110

Clare would say she had given the watch to Rutley, and it would be additional proof that I am he."

"I never thought of that."

"You don't have the criminal mind Clare has."

"And you." He flicked a disapproving glance at her.

He said as soon as they were out the door that he would like to forget the whole messy business for a few hours and enjoy himself, so it was difficult to tell him about her visit with Clare. He handed her up to the seat of his curricle while the team chomped eagerly to be off, and once they were given their heads, conversation was not easy. The team was as fast as its owner had boasted, and maintaining a seat as difficult as Lady Alice had predicted. Till they reached the village, they kept up a hot pace, but slowed to go through it, of course, which allowed a little conversation.

"I see the Blodgett store is shut down," he said. "Bernie and I used to stop in there and fill our pockets with sweets when we came to town with Papa. He was always awfully good to us."

Rorie tried to remember whether Bernard had ever mentioned this, but though he had harboured a sweet tooth till the day he died, she could not honestly say he had ever told her about buying sweets at Blodgett's.

"Old Ernie is still shaving and cutting hair," he remarked as they went past the barber's. "The Beckstead speciality—sugar-bowl style. We never went to him. Kravits, the senior footman at the Hall, used to do it when we were young. Is Kravitz still there?"

"No, he was retired a few years before Bernard died. He was getting on."

"Yes, he had snow-white hair already when I was a boy."

Rorie did remember that little Charles had been sent up from the Dower House to have his locks shorn by Kravitz once when she had been visiting Marnie and Bernard over a Christmas holiday. Would outsiders know Kravitz did the family hair? It seemed unlikely, but then the doings at the Hall were common gossip, and it might have been discovered by a curious questioner. She racked her brain for some bit of family esoterica Horace Rutley would not know. The others had all tested the man, but she had not. She hadn't known *him*, but she did know things about the

111

family, things Rutley would presumably not know. A few items came to mind, only to be rejected for one reason or another. At last she hit on something she could consider good evidence; it was so trivial it would never have got talked about the countryside.

It had only been drawn to her own attention because of Mimi. She had sneaked once into her father's room and played with his razor when she was young, cutting her finger in the process. In an effort to hide it, she had come downstairs holding her finger so tightly that attention was drawn to it at once. She could remember Bernard scolding and saying, "Just like Kennie when he burnt his fingers learning to strike a light from the tinderbox. He raised a huge blister and never let on till it became infected. Knew he deserved a good hiding for playing with fire. Lucky he didn't burn the house down." But at what age had it happened, and was it significant enough that Kenelm might justifiably be expected to remember it? Most of all, how was such an irrelevant subject to be introduced, when her partner was busily pointing out the shops?

To ease the conversation around to pains and bruises, she said, "My fingers are cramped with holding on so tightly."

"Better get used to it. I like a brisk pace," he answered.

In her quandary, she missed reading any importance into this telling speech. "The thing is, I hurt my hand recently—cut it on Bernard's razor when Marnie and I were putting away his things." This was an outright lie, but, she assuaged her conscience, a white lie. "Like Mimi," she went on. "She did the same thing, but knew she shouldn't have been playing with it, and never let on to us she was cut. Children are so foolish."

"Did you cut yourself badly?" he asked. "I didn't notice any plaster on your hands."

"No, only a scratch. It was a few weeks ago."

"Odd it still bothers you," he said, with a questioning look, and indeed it was a strange enough thing to have said.

"It doesn't bother me. Not much. It was so cute the way Mimi tried to hide her cut. Afraid of a spanking for playing with the razor, of course. She had been told never to play with it, or knives or fire."

112

If he was to make the comment unaided, he would do so now. "Yes, it's pretty dangerous," he said, then looked to the other side of the street. "Good Lord, I believe that's Mrs. Evans with her hair turned gray. How it makes me feel old, to see everyone wrinkled and stooped that I remember as so much younger. No wonder some of them have trouble remembering me."

It had not come unaided, but perhaps she could joggle his memory into it. "Did you ever do that sort of thing, Kenelm?" she asked. "Play with sharp things, or fire."

He looked at her and shook his head, then smiled ruefully. "You still don't believe me! I thought I had got you convinced days ago. Yes, Aurora, I recall very well striking a fire with the tinderbox I borrowed from the study. And Bernard, whom I assume told you the story, didn't know the whole of it, either. I not only burned the flesh off my fingers, I also very nearly burned down the barn. I was making my experiment in the cow barn, up in the hay loft, sitting on a stack of nice dry hay. Clever rascal, don't you think? I always had the knack of causing trouble. I little thought at the time how useful the episode would be. I hope it has served to convince you *at last* that I am not my half brother, Horace. He could not know the story, I trust."

She felt foolish in the extreme to be found out in her trick, but still she was happy. He was Kenelm. He had to be.

"What has happened to cast you into doubt again?" he asked, as they drove out the far side of the village into the country.

"Nothing. Well, perhaps Clare gave me a little cause."

"Clare? Have you been seeing her? I thought she held herself aloof from the family."

"No, she *sees me*," she confessed a little sheepishly.

"She is up to anything. She wants to know what I'm doing. What did she say to reawaken your suspicions?"

"She thought Lady Alice had been discovering the secrets of Eton from her brother, Hanley, and coaching you. Hennie and Alfred are prejudiced, she feels, and the footman as well."

"Biased, not prejudiced. They know her pretty well. I see she has done a splendid job of undermining your judgement. But Hanley didn't know what schoolmates were to

113

be chosen. For that matter, he wasn't in my class at Eton. I had very little to do with him. He's only twenty-four, you know, whereas I am an old man of twenty-seven. And feel closer to fifty-seven as a result of my Indian adventures. God, what a place it is. It is like stepping into an icehouse to be back in England, to be able to walk along the street with your jacket buttoned, and not have your shirt glued to your back."

"Is it so hot in India?" she asked, relieved to have cleared her chest, and also curious to hear about his travels.

"Hot, humid, bug-ridden, filthy. I don't know why I stayed so long."

"Why did you?"

"I had to make my fortune. That's why I went. It is the haven of the disinherited—the misfits, younger sons, the disgraced, the adventurers and outright rotters. The most raffish collection of men to be found anywhere outside of Newgate, or in it for all I know. They say it was worse in the old days, before Warren Hastings cleaned things up, but there is still plenty of crime there, and plenty of gold to go around too."

"What did you do there? What sort of work were you involved in?"

"I was first a mere box-wallah—junior clerk for the East India Company. Well, green as grass, you know, when I arrived, still wet behind the ears. But I soon made friends, and in a few years got myself made British resident at the court of one of the Indian princes—the nawab of Bengal it was."

"What did you do?"

"Sort of liaison officer between the public and the prince. I was the prestigious gent who decided who my nawab would condescend to see. Also liaison man between the prince and the British. A good part of my time was spent in buying up European things for him, too. All the crack for the princes to surround themselves with the trappings of the British, in much the same way as we returned nabobs surround ourselves with Indian finery. In the true nabob's fashion I have toted home some cartons of ugly ivory carvings and brass pots and silken scarves. I don't now what I'll do with them—set up an Indian Room at the

Hall I suppose, to amuse posterity. I had sundry other duties as well—polishing up his English and manners. He didn't realize how poorly he had chosen for that latter job. The blind leading the blind, but at least I knew more than he did. There is a fortune to be made in these posts. Even without bribery a man can do very well for himself. One fellow, the resident of a nawab of Carnatic, is said to have made well over a million during his term of office. I must confess I wasn't quite bent enough to gross a million, but I am not complaining. I would be wealthy independent of my lawful inheritance."

"What was it like there?"

"Everything is controlled by the heat. The early mornings—and I mean before breakfast—are the only times cool enough to do anything active. Races, riding or whatnot all take place in the morning, then a little of what we jokingly called work in the forenoon. By noon every shutter is closed, and nothing more is attempted till evening, when we get down to serious entertainment. A trip to the New Playhouse or the Harmonic Tavern, followed by a *staggering* dinner where the food is heavily spiced you must accompany every bite with a glass of wine, then on to a ball or party. The balls last till morning. I have known ladies to die as a result of those balls."

"It sounds rather fun."

"Oh yes, they died laughing. The British make it as British as they can, import their horses and carriages and even wear their British clothing—a dangerous thing. Import their wine and some women, but still it is no place for a human being."

"And where did you live? In what city, I mean?"

"Calcutta for the most part, on the hot and humid banks of the Hooghly. My nawab liked the bright lights."

"Is that a river, the Hooghly?"

"Yes, a mouth of the Ganges, and what a sewer that is! The baths at Bath are nothing to it for communal bathing. Quite a family affair. I mean the large family, including animals. Calcutta is the finest of the cities. A sort of imitation British decor. The Esplanade is its showpiece, with Palladian buildings, the stucco already crumbling away and showing the brick beneath. All along the riverbanks from Garden Reach to Barrackpore the nawabs have built their mansions, resembling country gentlemen's

115

homes, with porticoes and pillars and invariably green shutters to keep out the sun and heat. The Maidan, actually a military place but used as a park for riding and racing, is the Hyde Park of the place. There is a wretched amount of drinking that goes on to make life tolerable. Three bottles an evening for the gentlemen, and one for the ladies. It has ruined more livers and complexions that you can count. I *think* I got out with my liver intact, but of course I have lost my maidenly pallor forever. I will no doubt look like a blackamoor for the rest of my days. My hide is tanned like a piece of leather. Even my back and chest, as I did quite a bit of swimming. But then I am not vain."

"That is why I took you for a gypsy the day I saw you in the woods," Aurora said. "You were so very dark, and wearing rough clothing too."

"You're no help at all, you know," he said, turning to her with a roguish smile. "I thought I was beguiling that episode from your memory with all my Indian tales, but you revert to it. I took you for a servant. A poor excuse for molesting you, of course, but I hadn't kissed an English girl since I left eleven years ago, Aurora, and was eager to try it."

"You got little enough pleasure from it, if memory serves."

"I wouldn't say that."

"You already have, sir. You advised me strenuously not to take up lovemaking as a career, as I hadn't the knack for it."

"But I didn't know you were a *lady* then. One expects a proper frigidity from a lady. I expect this whole conversation is not at all the thing. Swat me down if I pass the bounds of what is acceptable, won't you? I have not been properly schooled in how to disport myself with a well-bred female. However, there can be no harm in saying I still advise you not to take up lovemaking as a career, but as an avocation I recommend it highly." He took his eyes from the reins long enough to cast a questioning glance at her.

She felt some stricture ought to be delivered, but decided instead to reform him by turning the conversation to a more discreet topic. "I imagine the countryside looks unusual to you after India," she attempted.

116

"I find it refreshingly green, like the girls," he said, returning determinedly to his preferred subject, with a bantering smile.

"You didn't seem to find the gypsy girl green."

"No, she's half Indian, like myself, and a married lady to boot."

"Married!"

"She isn't awfully strong on monogamy. Has lost one husband already, and he was destined to be the gypsy chief, too. Sometimes they choose their leader on his abilities, and sometimes he inherits, like our present string of Hanoverian Georges, despite his lack of them. The present chief is Ghizlaine's papa-in-law. She was first married to his son, and thought she had herself set up to be queen, but the husband unfortunately died."

"How did he die? In a duel defending her honour, I expect."

"Possibly. I hinted around once, but she was coy with me. Maybe the new gent who bought her had a hand in it. She dislikes him for some reason."

"*Bought* her?" Rorie asked, astonished.

"You haven't been taken in by that old canard that the best things in life are free? A rumour started by those who already have everything."

"It seems hard that she should be sold outright to a man she dislikes."

"Don't weep for her. She is trying to convince me I ought to do him in and become the chief when old Killu ends his days. That's the chief, Killu. Do you think I'd make a good gypsy prince, Aurora? Or should I say gypsy baron, considering my own title? I wouldn't care to relinquish it entirely, after all the trouble I am having to claim it."

"You would make an extremely elegant gypsy chief, and have the complexion for it too."

"But then Ghizlaine is so dark she reminds me of the half-caste mistresses of Calcutta, and I hope to get away from all that. A nice blonde is what I'm keeping an eye out for."

As Marnie and Lady Alice were both blonder than herself, Aurora could read no compliment into this, and turned to another subject instead. "Did you and that old gypsy hag fix it up between you for her to come and read

117

Marnie's fortune? She came spouting off about a tall, dark stranger that Marnie should help."

"She was supposed to say dark and handsome," he confessed. "I told her to stress the need to help. Now had I known *you* were there, I would have sent a message for you as well. Did she read your fortune?"

"She prophesied a future as dull as my past. I think you might have done a little better by me."

"Had I known, you may be sure I would have consigned the dark stranger to your particular care. You were the only one who was a stranger to me, actually. But you might be nice to me without a gypsy's urging, you know. Now that I have remembered for you how I got my fingers burned, I hope you will stop staring at me as though I were a ghost every time I enter your door."

"I'm sure I didn't!"

"But you did. I always take careful notice of the reactions of all pretty young ladies, and you did not react at all well. I was unsure whether it was my brown face or my black behaviour in the forest that had got your hackles up. As they seem to be settling down, may I conclude I am forgiven—for both?"

"Naturally I wondered, and if you *were* Horace Rutley, I could not like to accept you as Kenelm."

"They do poor old Horace an injustice to make him out so crafty. He had a little devious twist in him, of course, but he was not at all a scheming fellow from what I ever heard. Well, his mother was not bright, and I fear he inherited a little of her paucity of brains. Father's main worry was that he lacked the wits to stay out of trouble. Here we are discussing the thing again; it's hard to stay off the subject, isn't it? Papa used to worry what was to become of Horace once he began growing up. He had some schooling and it was hoped he might be got a position in London, but he wasn't bright enough. The fact that he ended up in that grave with a bullet in his back pretty well shows it. Clare knew he was a near moron too, and for her to be pretending now that she thinks I am he, devising some elaborate scheme to snatch Charlie's title . . ." He stopped a moment and shook his head. "I don't understand the woman. Nothing she does makes any sense. She knows I'm Kenelm; knows bloody well Horace is in that grave, and likely put him there herself. She wasn't a bit sur-

118

prised at what she saw—the uniform, the rings. But still the rings make me wonder. I don't see her burying those rings. It would have been the last straw if the emeralds had been there too. I get the feeling she is dashing from pillar to post—from expediency to expediency, I mean—as things turn out differently from what she expected. I wonder what she'll do next."

Rorie cleared her throat and said nonchalantly, "Clare is going up to London tomorrow on some business connected with the case."

"To *London*? But her man Coons is here, and it will do her no good to go pestering the judge. Why the devil is she doing that, I wonder? How did you find out, by the way? I hadn't heard."

"She told me. I am going to Raiker Hall to mind Charles while she is away."

"Oh," Kenelm said, and looked at her in open astonishment.

"She does not like to leave him alone because of the gypsies—alone with the servants, I mean ."

"I see," he answered automatically, but sounded unconvinced. "Why doesn't she send him down to the Dower House? You will be lonesome there alone. I would offer to call if I dared, but it would be taken as unwarranted meddling. In fact, she probably asked you there to see I *don't* decide to pay her a call. The servants would gladly welcome me."

"I don't think you had better come."

"I shan't. How long will you be there?"

"Just two days."

"Two whole days!" he objected, frowning. "You could bring Charlie down to the Dower House for a visit if you were at all eager for my company," he suggested. "I shall undertake to neither kidnap nor poison him, and it seems the only way I might see you. I should like to see you."

"You will have plenty to do," she countered, blushing with this unexpected show of gallantry.

"Indeed I shall. Any spare moment my case leaves me will find Sally in my pocket too. I think you might help me extricate myself from her. It is damnably hard to set her down when I am accepting her father's hospitality. I'm likely to find myself compromised, but it is such a good base for me, housed so respectably with old Dougall, that I

119

don't want to give it up. It allows me to keep an eye on the competition too—Hanley," he mentioned with a quizzing smile. "Come now, let me be able to tell her I have an appointment at the Dower House tomorrow afternoon at three."

"You can go to the Dower House without my being there."

"I could, but it would not achieve my aim. Berrigan will take the notion I'm making up to Marnie too, and he's already so jealous he'd like to think I'm Rutley. I don't mean to turn a soul against me till I'm wearing my full title and dignities. Then I'll tell him he's an upstart, and none of his dashed business either if I want to help Bernie's family into a decent house."

"They have a decent house."

"It will soon be only half one, and never mind diverting me. Say you'll go, and bring Charlie. I'd like to see him. He's my half brother, and I'm never allowed a single peek at him."

"He'd tell her you were there. She wouldn't like it."

"That's not my concern. She has asked you to mind him, not lock yourself up in an airtight room. I won't hurt him."

"I know that. That's not why I refuse."

"I shall be there tomorrow at three, and if you can overcome your scruples, I hope you will be too, with or without Charlie. The servants could mind him for an hour. But enough of Indian manners. I *do* know better than to force my attentions on a reluctant lady, I hope. I haven't been gone that long. Ah, I see the Dinsmores have painted their barns. They used to be gray. I don't like them nearly as well in red. Stick out like a sore thumb."

The talk turned to mere chit-chat, and soon Aurora was taken home. Raiker did not again urge her to come to the Dower House the next day, but did make a point of saying to Marnie and Malone before leaving that he would be there the next day, if it was convenient for them.

"I'm sure we'd like to see you," Malone told him, casting a scathing eye on Aurora, who still had not offered to scour the Hall for clues or evidence, after being low enough to go to the place at all.

"We may appear very backward not to be helping you to the best of our ingrate abilities, but at least you're welcome to come and take a cup of tea."

"I shall be here at three then," Kenelm said, with a questioning look to Aurora, then he bowed and left.

"There's a lad that's ripe for the plucking," she informed Miss Falkner. "He'll be snapped up before the summer's out by some wide-awake thing. A pity you're half asleep."

Chapter Eleven

Lady Raiker was up, dressed and had her carriage standing ready at the door when Aurora Falkner arrived the next morning. "Just make yourself at home, my dear," she advised her. "You must not feel you have to be with Charles every minute. His tutor has him in the morning, and he amuses himself pretty well in the afternoon. It is more for the night that I wish someone in the house. With the gypsies about, I do not like to leave the house without someone I trust." She narrowed her eyes at Aurora in a suspicious manner as she said this, causing her trusted friend to wonder if she had heard so soon about the outing with Kenelm—as indeed she had, and a pretty underhanded stunt she thought it, too.

"I do not let Charles out alone," she added. "Oh, at the stables or whatnot is allowed, but I have warned him he is not to go beyond the immediate area of the buildings alone. Well, I am off. Wish me well."

"I wish you a pleasant journey," was the farthest Aurora could stretch her duplicity. She went into the house, to face two days' isolation from her friends and family. She had brought books with her to read, some needlework to busy her fingers, letter paper and her own favourite pen, and long before lunchtime had had a go at these occupations. All were equally tedious when carried on in a still house, disturbed only by an occasional servant entering a room

122

on soft feet. To have some company, she had Charles down to lunch with her, a diversion from his usual habit of eating with his tutor. She liked Charles, a handsome and clever boy approaching twelve years; she discovered traces of both Bernard and Kenelm in him.

"May we go out for a ride this afternoon, Aunt Rorie?" he asked. She was not actually his aunt, but from confusion with her sister he had addressed her so from his early years, and continued to do so.

The day was fine. The sun shone in through the mullioned windows to the table where they ate. The trees waved languorously in the breeze, and most of all to lure her, there was the knowledge that Kenelm would be at the Dower House at three o'clock.

"It might be best not to, with the gypsies camped nearby."

"We would go by the post road. They wouldn't bother us on the public road. We can take a groom if you're afraid. You shouldn't be afraid with me, Aunt Rorie. I would defend you," he said, in all seriousness.

"In that case, we shall go for a ride," she agreed, suppressing a smile.

"I haven't seen Aunt Marnie and Mimi for ages. Are they angry with me? Mama says they're angry, but you aren't. Why are they?"

"They are not angry, Charles. How foolish."

"Mama says they're angry because the courts made me Lord Raiker. I would rather be their friend than Lord Raiker," he said a little sadly.

"I don't think your mother would want you to go to visit them."

"I asked her if I might, and she said you wouldn't take me. She didn't say I shouldn't if you *would* take me," he added with the winning smile that seemed to run in the males of the family. "Will you, *please*?"

"Very well, baggage," she answered, laughing. "And if your mama has my scalp for it, remember you are to defend me."

"I will. She must do what I say. *I* am the head of the family now," he said happily, and applied his fork to his meat.

It was barely half past two when the two headed their mounts down the road to the Dower House. This was due not only to eagerness. Rorie salved her conscience by plotting to get Charles off to the nursery with Mimi and Malone, so that he would not be exposed to his half brother. She felt Clare could have no real objection to his visiting his other relatives, and did not like it that the boy was being led to believe the family was angry with him. Her plan worked well. Mimi met them at the stable and ran into the house with Charles. Both children lacked for suitable playmates and enjoyed each other's company.

Malone met Rorie at the door. "Well, have you found out anything?"

"Yes, I have found out Clare must be bored to flinders all alone at that house for days on end. The morning seemed sixty hours long."

"Did you find the receipt?" Malone asked more pointedly, meaning the receipt for sale of the emeralds. Just why this incriminating document should exist, and be left lying about if it did, was of course a mystery.

"I haven't stumbled across it, Malone. It wasn't left out in the saloon with the latest papers. I'll let you know if I find it."

"No cause to be sartorial about it. It wouldn't hurt you to bestir yourself while you're there, right in the liar's den. Your sister's gone out with Berrigan, to take tea with his sister. He's nearly screwed up his courage to pop the question. This is the first time he's taken her to be approved by the sister, at least. Said when she mentioned the Gypperfield place, as she always makes a point to do when he's around, that if it was the leaded windows she liked so much, *his* place has leaded windows. Flat. Him six and thirty, and not the gumption to ask a lady proper."

"What did Marnie say to that hint?"

"Said she didn't realize his place was up for sale. As bad as he is. She ain't giving him an inch. Well, it's a good thing you came, then; young Kenelm is to call this afternoon, and would have had to make do with me for a flirt if you hadn't showed up. Figured you would," she added knowingly. "Better run a comb through your hair and sprinkle on a bit of scent. You smell of horse." She strode off to ride herd on her two charges, while Rorie flew to her room to make a fresh toilette.

She had not thought to meet Kenelm alone, but as a part of the family group, and felt foolish to be sitting in

124

state, obviously awaiting his call, when he came, but he found no fault in the arrangement.

"Good girl," he said when the butler showed him in. "Did you bring Charlie?"

"Yes, he is upstairs with Malone and Mimi. I ought to call Malone."

"I have some Indian toys I want to give him—a carved set of animals in ivory. But if I do it now it will reveal clearly to Mama that I was here. I collect you don't mean to bring him down to meet me?"

"I would rather not, if you don't mind. But I ought to fetch Malone."

"What for?" he asked.

She looked down primly. "We ought not to be alone," she said.

"Oh lord, am I a menace to *you*, too? Is the fact of our being connections not sufficient chaperonage?"

That this irrelevancy added any propriety to the situation was news to Miss Falkner, but she had no real desire to have Malone on her hands and pretended to consider the matter settled.

"Did anything of interest occur this morning?" he asked her.

"No, Malone is disappointed in me. Thought I would have the receipt of the emeralds for her."

"They weren't sold. They probably *are* there, hidden somewhere around the house."

"Do you really think so?"

"*I* didn't steal them; poor old Horace is cold in his grave, or out of it at the moment, with no more than my two rings to his name. They must be there. I wonder where she hid them."

"Have you any suggestions?" Rorie enquired. She was coming to think that she might do the unthinkable and have a look around in a surreptitious manner.

"Not the obvious places—the safe, under the mattress and so on. They might be hidden in any nook or cranny."

"They wouldn't be in any of the public rooms. They would probably be in Clare's own chamber, don't you think? I mean, the servants are more about the rest of the house than she is. And she wouldn't have them in Charlie's room. They must be in her own."

125

"Yes, but that is *not* why I wanted to see you, to bludgeon you into helping me."

She heard this with satisfaction, accompanied by an urge to render her services, as they were not being sought. Had he asked it of her, she might well have refused. "As Malone says, we might not get into the 'liar's den' again. It is an excellent opportunity."

Kenelm regarded her levelly. "Don't put me in a corner like this," he said, and changed the subject. "Sally McBain is twisting old Dougall's arm to have a party. You will be coming, I trust? She tells me Hanley always insists on asking Miss Falkner."

She was surprised at his not leaping at any chance to prove his case; not so surprised, however, that she failed to remark Alice's trick in intimating she and Hanley were good friends. "Marnie and I are usually invited to Lord Dougall's parties," she said. "Kenelm, I was saying—do you have any idea where I might look for the emeralds?"

"Persistent creature. I am not uninterested enough to refuse your help if you are offering it freely, Aurora. Are you?"

"Yes, I'll have a look around. I don't suppose I'll find anything."

"Probably not. They might be anywhere from attics to cellars. Clare used to be a great one for the attics, now I come to think of it. It's full of old lumber. She had a spree of dragging down broken chairs and whatnot and having them gilded."

"I can't say I relish going to the attics, especially as it will be dark before I have got Charlie home and fed. Nighttime would be the best for secret rummaging. The servants have a habit of sneaking up behind me. I suppose she told them to."

"Your criminal bent is coming on rapidly. I wonder if it is her influence or my own. Yes, night would be best. And there is her studio—that might yield something. She had a room renovated and turned into a studio. She still paints, I know. There were several pictures of Charlie in the saloon. I wonder what she did with the good Canalettos that were there."

"I don't know, but I'll try the studio and bedroom. Her woman went with her to London, so I should have easy access. If she didn't lock them," Rorie added with a wry smile.

126

"*One* of us is fast making you an expert. She will most certainly have locked them if there is anything worth seeing. Do you know how to pick a lock?"

"Good gracious no! How should I know that?" she asked.

"You are coming on so rapidly I thought you might have taken it up. Your education as a ken nabs wants bringing up to date, my dear. Pity I hadn't brought my passe-partout." She looked a question at him. "My master key. Regulation issue for us resident bigwigs in India. You never know when you might want to do a little discreet breaking and entering."

"Do you have one?"

"Most assuredly. Not that I would need it to open Mama's door. If it is like the other bedroom doors in the house, and it is, or *was*, it can be jimmied with a piece of wire. Bernie showed me the trick. Papa used to lock our birthday presents in the gold guest bedroom. We usually went in to see if we approved his choice before the great day. I never cared much for surprises," he explained.

"How odd. I adore them."

"So do I, really," he admitted, with a smile not so different from little Charlie's. "But I was always impatient, and broke down the doors."

"Too bad you couldn't come and give me a hand," she said, but in a joking spirit.

"I would be happy to. It's my house, after all. She is the intruder. Shall I join you, after the servants are in bed?"

This went a long way beyond what she had had in mind. It was no more than rifling a drawer or two she had thought to do, and felt extremely criminal to be doing even that much. She looked up to see Kenelm observing her with a lazy smile.

"Frightened?" he asked.

"Yes."

"It was a poor idea," he said at once, but she took the meaning that he was disappointed at her lack of daring. She was disappointed with herself. Lady Alice, Marnie—the others were doing their best for him, and this was her one chance to help. She *knew* he was Kenelm now, knew Clare was a sneak. Why should she not help him? Might it not even be a duty?—Marnie's favourite word. What could Clare do, if she found out? To raise a fuss would be tantamount to admitting she had something to hide.

127

"We'll do it," Rorie said, summoning all her courage.

His smile turned warm, approving. "Only if you want to. I put all the onus on your shoulders. A trick I learned from my nawab."

"I draw the line at luring you into it."

"I'm lured already. I was always susceptible to blond ladies. You talked me into it," he said, and laughed recklessly. "Tell me, guru, how will it be best for me to enter the door of bliss? That's probably a profanity against the Upanishads. One ought to respect other people's religious beliefs."

"What has bliss to do with religion or with Raiker Hall for that matter?" she asked in total confusion.

"I never got on to the bliss of the Hindu faith, but I begin to foresee glimmerings of it at Raiker Hall. But about the door, I have a key and am strongly tempted to use it, to enter like a gentleman."

"No, I think you had better enter like a thief. The door has a chain, and Wilkins will have it put on. I'll let you in at the library French windows."

"The servants sleep downstairs. It would be better for me to go in by the upstairs. Make less of a furor. Open my bedroom window. The beech tree will let me slip in, unless someone has lobbed off my favourite branch."

"Which was your room?"

"The far end of the east wing. A paneled room, adorned with a garish display of female pulchritrude, if Mama has not had the walls stripped."

"The walls are now adorned with a very proper display of military heroes," she informed him. "Nelson, Wellington, *et al.*"

"I wonder what she did with my gallery of beauties. I had an excellent set of Emma Hamilton I cherished. Copies of Romney's series depicting her as Venus, Circe, Mary Magdalene and herself, all the more interesting varieties of seductress. She was gorgeous, don't you think?"

"Yes, if you favour brunettes. We seem to keep hearing of your penchant for blondes."

"It was the unrelieved company of dusky ladies in India that made me hanker for a blonde. You know the room I mean?"

"There's only the one paneled room upstairs."

Kenelm's face took on a figuring look. "I wonder if she

would have hidden the emeralds in *my* room—a nice incriminating touch if they should happen to turn up there. I'll have a look around. A strip of panel behind my bed used to lift up. Many is the mouse and frog secreted there in days gone by."

She was no longer surprised at the wealth of information he had about Raiker Hall. She knew now he was Kenelm and assured herself there was nothing wrong in the owner entering his own home, even if he chose to do so by a window.

"I'll be there around midnight. I'll watch from the outside to see when the lights are extinguished in the servants' quarters. We'd better give them an hour to settle into sleep. You'll know when they retire. With her dresser gone, there will be only Charlie on that floor, and a child will sleep soundly, I trust. I am looking forward to our tryst. I always wanted to have a tryst with a lady at midnight."

Aurora found that in spite of her lingering fears and doubts, she was looking forward to it too. He stayed an hour, discussing other things than the night's activities. He was led to expand in more detail on his doings in India, of which she believed somewhat less than half, and if a quarter of them were true, the entire British population there ought to be behind bars. But still it sounded so very jolly that she could not think he had been entirely miserable. She thought he was the kind to find amusement wherever he went. She suspected he even enjoyed his little game with Clare.

"I've only been telling you the good parts," he told her when she charged him with having liked it. "I have omitted the monsoons, the diseases, and *much* worse, the cures." That a red-hot iron ring placed over the navel should cause the intestines to revolve and cure cholera she mistakenly assumed to be a joke, but believed that typhoid and malaria had no real cure and little treatment when she heard the number who had died of them.

"You were fortunate to leave there alive," she congratulated him.

"Only the good die young. I'll reach a hundred. Imagine, I survived all that, and Bernie died of an ear infection. I'll take good care of my ears now I am home. So, we shall rendezvous at midnight or thereabouts in my bedroom.

129

Sounds marvelous, doesn't it? I trust you will be wearing your most dashing peignoir, Miss Falkner. And I shall be wearing my passe-partout and a piece of wire. And a shirt and cravat, of course. I mean to observe the formalities. I have suspected from time to time—just a certain way you have of looking at me askance—that you find me lacking in formality. You mustn't feel because I masqueraded as a gypsy and attacked you and have embroiled you in this questionable spree that I am anything but a high stickler. I have already asked you to be my instructor in matters of form. *Do* let me know if you object to anything."

He arose to take his leave, bowing formally, but uttering his usual offhand comments. "*À bientôt*. I can hardly wait. I haven't had such fun since I caught my nawab's favourite mistress, and mine too, with her hands in the diamond jar." As her eyes widened in shock he rushed on with an explanation she doubted. "I *mean*, I favoured her for *his* mistress. She wasn't nearly as bad as the others."

"I see," she said, still stunned.

"Yes, I'm afraid you do. Good day, Miss Falkner," he took a hasty departure, muttering to himself some words that sounded like "damned fool."

Rorie soon took Charles home, and while he had a bath—for he had managed to get well soiled crawling under the furniture with Mimi—she made a seemingly innocent trip to Clare's studio, ostensibly to admire her paintings, but actually to go through cupboards, closet, boxes and paint chest for emeralds or clues. She found nothing of either, but did come across some sketchbooks that must have been over eleven years old, as they contained paintings of her husband, and one of Charles as an infant in his crib. In the same book, there were two sketches of young men, one she thought must be Kenelm. The man—boy, really—was fuller in the face, the nose less sculptured than now, but the eyes were similar, the shape of the head, and the mouth. She recognized the man in the picture of the boy, and wondered that Clare should deny it.

The other young man she did not recognize. He too was young, dark-haired and dark-eyed, with a swarthy complexion denoted by shading. She wondered if it could be Horace Rutley. She thought not—there was a foreign look about him—but she would show it to Kenelm and ask him. She put the books back and went to dine with Charles, and wait for midnight.

Chapter Twelve

Aurora's evening passed more quickly than her morning. She enjoyed dinner with Charles, a pleasant and conversable companion. A ceremonious round of the doors was made with the butler, who eyed her with scanty approval; he had used to smile on her when he was only an upper footman and she a guest in the house.

With the mistress away, the servants retired early. Already at half past ten there was not a sound in the house but the ticking of the clock. Rorie tiptoed down the hall from her bedroom and surreptitiously tried Clare's bedroom and sitting-room doors. Both were locked. This augured something worth hiding inside, but her hairpin proved an inadequate passe-partout, and she could not get in. To pass the time till Kenelm came, she took her branch of candles into some unlocked guest rooms to rummage through drawers and under mattresses, but discovered nothing. She did some preparatory exploring in Kenelm's room too, curious to see where he had passed his youth, but the chamber, stripped of personal effects, was uninteresting, gave no secret clue to his character. A paneled room with indifferent window hangings and rather nice campaign dressers, cornered in brass. Wellington and Nelson surveyed her with cold, haughty eyes from the walls. In a cupboard she found Kenelm's cherished copies

131

of the paintings of Emma Hamilton, the frames stripped away. Horace Rutley would not have known about these, she thought with satisfaction. How pretty the girl was. And how typical of Kenelm, that prodigious flirt, that his only belonging should relate to women. Marnie, Lady Alice, Ghizlaine, Millie and herself—he had made up to them all. Every female in the place except Clare.

As she looked at the pictures, she was startled to hear a tap at the window, and looking toward it she saw a form crouching in the branches beyond. In an instant she knew it must be Kenelm, come early, but for that fraction of a moment she was terrified. A frisson ran down her spine, but soon she was hurrying to the window, unlocking it and throwing it open. The branch was not so close to the window as she had thought it would be. In fact, it would take something of an acrobat to negotiate the leap, but Raiker proved up to it. He pounced unhesitatingly forward and landed on the windowsill with only a soft thump. She grabbed his arm lest he fall, but he was in no danger of it.

"Did I frighten you?" he asked in a low voice. "I have been there this half hour. The lights have been out since then, so we might as well get on with it. I have Mr. Passe-partout here, but I see you decided against your peignoir," he said, with a glance at her gown.

"I have been looking around here," she said, disregarding the mention of the peignoir.

"I've been watching you. You'll make Emma Hamilton jealous, flirting with her Admiral Nelson."

"Oh, yes, I found your pictures." She handed them to him, but he barely glanced at them. "Where is the loose panel?" she asked.

"Right here," he said, and climbed on the bed carefully, making a grimace as it let out a little squawk beneath his weight. "It always did that," he said, laughing. He slid his hand down between the bed and wall to pry up a loose board. He felt around with his fingers, but they came up empty and dusty. "No—not there," he told her, and hopped off the bed. Though his movements were rapid, brisk, he made very little sound. He went to the clothespress, felt the jacket pockets, top shelf, in the the toes of boots and other likely hiding places, but found only a couple of fish hooks and a bill for a pair of boots.

"Go through those drawers, will you?" he said over his

132

shoulder while he searched the clothespress. The drawers were empty. Clare had done away with his shirts and linens. The room searched, they looked into the hallway and walked stealthily to Clare's room, down the shadowed way with only a brace of candles. The master key did the trick, and they were soon in a lavish room, done up in white gilded furniture, with opulent appointings.

"This has been redone since Marnie lived here," Rorie mentioned, looking with distaste on yards of swathed satin on the canopied bed.

"Bordello," Kenelm muttered in disgust, then became more businesslike. "Start on the dresser; I'll take the desk." They both whisked quickly through the drawers, taking care to disturb nothing. There were so many possible hiding places—any jacket or hat or shoe might hold the gems—that it was really a hopeless task, and there was still the sitting room to go. After half an hour they had done what could be done without ripping open the mattress and pulling up the floorboards, which Ken considered more likely places, and stopped to discuss the next move. Other than the natural curiosity of examining another's personal effects, Rorie found the evening actually close to boring. She had expected more of it.

"I've been through the studio," she told him. "There is nothing much, but one picture I would like you to look at. I think it might be Rutley. I never saw him, but it is a young dark-haired man. If she knew him well enough to sketch him—well, then they were sort of friends, I assume. There is one of you too."

"Wearing an open-necked shirt?"

"Yes. At least I thought it was you. You remember posing for it?"

"Very well," he answered, with an inscrutable expression—not a smile, but not quite a frown either. "Let's go. I'll put out the candles."

This was done, and they left, with Kenelm twisting the key again behind him to conceal the fact that they had been there. They went along to the studio and relit the taper, and Rorie found the book again. Ken looked at it, pausing over the drawing of his father and himself, then turned to the other man. "This isn't Rutley," he said at once. "It looks like one of the gypsies."

133

"It is swarthy, and the features rather un-English. But would she have a gypsy pose for her?"

"Possibly. This next one is a fisherman from the wharf, you see. She was doing character studies at the time. She might have paid one of them to pose for her."

Rorie studied the picture closely. "Odd she didn't put in any detail to tell us—tell anyone, I mean—that it *is* a gypsy. No kerchief or earring."

"He's a handsome buck. She liked painting young men." There was a look of deep concentration on his face.

She had painted himself, Rorie thought. She was said to like more than *painting* men. The sittings no doubt were the scene of a flirtation. And it was said that Kennie was fond of his stepmama too. Hennie had mentioned it.

"I fancy she had a flirtation with this one," Ken said, returning the book to her. In Miss Falkner's mind this was as good as a confirmation of her suspicions. "It's not Rutley in any case. Now, what about the safe? I might as well have a look while we're here. Not that we'll find anything."

The safe was downstairs in the study, and the trip below was carried out with the greatest stealth, the candle extinguished. They went down hand in hand, lending a little excitement to the proceedings that had thus far been futile and unadventuresome. The lock on the safe had been changed. The passe-partout did not perform its magic, but Kenelm seemed undisturbed. "There wouldn't have been anything there anyway." He looked perfunctorily through a few desk drawers, again without result.

"Shall we tackle the attics, or call it a night?" he asked.

"It's early. We have lots of time, and no one is up. We might as well search them while you're here," she replied, not liking to have her first adventure finished so soon.

"I'll go alone if you like," he offered. "You won't want to be up there with the mice and dust."

"Will there be mice?" she asked, her craving for excitement diminishing.

"The cheese room is right below it."

"I think I won't go," she added.

He laughed aloud—much too loud, considering the secret nature of their enterprise. "Aurora Falkner, do you mean to tell me a big girl like you is afraid of *mice*?" he asked, and taking her hand he assured her the best way of overcoming her aversion was to confront them head on. Her low-pitched protests were to no avail. She was led up the stairs and down the hall to the attic door, and soon it was quietly closed after them.

The aura of stale air and disuse added gloom to the eerie darkness. It was extremely uncomfortable. If Clare's bedroom had been difficult to search, the attics were clearly impossible. Five large rooms, with hardly a square yard of uncovered floor space anywhere. There was scarcely a pathway through them. Chests, boxes, racks, battered furniture, discarded lamps and bowls, toys, cribs and beds—there was the debris of several generations of hoarders here. They made only a cursory look around. It would take months to go through it all. It was gloomy and unwelcoming—their one brace of candles doing little to dissipate the long black shadows and darkened corners that invaded nearly to the centre of the room. Once Kenelm entered a door a few steps before her, leaving her in nearly total darkness, and she dashed to his side, to clutch his arm in fright. He held the candles high and looked at her in surprise. "I'm sorry," she said, letting go of his arm.

"Don't apologize. I like it," he answered, and took a firm grip on her elbow. There was suddenly some excitement in the air between them that had very little to do with the darkness and possible danger. They went on into the last room, which was somewhat less crammed with lumber than the rest. There was the quietest of a pattering rustle in a corner, hardly audible. "What's that?" Rorie asked, her heart pounding. He took a step toward it, holding up the light to gleam on a mouse, which halted as the light struck it. It was not three inches long, but looked loathsome, its eyes like glittering bugle beads staring at her, its tail curved over its back. She emitted a stifled shout and clapped her own hand over her mouth to deaden the sound.

"Hush!" Kenelm warned, and instinctively put his arm around her waist to protect her. "What is it?" he asked.

"A mouse," she said, in a failing voice.

"I thought it must be a herd of rats at least," he said, scanning the floor, but the intruder had vanished behind a trunk. He went toward the furniture and set down the candle holder, still holding her.

135

"Let's go," she said in a breathless voice. "There is too much to begin searching here, and in the dark."

"Yes, we'll go," he said, "as soon as I've kissed you." There was a strange light in his eyes, curious, intense. He tightened both arms around her and lowered his head, examining her face closely the while. Just before his lips touched hers he said in a soft, caressing voice, "May I?" She tried to speak, but found no words came out, and in an instant he was kissing her ardently, holding her tighter and tighter till she could scarcely breathe, or even think, for the blood pounding in her ears. In her mind, she remembered him kissing the gypsy girl in much this same way, and she felt something of the gypsy in herself respond.

When he released her he lifted his head, and he was smiling. "I was wrong. You *do* have the knack for it. But I still don't want you setting up as a professional. A talented amateur will be good enough for me."

"We—we'd better go, don't you think?" she asked.

"You are the guru. I *feel* I would like very much to stay, but *think* I had better follow your advice, before I follow my own inclination. I don't want to do anything improper," he added quite seriously.

He took up the candle holder in one hand, still holding her tightly to his side with the other, and they walked back through all the rooms to the staircase. While still at the top, they heard a sound at the door leading to the hallway. There was a metallic click, then the door was tried, and steps were heard retreating softly down the hall.

"We've been locked in!" Rorie said in a muffled squeak. "What will we do?"

Kenelm made a strangled sound in his throat. Glancing at him, she was amazed to see he was trying to hide a laugh.

"Ken, it's not funny! I'm going to bang on the door and get help. You stay up here."

"No, not yet," he said, pulling her back.

"There is a sliding bolt on the other side. Your key can't open it. We're *stranded*."

"There is no one I would rather be stranded with," he answered, undismayed.

"I must hurry. Whoever is there will be gone. I'll have to

136

admit I was snooping. I'll let you out later." She tried to pull free, to hasten to the door.

"I can get out a window."

"We're three stories off the ground! You'll kill yourself."

"The beech must nearly reach these windows."

"You're not going to jump from the attic windows! You'll certainly fall."

"Wait—there's no hurry."

"There is! He'll never hear me knocking. I must go at once."

"You don't suppose she's come home?" he asked, pulling her down by his side. The tone of his voice alerted her to some chicanery—he was trying not to laugh, was enjoying their predicament and her efforts to break free.

"She can't have! I'm disgraced."

"No, sweet. I was teasing you. There's a trapdoor from the last room into the cheese room. It won't be locked from the outside, I trust, the cheese room. We'll give it a try. Anyway, we won't starve to death. Come along."

She was too relieved to be as angry as she wanted to be. They went back through all the rooms to the last, and there in the corner was a square of floor cut loose, with a handle to allow easy lifting. Kenelm sat on the edge of the hole, slid his legs through, grabbed the rough edge and swung down. She heard a little thump as he hit the floor beneath, then the sound of his opening the door and closing it again. She relaxed, not realizing till then how frightened she had been.

"Hand me down the light," he called up, and she did this. "Can you ease the cover into place as you come down—hold it over your head?" he asked.

"No," she answered unhesitatingly.

"I'll roll a barrel over for you to stand on." There were the rumbling noises, very loud, of this being done, and she lifted the square of floor over her head. It was by no means easy, but she got it up, swung her legs into the cavern and eased herself down. Kenelm was balancing on the barrel and caught her as she came, steadied her while she jiggled the trapdoor into position. They were both in imminent danger of toppling over, with the barrel wobbling on an uneven floor. When Rorie got her feet on the barrel top, Kenelm hopped down to the floor to swing her down in his arms. He was smiling recklessly in the dim light. "This is

137

too good a chance to miss," he said, and crushed her against him for another kiss, while her feet were still six inches from the floor. "Did I happen to tell you, my little sweet, you are a very competent partner in crime, and everything else?" he asked when he was finished.

"No, I'm not. My nerves are shattered," she confessed.

"Ah, but the excitement adds a dash of zest. It is the best time for romance."

"This is too much excitement for me. You'd better go, Ken. And we haven't accomplished a thing."

"What, you didn't really think we'd find the emeralds, did you?" he asked.

"I hoped we might find something."

"We did. We found each other. The right girl is harder to find than an emerald necklace any day."

Being no adept at flirting, Rorie did no more than smile at this meaningful speech. "No reassuring hint that you have at last found your soulmate too?" he asked in a light way. And still she didn't know what to say.

"Am I going too fast?" he asked, frowning. "I'm not doing something *wrong*, am I?"

He had gone not only faster but a good deal farther than she had ever been down this particular road before. "You do seem to be in rather a rush," she said. "There's no hurry, is there?"

"Oh no—I want to do it right," he said, then smiled again. "I'll give you till I get back to my bedroom window to think it over. We'll walk slowly—two minutes should be enough, even for a slowpoke like you to make up your mind."

He opened the door stealthily, and in the hallway with his arms crossed stood Wilkins, the butler, waiting with a poker in his hands.

"Oh!", Rorie gasped, and fell back against Kenelm.

"Steady on, old girl," he said, and turned to the butler. "Shame on you, Wilkins, frightening a lady. Where are your manners? By the by, congratulations. Butler now, eh? You're coming up in the world. I didn't think to mention it on my first visit."

"Good evening, your lordship," Wilkins said, and bowed sedately, using a lowered voice. "I thought it was you, and when I heard the noise in the cheese room, I knew it. Can I help you with anything?"

138

"You wouldn't happen to have seen an emerald necklace lying about?" Kenelm asked.

"It's never been seen since your father, God rest his soul, died, sir."

"Was it seen between my leaving and Papa's death?"

"I don't believe it was, sir, but it was so seldom worn that it means nothing. It was never said to be missing till his lordship died."

"Then I guess you can't help me, Wilkins. Well, my dear, it's time I be off," he added, turning to Aurora.

"I'll see you out, sir," Wilkins said with a punctilious bow.

"Don't be indiscreet, my good man. Miss Falkner will see me out the window."

Wilkins held his lips firm, but his eyes crinkled up with the effort of it. "As you say, milord. As to my overhearing you, I don't believe anyone else did, and I have a lamentable memory now I am growing old."

"Thank you. My own is still excellent. I shan't forget this."

Wilkins nodded. "If there's anything I can do for you, sir, I fancy I could be reached without too much trouble. My nephew, Sam Friggins, works at the tavern. You mind Sam?"

"Very well indeed, the rascal. You may be hearing from me then, Wilkins. Goodnight."

"Goodnight, milord, Miss Falkner." He bowed and strode off, swinging his poker.

Kenelm and Aurora went to his bedroom and he threw up the window, perched on the ledge and said in an oratorical way, "Parting is such sweet sorrow, That I shall say—goodnight, till it be morrow."

Then he assumed a more down-to-earth tone and went on, "But tomorrow I shall expect to hear your words on the subject of soulmates. I am giving you an extension to think it over."

While she stood preparing her farewell, he leaped to the branch and disappeared into the tree's foliage. In a minute he sprang to the ground, waved up at her, and was soon swallowed up into the night.

She was trembling when he left, although the breeze coming in at the window was not at all cold. It was reaction from the night's harrowing adventure. She felt as

139

if she had fought a war, and how calmly *he* had taken it. She smiled as she closed the window and took up her taper, burning low now. Was smiling still when she had undressed and crawled into her bed. She considered the lack of success of their search, and more curiously the fact that Kenelm hadn't really seemed to expect to find anything. Why had he come, then? Only to be with her? This unusual manner of conducting a romance seemed odd to her, but then it was so odd to have attached a beau at last that she was not severe in her judgement. And what a beau he was—surely the most dashing, handsome, satisfying beau ever to have kissed a lady. She had had her answer ready within a minute of hearing the question, and would make sure to give it next time they met.

Chapter Thirteen

In the morning, Aurora was greeted by the unsmiling Wilkins with no open intimation of the evening's activities. She found her thoughts so full of them herself that her time passed quickly. She made the gesture of sitting in the garden with a book, but her eyes had a way of straying to the beech tree and her thoughts of going past its protruding branch to the paneled room beyond. It was at lunchtime that Wilkins solemnly handed her a note, without a word. She opened it and read: "Darling, I have become worried about Mama's sudden bolt to London and have decided to give chase and see what she's up to. I will see you as soon as I return, and miss you every minute I am gone. Destroy this *billet doux*, like a good soulmate, and keep looking. Love, Kenelm."

She could not like to destroy her first *billet doux* ever, but folded it carefully into her pocket. His other order was followed, but a continued search revealed nothing new. At half past two she took Charles down to the Dower House again, and learned a piece of news of gratifying significance.

Malone greeted her at the door. "He's finely done it," she said. The tone was severe, but the Irish face was soon split wide with a smile.

"What, has Kenelm been here?"

"No, Berrigan has, and left not fifteen minutes ago. He's screwed hisself up to the sticking point at last. Your sister's engaged. Come in and she'll tell you all about it. The lad's an awful laggard and a smoke fiend, but *partis* don't grow on trees after all, and she's took him." Then she turned to Charlie and chucked him under the chin. "Back again, eh? You've got your eye on one of the kitchen girls if you're anything like your half brothers. Liberties and rakes, every last one of you."

Rorie had already darted into the saloon to congratulate her sister. "You have beaten me to it again!" she said, throwing her arms around Marnie to embrace her on her good fortune.

"Oh my dear, it is *much* too soon. We are not to be married for ages, but John insisted we become engaged now so he can forbid me to accept the Gypperfield mansion from Ken. That is the only reason he asked me. I know it well."

"Of course it is! Men are all alike. They would do anything to keep us from acquiring a property and becoming independent. Having snatched the mansion away from you, he will now be stuck with the unpleasant duty of housing you himself."

"Not for six months at least," Marnie said.

"Unless Kenelm moves into Raiker Hall before that time, in which case you will have the honour of sharing this roof with Clare. I give you two months on the outside."

"You are to stay with us," Marnie informed her sister. "I have already told John I cannot part with you."

With some notion that she might be making a match herself, Rorie did not immediately mention leaving. "We'll see," she said contentedly.

"I wonder what Kenelm will say," Marnie ran on. "He will think it too soon, I fancy, but then it will save him buying the place for me, so he won't object too strenuously. I shall tell him today, if he comes."

Rorie knew he would not come that day, but did not like to reveal how she knew, so said nothing. "*He* will be making a match too before long," Marnie continued. "He is seen every day with Lady Alice, and appears very particular in his attentions. It is an excellent connection, just what one would wish for him. I will be happy to see

142

him settled down. The fact of the matter is, Kennie was always just a bit of a philanderer."

"He was only sixteen when you knew him," Rorie pointed out, anxious to defend him.

"That sort of behaviour does not improve with age, my dear. Quite otherwise. I think I might have had an offer from him myself if I had half tried. But I would not want to be married to a man I had to worry about seven nights a week. I had some fear he might take it into his head to set up a flirtation with *you*. I am glad he has not."

"Whoever makes the sad and sorrowful mistake of marrying that one will have her hands full," Malone added. She stood at the door listening, but did not come in. "There is Millie broken-hearted in the kitchen now she's found out who he is, for he let on to her he was a gypsy. Let it be a lesson to her. You don't tell a sausage by its skin, and you don't tell a gypsy by a black hide. Come along, then, you two." She turned to herd the children upstairs, allowing the sisters a private discussion of Marnie's match.

Rorie took Charles back home for dinner and spent a quiet evening before the grate alone, looking a pathetic sight, but with her heart full to the brim of plans and memories. Life had been slow to get started, but was rolling along with a vengeance now—romance and adventure enough for anyone.

Clare returned the next day around noon. Inquiries as to the success of her mission were met with evasive replies. "Yes, it went well. I foresee no difficulty," she said, but Rorie thought she looked worried. There were fine lines etched around her eyes, a little pucker between them.

"Did you have time for any shopping, Clare?" she asked. It was unusual for Clare to go to the city and come home empty-handed.

"No, I hadn't time for that. What minutes I had free from business I spent at the house. It is in a sad state after being empty a year, and even when Bernard was alive, there was little done to keep it up. Your sister is not much good along those lines."

"I took Charles down to the Dower House for a visit twice. I hope you don't mind."

"No, no," Clare said absently. She hardly seemed to be listening.

143

With nothing to be gained from her in the way of news, Rorie was happy to be getting home again, with someone to talk to other than a child and the servants. Berrigan came for dinner. The conversation did not indicate in the least a lengthy wait before their marriage. Already he had been to see the minister, and spoke of a honeymoon to Brighton. As established fiancés now, John and Marnie required no token chaperonage, and Rorie felt more than ever that her presence was not wanted. She went early to her room to reread her note, and to wonder how soon she might expect to see Kenelm in person. She was a little dissatisfied with the manner in which her sister and Malone spoke of Kenelm, as a philanderer, but that would stop once they knew of her engagement. An engaged man would settle down, and she would be formally engaged as soon as he got back. He meant to marry her, she assumed—he would not speak of her giving him an *answer* unless he was to ask the crucial question.

He came the next day just after luncheon, and with the excitement of an engagement to be told him, no one mentioned his own absence the day before, nor did he. He was less than ecstatic—thought it too soon perhaps, as Marnie had feared he would, and as she knew very well herself it was. After a quarter of an hour's discussion, he asked Rorie to go out for a drive with him.

She felt his first words would be about his trip to London; she was prepared to hear that before he asked her the question of more importance. But what he said was, "What will become of Mimi?"

The question surprised her. "She will live with her mother and John, of course. Why do you ask?"

"I don't want him adopting her. She is a Derwent. I think Marnie is rushing into this without giving it enough thought. A widow usually waits a decent two years."

"She has known John for years, and with the likelihood of Clare's joining us, it is best for her to have some other plans made."

He shook his head as though trying to rid his mind of the matter. "It would be better if she waited. That would be the more proper way—but then *she* should know more about it than I. Who am I to be giving a lecture in propriety? Oh, I have some news to tell you. I think it will surprise you."

144

"I am dying to hear what Clare was up to. She wouldn't tell me a thing."

"When did she get back?"

"Around noon yesterday."

"She was not in London at all."

"Not in London! But she said she was at the London house. Where was she, then?"

"I have no idea. I inquired at the house. Oh, discreetly! I drove around to the stables. One of the old grooms recognized me, but her carriage wasn't there and hadn't been. Nor had she."

"Impossible! Could she have stayed at an hotel?"

"She *could* have—but she told you she was at the house."

"Yes, she definitely said so. And why should she stay at an hotel when the house is open and half-staffed?"

"I checked the larger hotels, the Pulteney and the Clarendon. I couldn't get around to them all, but I doubt she would put up at any little hole-in-the wall establishment. She made no secret of the trip. There was no reason to hide her presence. No, she wasn't there at all, and where the devil was she? That is what I must discover."

"You'll never find out."

"Induction—that is how we must set about it. Now, let's see where she stands. She has Rutley dead and buried—again. They put him back in this morning, poor soul. She has me, whom she hopes to pass off as him. And she has the emeralds. What would she be doing? She wants to prove I'm Rutley. Who could help her?"

"She's already been to Rutley's, and in any case it wouldn't take her two whole days to see them. They live right in the village."

"There's Nel Rutley, Horace's mother. Would she have been to see her?"

"What would be the point? If Horace were with his mother, surely his grandparents would know. They raised him. He is more to them than to her, I should think."

"There was that fellow with Horace at the time of the horse trade, the business that caused Horace to bolt off. Carson was the name. Elmer Carson. Also local people. It wouldn't take her days to find them. No, it must be Nel she went to see. I can't think of anyone else. Horace could be there without his grandparents' knowing it. I doubt Nel

145

can even write, and the distance would seem great to folks without a carriage or much money. Nel was a poor girl, not bright. She is somewhere in Hampshire. The time is about right. Clare could have made it with a fast team and driving late into the night. I think I must go see Nel Rutley myself."

"How would you find her?" Rorie asked.

"Her parents must know her married name, and where she lives. If Clare found her, I can find her."

"We don't know that is where Clare went. It may have had something to do with the emeralds. Selling them, to get rid of them. or trying to get them back."

"You're slipping, my sweet, just when I had some hope you were developing into a useful partner in crime, too. She'd never risk selling them at such a crucial time, with the chance that they would pop up and be traced back to her. She's too sly for that. And how could she hope to recover them if she sold them years ago? They'd have been broken up and disposed of long ago? It has to do with Rutley—it must."

Rorie sat thinking about this, and could not feel it at all likely that Clare had gone to visit Nel Rutley. "If Horace is dead, what Clare wants is silence. Why should she go to his mother, to stir up talk and gossip?"

"That is the stumbling block," he said, thinking deeply. "I can't think when I'm driving. Shall we pull off the road and take a walk into the meadow?"

They did this, and after walking into the meadow a hundred yards, sat on a large rock to cogitate. It was comparatively private here, private enough to do more than discuss Clare's trip, in Rorie's opinion, but today Kenelm's mind was on business. He wrinkled his brow and sat with his chin in his hand.

"I find myself coming to an utterly absurd conclusion," he said at length, lifting his chin to look at her.

"The whole thing is absurd. I can't see that Clare would go muddying the waters when she knows perfectly well Horace Rutley is dead. Surely she isn't thinking of trying to get Nel to say you are her son?"

"That occurred to me. That is possible, but then Nel was not very close to Horace. The Rutleys in the village would be the more likely people to use for that scheme. No, if Horace were indeed dead, she would have no reason to go

146

to Nel, but if he were alive—if she weren't sure he is dead, I mean—there is just a bit of a chance he might have gone to his real mother for help, being unable to come home here because of the trouble he was in when he left. She couldn't take the risk that he might turn up, giving the lie to her theory that I am he. She went to Nel Rutley to see if she has heard anything from her son, and that means she doesn't know he's dead. Doesn't know for a fact that the body in the grave is Horace."

"Who else could it be?"

He tossed up his hands. "Anybody. Any six foot black haired gent with good teeth who happened along eleven years ago and fell into a scrape of some sort with Clare. She's involved with it. She didn't turn a hair to see my uniform and rings on that body. She knew what to expect."

"Could it be that it was Nel's husband and not Horace Rutley who got rid of the emerald necklace for Clare? It is a pet theory of Malone's that Horace was shot for trying to diddle her over the emeralds."

"How could she use Nel's husband? In Hampshire, miles away. How would she know him? She's from Somerset herself, quite a distance away, and while Clare may not be quite top-drawer socially, she is a step above a fellow who would marry a halfwit who had already had a child. She would not have been a friend of such a man."

"If Nel is helping Clare in some way, she won't help you—won't tell you anything."

"I must go to Hampshire all the same and see what I can uncover. Like Malone, I have my own foolish theory. I don't think Nel is working with Clare. She went on a hunt for facts, and I'll do the same. I'll hint to Nel I mean to help the boy, and so I shall, too, if he's alive. Papa always paid him an allowance. No doubt Clare said the same thing."

"You are hunting mares' nests," Rorie told him, shaking her head.

"I'll find one, too. There's nothing to be done here in any case. The case will sit gathering dust for weeks yet. I have time to burn. But it is a pity I must dash off on *you* again so soon," he said, turning to face her. "I really have to get this business cleared up, though. I shall console myself that absence makes the heart grow fonder, and to overcome the possibility that my being out of sight will put me out of your mind, I shall write you, if I may. Would that be all right, considering we are now confirmed soulmates? You can keep my *billets doux* this time too, if you care to. You got rid of the other?"

"I was very careful of it," she answered vaguely. It was at home pressed between the leaves of a book, where Clare would never see it.

"Good. We wouldn't want Clare stumbling across it, and finding out that we are in league. Your relationship to her is too valuable. I sometimes feel I ought to cultivate her myself. The fact is, she is in the devil of a bind. I can almost pity her. I wonder if she would be interested in coming to terms—amicable terms. If Rutley is alive, she must be on the anxious seat. What do you think?"

"I doubt she would come to terms with you."

"She used to like me well enough." He laughed. "Very fond of Papa's younger son."

Rorie had already felt a little twinge of dissatisfaction at his mention of her relationship with Clare being valuable, useful. The dissatisfaction turned sharply toward anger at his last remark. "Odd she should have been attracted to a youth of sixteen years," she said.

"She was only twenty herself when she married Papa. And a very appetizing armful she was, too. Well, she was about thirty years closer to my own age than Papa's. The marriage was ludicrous. There is only five years' difference in our ages, and it seems less now than it did at the time. Once people are grown up, a few years is nothing. I am six years older than you, Aurora. I hope you don't find me quite an old man."

"No, but when the *man* is five years younger . . ."

"I was precocious," he said, and turned to her with a teasing smile. "All the ladies found me so. Quite the blade of the county. Of course I am all reformed now, ready for the bit and bridle."

With Clare now added to the list of Lady Alice and the others, including Marnie, who thought she might have had him had she tried, Rorie could not feel he was one hundred percent tamed yet. And never a mention of her giving him any answer today.

"Now don't sulk, Aurora," he said, taking her hand. "I mean to leave this afternoon. Shan't see you for a few days, and I don't want to carry off with me the image of

148

you in a pique. I like to leave my ladies smiling." Ladies, in the plural, she noticed.

They walked back to the curricle and returned immediately home. "I'll drop down to Rutley's in the village and see if they can give me Nel's direction. See if Clare preceded me there too. That would be substantiation of my theory. Meanwhile, if Clare makes any overtures of friendship, don't turn her off. It would be interesting to discover if she had a beau at the time of Horace's leaving. Of course she won't mention that, and you'd better not ask her directly. I wonder if Wilkins would know. That's an idea. I'll send a message with Sam from the tavern."

He walked her to the door and stepped inside. The hallway was deserted, and before leaving he leaned down and kissed her cheek. "That will have to do you till I get back," he said, teasing. He regarded her a moment, then the reckless gypsy smile slowly formed on his lips. "Oh, but it won't quite do me," he added, and began to draw her into his arms, just as Malone came trudging down the stairs.

Her hands went to her waist, and she stood glaring. "And just what do you think you're up to if a body might ask?" she demanded of them.

"You amaze me, Mrs. Malaprop, that a woman of the world like yourself doesn't recognize an embrace when she sees it," Kenelm told her, unperturbed but for the annoyance of having his embrace interrupted. He didn't quite let go of Aurora either, but merely loosened his hold a little.

"Embroglio is more like it," she charged, well pleased with this grand near word.

"That's truer than you know, ma'am. Do you intend to turn voyeur on us, and observe my leavetaking?"

"It's yourself as does all the voyaging. I've no mind to go and mix it up with a bunch of Moslemites. Where are you off to?—as you mentioned taking your leave."

"What would you expect of one of my kidney? I am off to pay my respects to another woman, naturally."

"You're a brass box if there ever was one. Bernard never talked so impudent to me."

"He was always a bit of a slow top. Were you about to leave, Malone?" he asked, a trifle impatiently.

"I'll give you just exactly one minute, and then I'll come and fetch her, so you'd better get busy." The warning given, she went into the saloon and stood counting off the minute on the long case clock.

"I hope she is equally strict with all your callers?" Kenelm asked, and put the remainder of his minute to better use.

Malone, true to her word, was back in sixty seconds, and promptly showed Lord Raiker out the door. "You've got a bit of explaining to do, missie," she said to her charge when he was gone. "Haven't I been warning you what he's like?"

"Yes, when you are not advising me to make up to him," Rorie answered pertly.

"It'll be yourself with red eyes next. I gave you credit for a little self-respect. You shouldn't be holding yourself so cheap. It's marriage or nothing."

"I wish you would not make a great to-do about it. He is a connection, after all."

"Oh ho, *connection*, is it? I don't see Mr. Berrigan taking such a warm leave of you, nor did I ever see Bernard, nor anyone else that calls himself a gentleman. And he as well as saying to your face he was running right back to Lady Alice, the villain. What he sees in the vixen is beyond me. Is he sweet on you then?" she asked, unable to contain her curiosity longer.

"Yes, Malone, I think he is, and I am very sweet on *him*, but nothing is settled, so pray don't feel obliged to run to Marnie with tales of what you have seen."

Malone regarded her with narrowed eyes. "I hope you know what you're about. He shouldn't be taking such liberties till it *is* settled. He's as sly as a weasel, that one. Still, he's been abroad, and don't know the right way to behave, I suppose. You'd oughta teach him. Who is he going off to see now?"

"It has something to do with the case," Rorie answered unhelpfully. Malone thought she didn't know, so didn't press her. She was in two minds about Kenelm. Certainly she considered him an indelible *parti*, but a little raffish for one of her girls. He'd bear watching, and there was little dearer to her soul than keeping a sharp eye cocked on her girls, unless it was spying on their beaux. To find the latter had run amok was heaven.

Chapter Fourteen

The two days of Kenelm's absence were full days for him, and not entirely without incident for Aurora. Lady Alice came fishing for news at the Dower House, as Raiker was fishing in Hampshire. It was clear from the outset she had no idea where he had gone, and becoming clear too that she realized she had an archrival in Aurora. She dropped a million hints that she and Kenelm were more than friends, even using the word "soulmates," which caused Rorie's brow to rise and her heart to sink. He had shown her all his treasures from India, discussed his plans for them, had given her a shawl and a book on Indian customs. She had been teaching him to waltz. "He *adores* the waltz, and how well he does it! He says he would have come home sooner had he realized it was the style now to hold all the young ladies in your arms with public approval. He is teaching me to drive his curricle. What fun we have, out every day. He took *you* out once I think, Miss Falkner? He mentioned he ought to do so, as you are Lady Raiker's sister."

"Yes, more than once," Rorie answered, not telling the number.

"He is very concerned about behaving properly, doing the right thing. He would want to show you respect, because of family."

Rorie began to wonder how he ever found a minute to

pursue his claim to Raiker Hall. It was a highly unsatisfactory visit, leaving Rorie drained and doubtful of her lover's constancy. He had not behaved properly at all, despite several mentions that he would like to. What he was doing was making up to all the girls, as hard as he could. He wrote no letter, despite saying he would do so. Malone, who had audited Lady Alice's visit from behind a chair, took to dropping a setdown every time she opened her mouth. At least she did it when they were alone. "When the cat's astray he's bound to play," she would say cryptically, and peer at her victim for a reaction. "He's using *you* to be rid of Sally McBain. I wonder who he's found to be rid of *you*."

When morning of the third day came and still he had not returned, Malone began saying he must be having a good success with the woman he'd gone to call on, and she'd get the backhouse boy to chip her off some ice to make up cold compresses for the eyes. She did hate to see a girl with red eyes. The only saving note was that the two of them were alone. Marnie was a good deal absent. She went frequently to Berrigan's home to see what it would require in the way of improvement before she would move in. She was so wrapped up in her own concerns that she took little note of Rorie's decline.

It was just past noon of the third day, and there was some fear the cold compresses would be required, when he came back, big with news. Malone took up her post behind the chair, which caused Kenelm to suggest a drive, in spite of a brisk wind and gray skies, presaging a storm.

"Rutley's alive," he said, the minute they were beyond Malone's ears. "At least I think he is. He *was* alive well past the time that body in my uniform was buried, in any case. Nel had a note from him, just one, in America. She showed it to me. Had it right out in the parlour, which gave me a good idea Clare had been there before me. It was dated five years ago, and in it he complained of conditions there, spoke of coming home as soon as he could save up the money. Five years—he is likely back long ago, but I am convinced the mother hasn't heard of him since. She sounded genuinely worried."

"You don't actually *know* Clare was there, though?"

"I am morally certain of it. The Rutleys in the village

152

confirmed she had been back to them, enquiring of Nel's name and address. She didn't know the husband's name at all, so we can eliminate him from the case. Nel wouldn't be likely to have a five-year-old note on the mantel if she hadn't had reason to show it very recently."

"What about the husband? What was he like?"

"He's the one I'm worried about. As shrewd as a horse dealer, which he is, incidentally. I think he married Nel only because Papa gave her a settlement. He hinted they could use more. There is no love lost between the two of them, but if Clare was there, she has bought their silence. He said nothing. I finally asked outright, and he denied it, but with a very guilty look. I'm glad I went. I don't know exactly what she's up to, but I was right in thinking it had to do with Nel and Horace. She's trying to find Horace—that must be it. The thing to do now is to keep a sharp eye on Clare, follow her if she goes to London or elsewhere again. If she leaves, it is to get hold of Horace, that's certain. The husband may have told her something. I don't actually believe he did. I don't think he knows, or the information would have been for sale."

"Surely what she wants at this time is to keep Horace well out of sight."

"Yes, and she'd be more sure of doing it if she knew where he was. If he is floating at loose ends, he might make an untimely appearance in the village and her story is shown to be false. He can read, and it has been in the papers that I am back. They made a big thing of it in the London papers. There were some articles in the *Observer* when I was there. The next thing we have to discover is the identity of the gent in the grave."

"Wilkins could tell you nothing?"

"Nothing helpful. He gave me some names, but they are both very much alive. Neither one fits the remains that wears my uniform either. Someone who wasn't missed or spoken of locally as missing. An outsider, in other words. He'll be hard to trace. I'm tempted to have a go at Clare. She apparently thought it worth her while to challenge me, but she must know now after the questioning and all that I mean to have my rightful place. And with Horace alive to worry her, she might be happy to come to terms. She can no longer twist me round her thumb, if that is what she was counting on."

153

"Did she use to?" Aurora asked, her heart plunging.

"Lord yes. I was putty in her hands. I had never seen anyone so beautiful and sophisticated—worldly. She was like a creature from some rarefied atmosphere to me. Well, a green boy of sixteen who had had no doings with anything but country girls. And Papa's wife. There is nothing like unattainability to make a lady more desirable. The feeling of sin and damnation that hung around her was irresistible. No, I shouldn't say that. You'll think me worse than I was. I resisted, coveting her every second of the day. What a fool I was! Things are different now, however," he said in a cold voice. "I know what she is now."

"Did you love her?" Rorie asked.

"Madly. An apt word—I was insane, infatuated, and too inexperienced to recognize her for the well-dressed trollop she was. I've met many of her sort since. You must think me an utter ass, but I was a child, and she played with me, my feelings. She is an unconscionable woman."

"She's still attractive," Rorie mentioned unhappily.

"Not to me! I find her physically repellent. Oh, I know she has kept her looks well. Objectively I know it, but there is too much between us now. However, she *is* Papa's widow and my stepmother, whatever else she is, and I ought perhaps to give her the opportunity to unburden herself. It would save a deal of bother and disgrace, very likely. Best to wrap the family laundry up in clean linen when it is possible. She is a woman. It is a man's instinct to protect a woman in trouble."

"She won't even see you."

"She'll see me, if she's approached in the right way," he said confidently. "I haven't had the stomach for it till now. Now I begin to feel I have enough of a grasp of the situation to deal with her. You haven't seen her during my absence? She doesn't know about us?"

Rorie was feeling there was nothing to know, except that he had made a fool of her. He had not written the promised letter, nor ever asked for her answer, ready now for several days. "No, Lady Alice called, but not Clare."

"Sally called? What did she want? She was not pleased with my leaving."

"Just a social call."

"Hanley with her?" he asked, with what could not possibly be jealousy, though she tried to imagine it was.

"No."

They were soon back in front of the Dower House. "No point in going in with Malone to clock me. I didn't write you, by the way."

"I noticed."

"I started to, but realized the futility of it. I would be home before my letter, to tell you in person how much I missed you. Very much," he said, with a searching look into her eyes, and an intimate smile. But that was all the affection she had from him before he was off again, to call on his beautiful stepmother, with whom he used to be madly in love.

For two days nothing more was seen of him. Rorie remembered his asking whether Clare knew about them, and assumed he stayed away from her to lull his stepmother's fears. And why should he do that, unless he was carrying on a flirtation with Clare? Marnie, busy with her own plans, didn't notice his absence, but of course she did notice when she saw him drive quite openly into the village with the dowager Lady Raiker, and she was furious.

"He's back after her!" she said, coming in from a drive with Mr. Berrigan, her eyes flashing with anger. "Driving with Clare beside him in his curricle, and he has left Dougall's house. Has taken a suite at the inn, to be closer to her no doubt. Or more likely Lord Dougall kicked him out. It is said in the village he has been twice at Raiker Hall. Oh, it is *scandalous!* John is furious."

"It has nothing to do with John," Rorie said, trying to trust her lover, trying not to be angry and jealous, but it was a very large order.

"Nothing to do with John! Indeed it has. Raiker is my brother-in-law, the same name. To see him *courting* his stepmother—for that is *exactly* the impression left in the village—is infamous. And they had Charlie with them."

"The brute!" Malone said. "Oh, the unnatural man. He'll be his little half brother's stepfather, and his mother's husband. He'll be his own father is what he'll be! It must be illegal!"

"Of course it is. He can never *marry* her," Marnie said. "And after he came here telling us he *hated* her. But he

155

always liked her. And he liked *me* pretty well too, I can tell you. We are not to see him again. John says we are absolutely not to let him in if he calls."

"I should say so, the abominable corruptor!" Malone agreed. "Oh, this is worse than the Bible. Solomon and Glocamorra is nothing to it. I've never heard the likes. It'll be an infamy throughout the land, and the sooner you change your name the better, my girl," she advised Marnie.

Rorie listened, silent, and began to perceive that Kenelm's behaviour was indeed seriously at fault. Even if he was only buttering Clare up to see what he could discover, the scandal he would cause was serious. It was ill-judged of him to do it.

"It is an outrage!" Marnie agreed. "And you may be sure Lady Alice won't stand still for it. He has lost her, such an eligible match in every way. Why is he *doing* this? Has he run mad completely?"

"You must see he is trying to get Clare to accept him," Rorie said. "*She* has been the stumbling block all along to his inheritance. For her to be seen with him in the village must mean she has given up opposing his claim."

"No such a thing," Marnie contradicted. "I wouldn't mind if that were it. She is not giving up her opposition. And what is *she* up to, to befriend him when she says he is not Kenelm? Her behaviour is even more bizarre than his, but she never could resist a handsome man, and hasn't had one for a long time."

"She's been man-hungry for a year," Malone told them. "Ever since Bernard's death she's been trying to act half decent, to give the devil her dues. But if she must break off her celibating, it's a shame and a pity she had to choose *him* to do it with."

"And to do it in public," Marnie added, sighing.

"If Charlie was with them, I can't think it was so horrid as you say," Rorie tried.

"Corrupting that young innocent is the worst of it all," Malone corrected her. "And never mind trying to defend the heathen. That's what comes of him going off to India. He's worse than a warlock. I wouldn't be a bit surprised to hear he's turned into a full-fledged Hindustani. He'll be worshipping holy cows and refusing to eat a bite of beef the next thing we hear. Bernard would turn over in his grave if he were alive to hear of it," she finished off, too excited to find any inconsistency in this opinion.

"Charles is his half brother. It is only natural he should want to see him," Rorie tried again.

"He didn't have to see *her* with him," Marnie pointed out. "I can't think what Clare is up to."

"Hedging her bets," Malone decided. "If Kenelm *does* win—and I suppose he will, for he's Raiker even if he is a rake along with it—she's got him in her pocket, set up for life. It'll be her ends up in Gypperfield's mansion, mark my words if it ain't."

"*That's* what she's up to!" Marnie exclaimed, and her pique knew no bounds. That John had forbidden her the Gypperfield mansion was a bitter pill, made palatable only by her marriage, but if Clare were to get it, even a marriage was not sufficient to coat the pill.

"They're a fine pair is all I've got to say," Malone declared, then went on at once to say a deal more in the same vein, as did Lady Raiker. Rorie was wilted with it all, and went above-stairs alone.

Kenelm had told her he meant to see Clare, but she had not foreseen his doing it so publicly or so often. Nor had she foreseen how little she trusted him. She felt a strong suspicion that if he befriended Clare for his own ends, he enjoyed doing it. And of course she was curious to know how far the befriending went. "Courting" was the word used by Marnie. But then he was said to be courting Lady Alice too, and he did not love her in the least. He admitted quite shamelessly he was using her and her father's prestige. He used everyone—Marnie to bolster his claim, Millie to discover information. Had he used herself too? She had let him into the house to search it—had helped him. Yes, it was only after he discovered that she alone continued on terms with Clare that he had showed any partiality for her, that he had kissed her, and spoken of soulmates. The same word he used with Alice. He never had followed up on his question of whether she had found her soulmate. Hadn't even written her as he had said he would. Never had made any public gesture or announcement of his relationship with her. He was as wicked as they said, and she shouldn't see him if he called. She *wouldn't* see him. She had that much self-respect. And if she met him in the village she would cut him dead.

She pulled his unsubstantial *billet doux* from its hiding place between the leaves of the book, read it one last time and consigned it to the flames, as he had asked her to in the first place. He didn't want any evidence of his philandering. He needn't worry. There'd be no evidence, including red eyes.

Chapter Fifteen

The next day word came to the Dower House that Kenelm had not been to Raiker Hall that day, but had been in the village again with Lady Alice. He was not giving up that helpful connection, and apparently Sally had not quite given up on him either. Another message was also received, this one in writing holding an invitation to a party at Lord Dougall's two nights hence. Marnie received it and sent a reply back with Dougall's footman accepting for her sister and herself. Of course, Kenelm would be there—that was inevitable, as Lady Alice was still after him. This, however, was no reason why the ladies should miss one of the better parties of the season.

Along with their Irish mentor, they laid plans for their reception of Raiker. "*I* mean to cut him quite openly and publicly," Marnie said with relish. "I shan't say so much as good evening to him, and I hope you will do the same, Rorie."

"I wouldn't satisfy him," Rorie answered. "I shall say, 'Good evening, Lord Raiker,' and not another word."

"Maybe that would be better," Marnie said, considering this alternative. "Malone, which is more degrading—not to speak at all, or to address him *very coolly* as Lord Raiker?"

This important matter was given deep thought, with

Malone's head resting on her bosom while a frown furrowed her brow. What she desired was to say nothing, and still call him Lord Raiker very coolly, but as this was impossible, she decided on total silence, and was voted down by her rebellious charges. They agreed on "Good evening, Lord Raiker," and spent a few minutes practicing up the chilliest tone possible in which to deliver their slight. They would say not a word throughout dinner if it fell out that one of them drew him for a partner. They would refuse to stand up with him to dance if he asked, and would remain deaf to any questions or speeches he might put to them. They looked forward to a marvelously interesting evening. Rorie hadn't realized losing a beau could be so entertaining. Her entertainment was of course heightened by the hope that he would override all her ill manners and ill humour and force his attentions on her in some dark and private spot. She quite expected it, but was less certain that in some corner of his heart he still harboured a regard for her when she chanced to see him that afternoon while gathering flowers in the meadow. She thought the gypsies were gone. Nothing had been seen of them for a few days, and she wandered close to the woods, not actually entering.

She didn't have to. Through the trees she saw a red dress, and recognized it for Ghizlaine's. She had seen her once in the village, and would have recognized her in any case from having observed her with Kenelm. She was with him again. They were not embracing quite so passionately this time, but sat together on a fallen tree. Kenelm has his arm around her shoulder, patting it tenderly, while her head rested on his chest. The familiarity of it was worse than a kiss—and the woman was married, too! He would draw the line at nothing. Rorie was so angry she was nearly sick with it. She went home at once, and that evening Kenelm came to call on her. Not Marnie, but herself he asked for when he came. She sent down a message that she had a headache, and after listening to Marnie and Malone deride "the gall of the creature" for an hour, she had. But still her hopes were high for the party the next evening. He hadn't quite forgotten her. While making up to Clare and Lady Alice and the gypsy, he had at least come to call on herself, for what it was worth.

Both the ladies dressed with particular care for Dougall's

party the next evening. They wished to be outfitted in the highest kick of fashion to insult Lord Raiker. Marnie wore a blue gown and her sister went in her finest cream, with dark-blue velvet ribbons. Their eyes glittered with excitement, and their colour was high.

"Mind you don't let the heathen be making up to you," was Malone's parting shot. She had Mimi at the doorway with her, to give her a glimpse of her mama in her party splendour. Each lady thought the warning was directed at herself, and both replied in reassuring tones that indeed they would not.

Before ever the carriage got a mile down the road they had a new topic to discuss. Clare's brougham pulled out of the drive of Raiker Hall just as they approached it, headed in the direction of Dougall's place. The girls looked a question at each other. "She can't be going there," Marnie said.

"Oh no," Rorie agreed.

"She's driving down the road to see who is going. She is out spying," Marnie decided. This seemed very Clare-like, but when the brougham turned up the curved sweep to Bradhurst Hall, the explanation seemed inadequate. Even Clare would not be so brazen and ill-mannered as to drive her carriage to the door of a party to which she had not been invited, to spy out the guests.

"She's got Kenelm to get her invited," was Marnie's next opinion.

"Would Lady Alice be so gullible?" Rorie wondered. It was beginning to seem the credulity of other ladies exceeded even her own where Kenelm was concerned.

"He'd talk her into it. Lady Alice is very eager to see his claim settled so that she might get on with marrying him. Much chance she has if Clare has got her talons into him. I have a good mind to turn the carriage around and go home. What do you say?"

"An excellent idea," Rorie agreed at once. She really didn't feel up to a party as overendowed with intrigue as this one promised to be, yet she would be sorry to miss it.

But still the carriage advanced along the drive toward the front door without any command being given to the driver. With a curiosity so rampant as to be consuming her, Marnie had no real thought of missing the party. The reception accorded Lord Raiker had been canvassed a

161

dozen times. Both ladies had their cool "Good evening, Lord Raiker" at their finger tips, but they had never foreseen the necessity of preparing a strategy vis-à-vis Clare. "Shall we speak to her?" Marnie asked as they dismounted from the carriage.

"I must," Rorie decided. How could she suddenly cease speaking after having spent two nights under her roof so very recently?

"See if you can get anything out of her," Marnie warned. "I'll speak, but coolly."

Clare was no real problem. She was no more interested in pursuing any friendship with the ladies than were they with her. The dowager's reception of them could hardly have been cooler had she rehearsed it as they had Kenelm's. She nodded her head a slight fraction of an inch and parted her lips in a vestige of a smile. Lady Alice received Clare with every polite attention. She showed her a seat beside Lady Spencer, who disliked her less intensely than most, and sat on her other side herself, giving confirmation to the suspicion that she was working in harness with Kenelm. Certainly he had put her up to this, and though she resented being used by him herself, Rorie found she resented even more that he chose to use Lady Alice. The other neighbours looked surprised in the extreme to find themselves under Lord Dougall's roof with the dowager Lady Raiker, but were too polite to do more than stare. No one cut her.

When Lord Raiker was announced, he showed not the least surprise and no chagrin to find his stepmama sitting in state in the Rococo Saloon. He bowed formally to her, and did it before bowing to Marnie and Rorie. They didn't even say, "Good evening, Lord Raiker," but only looked and tried to refrain from glaring. Marnie did not quite succeed, but Rorie felt she simulated polite uninterest rather successfully.

Lord Raiker was soon into conversation with some neutral parties on the far side of the room, and did no more than glance occasionally at all his female relations and connections. None of them exhibited any interest in him, including Clare. The sisters were nearly bursting with curiosity wondering if Clare and Ken had had a falling-out. At length, Marnie could contain her curiosity no

162

longer. "Lady Spencer has just left her seat. Go and sit by Clare, Rorie, and see what you can discover."

Rorie proved disobedient, so Marnie went herself. "Well, Clare, what a surprise to find you here," she said icily.

"I decided to come," Clare replied. "One cannot isolate herself forever." She wished to give the idea that her not being present would have no other explanation than declining the invitation.

"We quite forced her into it," Lady Alice said brightly. "Lady Raiker has kept to herself long enough. It is time she came out of hibernation."

She just glanced at Marnie at this speech, managing to convey a little of her distress at the haste with which the other widow had doffed her crape.

"I hear you have had a call from Lord Raiker," Marnie said, ignoring Lady Alice completely and turning full toward Clare.

"Lord Raiker? Ah, you mean the man who *calls* himself Kenelm," Clare replied, and laughed lightly. "What a bold rascal he is, but *très amusant*. I decided to let him call to see what he has to say for himself, to confirm my belief that he is *not* Lord Raiker, as some of you feel I acted too hastily. An impostor, of course. I become every day more sure of it, but he has at least the manners of a gentleman. He has been telling me some interesting tales of India. Whoever he is, he has certainly been in India."

"Of course Kenelm has been in India," Alice said at once. "He gave me the loveliest shawl, and a book. I saw all the things he brought back."

"He also gave Rorie and myself a shawl," Marnie said, not to be outdone.

"Perhaps he is a shawl merchant!" Clare laughed. "He gave me one too."

"Odd you let him call, if that's the way you feel," Marnie charged.

"What would seem sane at such a bizarre time?" Clare asked. "*You* let him call, and I had certain questions I wished to test him with."

Across the room, Kenelm saw the chair beside Rorie vacant, and advanced toward it. "I trust your headache is gone," he said, bowing and taking up the chair, unaware of the plans for his reception.

The rehearsed speech was inappropriate to the question,

163

so Rorie altered it, but still used the cool tone. "Quite gone," she said, then looked away.

"This affair will be enough to bring on another. I feel twinges myself," he remarked. "I had strong doubts she'd come. She has let me call twice, and once rode out with me, using Charlie as a chaperon, but I am not having much luck getting her to acknowledge me. I think I might as well give it up."

"Pity," Rorie said. He was beginning to look at her with the dawning of realization that she was in the sulks.

"I have to see you," he said next. "I found out something of interest. Can I take you home tonight?"

"No. I came with Marnie. We must return together."

"Berrigan is here. He'll take her home."

"Then I shall go with them."

"I'll call tomorrow," he said. Not a question—a statement.

"I'm busy tomorrow," she said hastily.

"Aurora, I want to tell you something *important*," he said urgently, a little angrily, and glanced around to see if the present circumstance allowed him enough privacy to tell her now. "I spoke to Ghizlaine."

Spoke to her! Is that what he called it? "How nice for you."

Lady Alice felt she had wasted enough time on Clare and went to join Kenelm, whom she did not like to see alone with Rorie. Their privacy ruined, they ceased talking to each other altogether, and Lady Alice soon had Raiker's ear. Rorie suddenly found a dozen things to say to a country squire on her other side. She became quite lively on the subject of rain and weather, and the likelihood of a good harvest. There was no danger of the conversation's flagging when she got him started on sheep. She sat through a lecture on the care and breeding of a proper flock till dinner was served, and went away not a whit more informed than when she had begun, for while she nodded at Squire Norman, her ears had been cocked to try to hear Alice rattle on to Ken.

At dinner, Raiker was placed between Lady Alice and Clare, so that the other two ladies didn't have to worry about speaking to him, but they worried considerably to see him in animated conversation with his stepmother. Despite her reputation as a man-killer, she appeared to be only toying with Kenelm. The advances were all on his side. She only smiled sardonically half the time, in a condescending way. Marnie and Rorie were seated across the table from one another. A good discussion would have to wait till they got home, but they more than once exchanged a furious glance, full of impatience to put into words all their frustration. A trio of fiddlers and a pianoforte player had been called in to provide music for an informal dance after dinner, and with this entertainment to hasten their port taking, the gentlemen sat for less than an hour at the table before joining the ladies.

Marnie would not dance. Daring enough to take off her last remnant of crape and become engaged only a year after her husband's death, she would not dance yet, but before going to the card room with John, she urged her sister to keep a watch in the dancing parlour. As Clare, too, chose to play cards, it was unlikely there would be anything to report other than that Kenelm opened the dance with Lady Alice—unexceptionable behaviour to all but Miss Falkner.

He came next to Aurora, who said in an arctic accent that she was already taken for the dance, and by judicious advancing to a new group the minute a dance was finished, she contrived to have a partner before he got to her for the next two dances as well. On to her tactic, Raiker stood out the next dance, and as its end approached, he walked onto the floor and took her arm. "The early bird gets the worm," he said unceremoniously, and led her off.

Before he got to the edge of the floor he was demanding an explanation. "May I know why I am being treated like the lowliest untouchable? It looks so very odd for my own family to be treating me disdainfully. Have you been seized again by the notion I am Horace Rutley? Search your mind for another question to try me."

"No, I know who you are," she replied, and refrained from adding, "and *what* you are."

"Is it my public venture into town with Mama that has you in the boughs? I thought it an excellent thing. I talked it over with Lord Dougall, and he saw no harm in it. I never dreamed she'd go on pretending she thinks I'm Horace after that. She knows I'm not, of course. In private she as well as admits it, and I think if I keep after her I'll get at the truth. I must, Aurora."

165

"No one's trying to stop you."

"What's the matter? Why are you acting this way?" he asked. They had reached the side of the room, and stood off a little from the crowd. He looked at her, frowning, regarding her intensely with his black eyes. "Don't you trust me?"

She no more trusted him than she'd trust an assassin. Hadn't she seen him with her own eyes in the meadow with Ghizlaine only yesterday?" I trust you to use anyone you think can help you, but you no longer require *my* help. You've got a direct line to Clare now. You don't have to bother buttering me up, Lord Raiker. We don't intend to challenge your claim, Marnie and I. We know you're who you say you are. We just don't approve of you."

"I see," he said stiffly. "In that case I shan't pester you again. You make yourself perfectly clear, ma'am."

"I trust I do," she replied, more stiffly still.

He turned to leave, then turned back, his eyes flashing with anger. "But I will say before I go, I think it extremely petty-minded of you. Others who are less to me than you and your sister haven't stuck at my behaviour. If Lord Dougall and his family can support me, I find it hard that Bernard's wife and her sister cannot. I won't forget this."

"Neither will we! Don't think to threaten us with withholding your largesse. We don't want anything from you. We never asked for anything."

"You *implied* you *loved* me! What sort of love is this?" he asked in a voice becoming loud, a voice that betrayed anger.

"The sort you will understand very well, I think. Inconstant," she snapped back, and turned to flee before she should lose the last vestige of composure. As she left, she bumped into Clare, come to the parlour to observe the dancing. Her curiosity could not let her leave the room without seeing how Raiker and Clare acted in this meeting. She stopped at the door and looked around. Kenelm was looking after her, but when their eyes met he turned quickly away and turned to Clare. "Mama," he said in a voice of delight. "Shall we dance?"

"I do not dance, sir, but if you can behave you may get me a glass of punch," Clare replied.

"I shall behave exactly as is expected of me, ma'am. Very badly," he cautioned playfully, then offered her his arm. The two walked away toward the refreshment table. Rorie went off to a private parlour to compose herself before going to the card room. She would return no more to the dancing room. The parlour had a French door leading to the garden, and to cool her heated brow, she slipped out and looked about for a bench. Her legs were trembling from her encounter. She sat down in a dark corner and hated the world. Had she done rightly? It was surely wrong of Kenelm to accept Clare publicly. He ought not to be seen with her when she had declared herself against him. Even more, Clare ought not to be seen with him. But that wily woman always had an explanation for everything. She was testing him, confirming he was Horace Rutley. Lord Dougall did not disapprove of Raiker, so perhaps she was wrong to, but she did hate it. It made her so angry her breath became short to see it. To see Clare smiling at him with an invitation in her eyes, and to see him return the smile. It caused severe doubts as to what had gone on between them before Raiker left. Kenelm was young then, might not have known better than to be led astray by an older, scheming woman, but he was no child now. He shouldn't do it. For five minutes she sat, then arose to return inside. Before she got to the French door, she saw someone enter the room and decided to return inside the house by a different way. She stepped quickly away from the door to avoid being seen, but from the shadows she took a peep inside, and saw the new-comers to be Kenelm and Clare. Each held a glass of punch, and after they had entered, Kenelm reached behind him and closed the door, bestowing a meaningful smile on his partner as he did so. She had seen that smile before. Rorie wished with all her heart she could hear them, but to see was really more than enough. They were talking with the greatest animation and familiarity. They did not touch, but every smile, every gesture bespoke the nature of their conversation. Clare's eyes were used in a manner that required no literal translation. There was coquetry in each flash from them, and it was returned by her partner. It was all soft smiles, teasing and playfulness, and it was disgusting when one considered all the circumstances.

Squaring her shoulders, Miss Falkner took the decision to enter the way she had come out, to let them know they had been observed, in spite of the carefully closed door.

She walked in, looked from one to the other and said, "Sorry to disturb you. I shall be sure to close the door after me, as I see you wish privacy."

"Thank you," Kenelm said, regarding her with satisfaction.

"Too kind," Clare flung after her departing back.

She was in no mood for a party after this, and went at once to ask Marnie to return home. They went together for their wraps, but a swift colloquy between them determined a course of action that would send Rorie home alone in their carriage, while Marnie remained behind to see what transpired, and to return later with John.

Malone heard with unrestrained joy that Clare had been there, and had been singled out for attention from Raiker. "What did I tell you? A regular sneak in the grass, that one," she adjured. "And don't think he limits hisself to you ladies neither. Millie saw him in the forest with a gypsy girl, making up to her a mile a minute. Upon my word, I come to think the fellow's unbalanced. He ought to be restrained."

"He's not mad. He knows exactly what he is doing. He has kept poor Lady Alice dancing on his string, but I trust we are not so gullible."

"And to think you let the heathen sully your lips. You want to rinse them off with carbolic acid, missie. You'll take an affection."

"Oh no, Malone. I am cured of my affection."

"That's the spirit. Never fear a thing. I'll say a decade of my beads to St. Anne and we'll find you a new beau in jig time. Did you make any headway with young Hanley at all?"

"Yes, I had a dance with him."

"Good for you. You're not so besodden as I feared, for there's no denying the Hindustani does have a tempting eye in his head. Still, Lord Dougall's son ain't to be sneezed at, even if he is only a younger son, and as dull as ditchwater."

"I am not tempted by Raiker's eyes."

"Well, I am," Malone said baldly. "Or would be if I was twenty-five years younger, which I ain't, thank the good Lord. He'll worm the truth out of that she-devil, see if he doesn't."

"She is not tempted either," Rorie was forced to confess.

168

There had been no sign of weakening in Clare. Flirtation definitely, but no capitulation. She was as cool as a cucumber, to judge from the scene watched through the window.

"How about Lady Alice? He still has her in line, you say, after running right out her door and putting up at the inn. She's easily cozened."

"No doubt she trusts her soulmate," Rorie said.

"St. Anthony could save us a deal of time if he'd get busy and find the emeralds. I've said a decade a day to him without a bit of results. Maybe I ought to make a novena."

Miss Falkner was familiar with the roster of saints called on in Malone's emergencies, and accepted this means of help. She sipped her cocoa till Marnie arrived some time after twelve to give them the end of the story.

Clare and Kenelm had both stayed till the party's end, had been seen talking together in a perfectly friendly manner, but had left in their individual carriages. "Kenelm had the nerve to hint if he might call on me tomorrow," she said. "Didn't come right out and ask, you know, but said he would like to see Mimi. I told him I always take her to church on Sunday, and he was welcome to *look* as much as he liked. He's quite shameless, but I think we gave society a fair idea what we think of him," Marnie declared, satisfied with her behaviour.

"You both did good. I'm proud of you," Malone complimented, in a rare mood of approval, and to reward them she had fresh cocoa made up, and let Aurora stay up for another cup.

Chapter Sixteen

Lord Raiker did not come to the Dower House after his Turkish treatment by the ladies, and from what they could discover, he had also ceased going to Raiker Hall. He was deprived of even a glimpse of his little niece on the Sunday, as she had a sore throat, and her mama kept her home from church. In the afternoon, John Berrigan came to call, as he did every day now, and Rorie had not even the child for company, as Malone had chucked her up into her bed to cosset her and tell her she wouldn't let her die. Life was becoming so tedious in the light of Marnie's new engagement that Aurora was beginning to think quite seriously about going home. She would not have to bear Marnie company after she was married, would be a definite nuisance in fact. With Kenelm taking her at her word and not pestering her (by his presence at least), there was no question any longer of a match with him, and it was preferable to go home than to stay and watch him marry Lady Alice. Sally was having clear sailing these days.

To have something to do with her afternoon, she decided to take flowers to Bernard's grave. It used to get a fresh batch every couple of days in good weather, but with the widow thinking so much of her new bridegroom, the old was rapidly sinking to the bottom of her thoughts, sometimes to be forgotten for a week at a stretch. She picked a large bouquet, but from the home garden, as she knew now the gypsies were still in the woods. She walked slowly to the family burial ground, trying to find some pleasure in the warm sun, the wild flowers, and the doleful somnolence of the surroundings. Kenelm disliked a graveyard, but Rorie always had liked one. It was so peaceful; all problems vanished here. Here was only the last reminder of those who had passed through life and gone on, perhaps to something better. She read the inscriptions as she walked along, shaking her head sadly as she always did at the number of small white stones marking the graves of infants. Bernard's plinth was ahead, ranged beside his father's. Till she got past the marker, she didn't realize the marble stone was hiding a live man as well. Kenelm stood beside it, staring at the ground with an impassive face. He looked up as she approached, not smiling to see her, but regarding her cautiously. She didn't say a word. She put down her flowers, stood with her head bowed for a moment, then turned to leave.

"Aurora, don't be so childish," Raiker said harshly, and walked quickly after her. "You've given me my lesson. Slapped my fingers like a bad boy for doing what you disliked, but I must say you might have told me *before* I did it. I told you I was going to see Clare, and you didn't say a word against it. I find it hard that you should turn on me after I did it, when you didn't ask me not to when we discussed it."

"We didn't discuss it. You told me you were going to see her."

"You didn't ask me not to."

"Much good it would have done! You didn't say you were going to parade yourself through town with her and Charlie. You didn't say you were going to go calling on her, and make a spectacle of yourself at a party, flirting with her."

"I wasn't *flirting* with her. I was trying to find out what she's up to, and I think I would have done it too, if *you* hadn't acted so foolishly. I haven't been back, haven't seen her at all since the party. I feel in my bones I'm doing the wrong thing. I could get it out of her, but as you dislike it so much, I have given it up."

"She's turned you off, in other words."

"Dammit, you make it sound as though I were courting her. She's my stepmother."

"Is she?" she asked in a sneering way, to show him what she thought of this relationship.

"Her credentials are not in doubt. I can only assume you have reverted to mistrusting mine."

"No, sir, it is not your *credentials* I mistrust."

"You have no cause to mistrust anything else. Certainly not my feelings for you. I love you. I haven't shown you in the right manner, I expect. I haven't had the advantage of a very proper unbringing, leaving home when I was so young. I don't know how to court a lady in the approved way. I am not a slow learner, however, and if you would direct me, as I have asked you before to do, I would not be long catching on to it." He stood looking at her with an uncertain, unhappy but withal impatient face.

It was impossible, but the daring, reckless, elegant gypsy was showing signs of discomposure. She was so astonished she could only stand looking while he continued talking, surprising her more with every word he uttered.

"I don't have any experience with ladies—real ladies, I mean."

"Lady Alice will be surprised to hear she is not numbered amongst the elect."

"There is no courting done there. Not by me, at least. I am becoming an adept at *retreating*. Now why are you so *angry* with me? Is it only my seeing Clare? I won't see her again. Or is it something else? What ought I to have done, or to do? Should I have gone to see your father—have written him, perhaps? I have been wondering if that was what bothered you, that I hadn't observed the usual formalities. You should have told me, if that's what it is."

That no sort of public gesture had ever been made of course had been subjected to scrutiny long ago by Miss Falkner. She concluded she had been no more than a useful flirt, and to hear him state in dead earnest his intentions were not only honourable but seemingly firm and immovable was heart-lifting news.

"You forget we never discussed marriage," she pointed out. "How could I ask you to write my father in that case?"

"Surely when you allowed me to make love to you it was understood between us. Things cannot have changed that drastically since I have been away. Ladies and gentlemen do not behave as we have toward each other unless there

172

is a commitment." He looked at her closely, frowning slightly in uncertainty, and she came to realize that he was actually at a loss as to where he stood. He didn't know how to conduct a polite courtship in his own country. Kissing gypsies and housemaids he obviously knew well, but with a lady he was at sea.

She had to smile at his ignorance, and he became even more confused. "I've done something wrong. I know that, but I didn't mean to," he continued earnestly. "I hope you haven't taken the idea I wasn't serious. I am. I want to marry you. I have dreamt for years of a girl like you. My manners are disgusting to you, no doubt, after my long exile. I am a near barbarian—I was told *that* often enough by Bernard before I left, and my female acquaintances since then have been demimondaines and worse. I can learn to be civilized if you will give me a chance."

"All right," she said magnanimously, "but the first thing you must learn is that you must not be making up to any other ladies. That is very much frowned on in polite company."

He grabbed her two hands and kissed them, then looked up. "Is this all right?" he asked, fearful of offense after being so lately forgiven. As there wasn't a living soul for a half mile around, and particularly as his ardour pleased her so well, Miss Falkner permitted it to be acceptable.

"Where can we go to talk?" he asked.

"What's wrong with here?"

"I hate graveyards. Let's go to the meadow."

"I hate meadows," she answered, teasingly. "I always see something I don't want to when I go there. Usually you carrying on with Ghizlaine."

"Ah no, that was the forest," he reminded her, and they began walking off.

"Not the second time. A few days ago I saw you with Ghizlaine, and though you were in the forest, I had an excellent view from the meadow."

"You saw that, did you? If you hadn't been on your high ropes, you would have had an explanation long ago. I tried to tell you at the party, but you gave me such a cold shoulder the words froze on my lips. And very odd it looked, to see Clare on good terms with me while you and Marnie all but cut me dead. I can't imagine what everyone thought. Yes I can, though. They'll think she's proved I'm

173

an impostor, and I have made some arrangement with her."

"Never mind that. Let me hear your explanation for sitting with your arms around that old gypsy."

"Young gypsy—she's only twenty-six."

"Already married twice. To say nothing of affairs on the side. Well, what is your story?"

"The story, and it is pure hypothesis, is that it is Ghizlaine's first husband that lies in the grave wearing my uniform. Not my rings, though. I talked them into leaving my rings out. Not that I could bear to wear them after what they've been through, but in a few generations it will only be an interesting story. Ferdinand—that's the gypsy's name—disappeared at the same time as Horace. The gypsies were camped in the forest then, you remember, after attending the gypsy fair. It wasn't their usual time for a visit. Anyway, Ghizlaine's husband vanished. He was tall, the right size and right hair. Well, it is more than hypothesis, I think. I got the picture of the man in Clare's sketch pad—you remember the one you showed me. I had Wilkins get it for me. It is very handy living at the inn. Sam Friggins is my contact with Wilkins, and I sent a message with him. Wilkins purloined the pad for me, and I showed the picture to Ghizlaine. It is her husband. He disappeared at the right time, and she still misses him, too. I was only comforting her when you saw me. Perfectly innocent. Clare knew him, of course—*vide* the sketch. Horace was still alive long after the burial, so it seems to me the corpse is what remains of Ferdinand. How he got shot and into my uniform I haven't discovered. Ghizlaine knew Lady Raiker was sketching him. It was done quite openly, apparently, with chaperon and all at Raiker Hall, but this is not to say there weren't more private meetings later on at night. Clare was doing a series of character studies and paid the gypsy to pose, so Papa would have suspected nothing. The gypsy returned in the late afternoon from his last sketching session but went out that night, to do a spot of poaching, he said. He never came back. He was a bit of a wild buck. The gypsies were afraid he'd been caught out in some illegal act, something more serious than poaching, I mean, and never reported him missing. He might have been stealing or pursuing some servant girl. I quizzed Ghizlaine about the emeralds, but she claims no knowledge of them. I can't tell whether she's telling the truth or not. She lies, but skillfully. He *might* have been actually after the necklace—or Clare. He clearly never got them in any case. I think if I went back to Clare and dropped a few dark hints about Ferdinand, I might frighten her into a confession. May I?" he asked, with a quizzical look.

Rorie shrugged her shoulders.

"This is a *discussion*. I am not telling you I am going. I hope I learned my lesson, but it would be interesting to hear what she has to say. I think I must go. End of discussion. Speak now, or forever hold your peace."

She had a pretty good idea he would go whatever she said, and of course she wanted him to force Clare's hand if he could. "No objection," she said.

Already he appeared to have forgotten he had asked for permission. "I'll call tonight and let you know tomorrow what she says. No headaches, please. You didn't have one at all, did you?"

"Of course not. There is a useful bit of information for you, savage. When a lady says she has a headache, it means she is in the sulks with you. A bouquet of flowers will often cure the headache, or a well-worded *billet doux*. Of course if you have caused a *migraine*, you might require a stronger cure."

"What is the cure for migraine?" he asked with great interest.

"Nothing less than a proposal of marriage. You want to be careful where you go causing migraines. And it must be in writing, the proposal, without instructions to destroy the evidence."

"Would you like your evidence in writing? I have no objection in the least, but would require a written answer. It is more likely *you* who will try to get out of it. Is it quite settled we are to get married, incidentally?"

"No, it isn't."

"What?" he asked, surprised.

"If you want a lesson in civility, sir, let me tell you, an offer of marriage is not to be thrown *incidentally* at the tail end of a discussion."

"But we were discussing a proposal."

"I still don't like the *incidentally*."

175

"Fussy!" I'm not at all sure a blonde is worth the bother. Shall I write to your father, or speak to Marnie?"

"Marnie is in charge of me, temporarily."

"And *I* am in charge of Marnie, temporarily. Till she marries John, I am the head of her family. I give myself permission."

"No, really, Kenelm, that is not at all the way to go about it."

He laughed, shaking his head at her gullibility. "I shall write to your father. Marnie might say no, the mood she's in."

"The mood she is in, she'll write to Papa advising him to withhold his consent. Let me talk her around. Wait a few days."

"You won't let her talk you out of it?" he asked, perfectly serious.

"No."

"Promise."

"She won't try to, so long as you don't buy Clare the Gypperfield place."

"How did you know she was hinting for it?"

"Call it woman's instinct. How should she do so, if she doesn't think you are Kenelm?"

"She knows who I am, and is beginning to give thought to a bargain with me. Ferdinand will lessen her bargaining power considerably. Well, here we are at your favourite meadow, and no sign of Ghizlaine. Whom shall I kiss instead?" he asked, regarding her with an anticipatory light in his eyes.

"Don't feel obliged to ravish some woman every time you walk through the place. It will be at our back doorstep when we live at the Hall, with dairymaids and berry pickers abounding."

"It sounds promising, but in the meanwhile the only ravishable woman I see is you." He reached out his arms toward her, but she stepped back quickly. "Indian manners again on my part?" he asked, surprised at her withdrawal.

"Hindustani manners, to quote Malone."

"I didn't find the Hindus so hard to get an arm around. You let me before, at the Hall."

"I didn't *let* you. You caught me unawares," she explained, finding it difficult to train this wayward suitor.

176

"Look at the fox!" he said suddenly, pointing over her shoulder. She looked quickly back, and found herself gripped firmly about the waist.

"If it's 'unawares' you require, I am happy to oblige," he said, and kissed her full on the lips, long and hard, before she knew what had happened.

"That was *not* a very nice trick," she said, blushing with pleasure after a long embrace, during which she made no effort to free herself.

"*I* thought it was nice. I may not be up on my manners, but I will require no help in dealing with a woman when I manage to get her alone."

"Try to remember I am a lady."

"*You* try to forget it, sweet. Only in company need you be a lady. When you are with me alone, you are a woman. *My* woman," he said possessively.

Miss Falkner, though she was thrilled at his high-handed manners, felt obliged to object to this bald assertion.

"I am a confirmed Indian in that respect," he told her. "Puttee, suttee and all the other Indian ee's. You had better take good care of me. When *I* go, you hop up on the funeral pyre and go with me."

"And if I go first?"

"Then I would break all the rules of the game and jump up and be roasted with you. I don't want to go through life without you."

She was well enough pleased with this ardent nonsense that she let him walk with her right to the gate, and thus laid herself open to a lambasting from Malone.

"I saw you," the Irishwoman said. "You've fallen under the Hindustani's spell again. You were holding hands with him! I'll get out the lye soap. If this keeps up I'll tell your sister."

"I'll tell her myself. I am going to marry him," Rorie said defiantly, expecting a rolling pin to fall on her head, for Malone had picked one up lest the Hindustani invade the house.

"You never mean it!" she exclaimed. Miss Falkner had the unexpected pleasure of seeing Malone speechless for a full ten seconds. "You've never got an outright *offer* from him!"

"Certainly I have, and I have accepted."

"Accepted! I should say so! Whoever thought you'd get him, and Lady Alice trotting as hard as her legs will carry her after him! He's the handsomest rascal that ever drew breath. I could love him myself without too much prodding. Why, Berrigan is nothing to him, a great lump of a lad with no sparkle or dash or conversation. Give me a good rascal any day. *We'll* keep him in line between the two of us."

"I thought you hated him?" Rorie asked, confused.

"I hated to see you mooning after him when I thought he was up to no good. He's the kind there's no getting over. Are you sure it's marriage he means?"

"I don't expect he is writing to Papa about a *carte blanche*," Rorie answered pertly.

"*Carte blanche* is it? It beats me how the young ladies nowadays get away talking like a parcel of light skirts, and never a word of retromand. Is he writing your father?"

"Yes, when I tell him he may."

"Think you've got him under your thumb, do you? He's too big a man to stay put, missie. Give him a good long leash, and never let him off it, nor out of your sight."

"I trust him," Rorie said, and wished she could mean it, for in truth she was not happy that he was going to see Clare again. But he would do whatever she said, and she should support him.

"You're either a fool or slyer than you've been letting on. Why is he going back there?"

"To try to scare her. He wants to brush the family scandal under the rug, where it belongs."

"The rugs will be a foot off the floor in that case," Malone advised, and walked away smiling happily.

Chapter Seventeen

Raiker waited till after dinner before going to call on his stepmother. He wanted ample time to prepare his bargain. At eight o'clock he was handing his curled beaver and malacca cane to Wilkins and being shown into the Blue Saloon, where Clare sat alone with a piece of writing paper on her lap and a pen between her fingers.

"Good evening, sir," she said, smiling tolerantly and offering her hand.

Kenelm raised the fingers to his lips and kissed them, before taking a seat beside her. "Good evening, Mama," he said with a sardonic smile.

"No need to call me so, sir. There is no one here to listen to your performance this evening."

"Which led me to hope you might give up your play-acting, Clare. It's time you and I got down to hard bargaining. You know I'm going to insist on my full rights. My boyish behaviour in the far past misled you into thinking you might make a fool of me again, but it is not the case. I took full blame for *your* misdeeds the night Papa caught you laying siege to me, but really, you know, when you accused me of beating him and him of shooting me in the back, you went beyond forgiveness. That was your undoing. I came prepared to be generous to you, to forgive and forget. You were young yourself in those days, and life

179

with an old man cannot have been easy for a lusty young girl, but you brought it on yourself, and I *do* think still you might have looked for more eligible lovers than your husband's sons. I don't know how you hoped to prove I am not Kenelm, when all my friends and relatives have recognized me. You thought they would not do so, perhaps, but you were wrong. It's time to give up the game, and strike the best deal with me you can."

"Do you think so, Mr. Rutley?" she asked, smiling serenely.

"Another mistake, claiming I am he, when we both know the man is alive, or was five years after his mysterious disappearance, in any case. A bit of a problem for you if he should turn up, *n'est-ce pas*?"

"You have turned up, Mr. Rutley. The problem would be if Kenelm turned up, but I don't think it at all likely, as he is dead and buried."

"Well then, let us say a problem if the gypsies began instituting enquiries regarding the disappearance of Ferdinand."

Her eyes narrowed, and she shifted uneasily in her chair. "Who is this gypsy you speak of?"

"How unreliable that memory of yours is! The one you sketched so prettily in your book just before Papa died. The one who is dead now, and buried in the unmarked grave wearing my outfit. Tell me, Clare, for I must confess those two points continue to nag. Why my uniform, and even more curious, why my rings? I thought that they, like the emeralds, you would have squirreled away for a rainy day."

"I don't have the emeralds!" she said quickly.

"I think you must, Mama. *I* don't have them. They were not buried with my rings and Ferdinand, and they are not among the heirlooms. Ergo, you have them."

"You overlook Horace Rutley," she said.

"Now this is more like it. You are beginning to talk sense."

She looked at him, a short, calculating glance, and he went on blandly. "No, no, I have not swallowed that nonsense that poor old Horace has the necklace. I mean the good sense of not bothering to pretend you think I am Rutley. You're at a standstill, Clare. Your plan has failed miserably. I can almost admire your nerve in attempting

180

it, but it has collapsed; let us get down to terms. How much for withdrawing your objections to my claim, and for returning the emeralds? I am pretty well-to-do, even beyond my inheritance. Business prospered in the east. You won't want to remain here when all this is over. I suggest Tunbridge Wells again, where you landed Papa. I'll give you sufficient to set yourself up in the height of fashion. You might even do better than a baron this time. You're not quite gone to seed yet." He looked her over assessingly, and she bristled.

"No time to show your hackles, my girl. There is still Ferdinand to be explained away. Better for you to do it privately. I am not eager to see my stepmother in the dock for murder. If you can give me a plausible story, I'll be quiet."

"Don't think *I* killed him!"

"You know who did. Let's hear it."

She sat a moment, drawing deep breaths and running her mind over a likely story. Events had turned out badly for Lady Raiker. She really had thought Kenelm was dead. Eleven years, and never a word from him outside of that card the first year. Dozens of Englishmen succumbed to fevers and liver in the east. Why couldn't he? It seemed hard that he should turn up on the *very day* she was presenting Charles as the lord, and herself as his guardian, with the estate and income in her keeping. She had hardly recognized Ken herself, and she knew him so very well, better than all the others who eagerly backed him up. She had had only a moment to make her decision, and had had to do it in a crowded room with dozens of eyes on her. It had seemed entirely possible that she might defeat his claim. There was the body in the grave pointing to him, and if that failed, there was his old infatuation with her to fall back on. But he had proved to the board of questioners that he was Kenelm Derwent, had proved impervious to her charms. She thought the worst that could happen was that she would be shown to be mistaken. She claimed no personal knowledge of the body in the grave. With her husband dead, she could impute any story to him without fear of contradiction, so that was all right. But now that the truth about the gypsy was known, she must reconsider. It had been a bad blow to find Horace Rutley not only alive, but possibly even in England. He

181

had disliked America, had spoken of returning. It seemed every step she took sank her deeper into trouble, till at last she nearly wanted to unburden herself. But she must move cautiously. She had to say either his father or Rutley killed Ferdinand. The father was dead, which weighed the scales in his favour. But then Kenelm had taken deep offense at her other charge of his father's having shot anyone in the back. Shooting a thieving gypsy would not be as bad as shooting a son, presumably, and might not it be wise to protect Rutley, to have that little edge over Horace in case he too showed up? On the other hand Rutley must be held accountable for stealing the necklace, and it would be easier to have only one culprit.

"I think it must have been Rutley," she said. "Of course, I wasn't there myself. Your papa *said* it was Rutley."

"Oh my poor father!" Kenelm cried, looking at her with a totally disbelieving eye.

"It happened in this way. I had been sketching that gypsy fellow, as you have apparently learned. From one of the girls in the caravan, I presume?"

"That's right." He smiled. "It was her happening to mention to me that I reminded her of Ferdinand that made me twig to it."

"He was here one evening when I was going to a party with your father, wearing the Raiker emeralds. I saw him looking at them, admiring them."

"What was he doing here at such an hour?"

"I had been sketching him, and they were feeding him in the kitchen afterward. He was leaving just as we came out of the house. That same night, about an hour after we had returned from the party and the emeralds were put in the vault, Rutley came to see your father. He was in trouble over that horse-trading deal, and wanted money to go abroad. Your father went to his study to the vault. There was a movement in the corner, and the gypsy made a run for the window. Rutley had a gun with him, and shot him as he tried to jump out."

"I take it the gypsy wasn't wearing my uniform at the time?"

"Gracious no! That was your papa's idea. He was afraid the gypsies would come back looking for him and dig up the grave some dark night. He thought if they saw an impressive uniform they would take it for someone else.

And the rings were put in as an added inducement. Even if they came early enough to recognize the dead man's face—and of course your father hoped they would not—he thought they would content themselves with stealing the rings. They couldn't very well report the death if they had stolen those rings."

"A posthumous bribe. It doesn't sound like Papa, Clare. Are you certain that wasn't your idea?"

"I may have thought of it. Your father discussed it with me. I don't really remember where the idea came from initially."

"Did it occur to you that early on they might also lead people to think the body was mine, should it be necessary to dig it up?"

"Certainly not! Both your father and Bernard were alive and well. I never foresaw the day *you* would be Lord Raiker."

"Just a happy accident, then. I daresay it weighed with your thinking you could palm the body off as mine. But you really should have made sure Horace was dead before doing it."

"He won't come back. We discovered after the gypsy was buried and Horace gone that the emeralds were missing. The gypsy had been after them, we assumed. Why else would he have been there? But he didn't get them. Didn't know how to get the vault open, I suppose. He must have spied around till we returned from the party, and seen your father put them away, for he was in the right room at least. But they were gone, and it must be that Horace pocketed them in the confusion of finding the gypsy here. Your father had the vault open to give him money—it would have been possible for him to slip them out."

"I hope you're telling the truth. I mean to find Horace, if I have to comb the world to do it."

"Well, as far as that goes, we don't *know* he took them. The gypsy could have got them out of the vault and closed it up again, passed them along to an accomplice who got away while Ferdinand looked around to see what else was worth taking. They were gone. That is all we know, and the rest is assumption."

"You know damned well Horace hasn't got them, in other words, and are beginning your explanations early.

183

You've told me this much, Clare. Why not be honest and give up the necklace while you're about it?"

"I don't have it, I tell you. It's gone."

"You know perfectly well I hadn't taken the emeralds, as I'd been gone six months. Knew all along I was Kenelm. How do you excuse that series of lies? Your foolish story that I attacked my father, and was shot in the back by him?"

"Oh, Ken, your father was dead and I truly believed you were too. What was the harm in telling a little story about two dead men, just in the greatest privacy? I didn't recognize you at all when you came back. You have grown so tall and handsome, so manly. You were only a boy when you left. How should I recognize that boy in you? Kennie used to like me, and you were so cold and hard. I had to do something to secure your brother's rightful inheritance. I could see at a glance you were so determined and clever and so handsome all the girls were ready to back you, whoever you were. I took you for some reckless adventurer, an impostor trying to seize the Raiker title and fortune from Charles. I had to make a very strong effort not to fall in love with you myself, for you *did* remind me a *little* of Ken, whom I always was fond of," she added with a speaking smile.

"Cut line, Clare. I'm older than sixteen now. You thought I'd changed enough that you might pull it off, taking into consideration my outfit and rings on the gypsy's body."

Clare looked closely, and decided he was not to be won by flattery. She assumed a wounded face, and remained silent to see what he would say or do next.

"Now where do we stand?" he asked himself. "Any loose ends, barring the emeralds? We've accounted for the body in the grave and the outfit on him, for your thinking you could oust me, and for Rutley's remove. Ah yes, my letter to Papa. What did you do with it?"

"There was no letter received, Ken. But the post from such an outlandish place as Karikal, anything might have happened to it. Why didn't you write again?"

"I don't recall mentioning that I wrote from Karikal." He looked at her with a triumphant smile. She opened her lips to offer some explanation, then closed them again. "Obviously you would have kept any other letters from me as well. Ah, one other detail. The grave—what did you do

184

with the Jenkins baby formerly occupying the spot?"

"Your father mentioned something about disliking having a bastard child who was not family there. He wished to have it moved—sent to the mother's own parish—and chose that time to do it, I assume."

Kenelm lifted a brow at this, mentally jotting down one more point for further consideration. "You must rescind that infamous story about Papa shooting me," he said.

"How can I do so?" she asked.

"Claim it was the delirious ramblings of a man *in extremis*. As I am alive everyone knows it to be a lie in any case. Say I have convinced you of my identity, so you have concluded Papa was delirious. You might dilute the story in stages. You will know how to do it better than I," he added with a satirical smile.

"I could say I only had it of Joe Miller," she suggested.

"Excellent! There is no one like a dead man for a witness. But I hardly have to tell *you* that. If only we could know Horace is dead, what a lot of worry you would be saved, eh, Clare? But I give you fair warning, if I find him freshly murdered, you won't get away with it. And I'll find him. Better get busy watering down tonight's story."

He arose, bowed punctiliously, and said, "Goodnight, ma'am. I take it my brother is already tucked up? I want to see him next time I come. If you're thinking of getting rid of him, I will be happy to take him on. He might be a bit of an impediment to a match at Tunbridge Wells."

"Leave my son! He is all I have left of your father."

"Nonsense, you have *me*, Mama. And the emeralds, temporarily," he said with a wicked grin.

"And what am *I* to get out of it?" she asked.

"You have your widow's allowance. If you can bring yourself to part with the emeralds, I'll throw in five thousand. Otherwise no deal."

"There's no profit in it for me, in other words."

"Try to think of something other than money, Mama. I could stir up a hive of trouble for you if I told who is in that grave."

"What you would stir up is a deal of scandal for your father."

"Ah, has *Papa* killed the gypsy now? Who will he take into his head to murder next? I thought we were to let Horace have the honour."

185

"Five thousand, and forget the emeralds," she said.

He regarded her levelly for a minute. "No," he said at last. "I might have, had you told the truth. Care for another version of this ever-changing story?"

"I've told you the truth."

"No, Clare, you haven't even told me a convincing lie. You have only confirmed the facts I knew when I came in here. I knew the body was the gypsy, and I knew Horace was alive. I still don't know how Ferdinand died, but I'll find out. This is your last chance to unburden yourself."

"I've told all I know."

"I think not. Now what I suggest you do, Mama, is to think of little Charles, and think of Bridewell as an alternative to Tunbridge Wells. You will find prison even more unpleasant than the Dower House. No company but females, for one thing! Well?"

"Twenty-five hundred," was her answer.

"Not a red penny, bitch," he said ruthlessly, and as he had her on the run, he left her to stew in her juice.

Her first move when he left was to dash for the sketch pad in the studio, and find it gone, and then to curse herself for not having gotten rid of it. Her second was to consider the safe-keeping of the emeralds. But he would never find them. They at least were safe. Her third thought was of Horace Rutley, and she could not agree more strongly with Kenelm that it would be better if he were dead.

Chapter Eighteen

In London, Horace Rutley had fallen on hard times. Having worked his way home from America two years ago, it was his intention to let his mother know he was safely back. He couldn't write her, or at least she couldn't read a letter, and it was too dangerous to have the vicar reading that he was back in England. From America, all the way across the Atlantic, he had risked it, but not from England. What he really wanted was to return in style, to give Nel a proper cottage with flowers around the front porch, and some chickens in the backyard. He could never go back to his grandparents, but he had always remembered the two visits he had had with Nel, as he called his mother. What a sweet thing she was, so easy to talk to. Never one to jaw and nag at him for a little spot of trouble or mischief. He was saving up all his money to buy a cottage to share with Nel, but an ostler didn't make much money. He should have better work—his Papa would be ashamed to know he was grooming horses, he who could read and write. But an ostler was what he was, earning a pittance. By the time a fellow had a bottle of gin once in a while and a game of cards, it took forever to save up a couple of hundred pounds. He would have to go to Hampshire with Nel. Clare had told him he mustn't show his face in Kent again, ever, after the terrible thing he had done. It wasn't safe, and he never thought of going there. He hardly ever even thought of Kent anymore, but he liked it.

He had brushed down the last of the horses and fed them. The stalls were full, and if any more people came they'd be turned away. He washed and went into the kitchen for dinner. There was a paper being used to hold potato skins, and he glanced at it. He could read very well, though he didn't get much practice these days. The servant girls were always amazed at how he could read anything after having gone to school. He looked, and was surprised to see the name Lord Raiker, right in a big black headline. How they'd stare if he told them that was his father. No, brother. Half brother. The old man had died. He'd read about that after he came back. This would be Bernard. A cursed rum touch, Bernard. Never let on to recognize him when they met in the village. Kennie now, he was a bit better. He always smiled and looked friendly, looked as if he'd like to say hello, but didn't quite dare. He glanced at the piece, and made little sense of it. Then he pulled it loose from the rest of the paper and read it more closely, forming each hard word with his lips.

He was soon possessed of the fact that Bernard was dead, and somebody who might or might not be Ken was taking over. This was vastly interesting. All the chaps had asked Ken questions and thought he was Ken all right. By Jove, if he was, he'd lend his half brother a helping hand. Wouldn't it be something if Ken gave him back the allowance his father used to give him? Those were the good old days— money every quarter to buy a new jacket or take out a girl. But he was older, smarter now. He'd take his allowance and buy Mama a cottage and some chickens. He ate up his mutton and potatoes, and by winking friendly at cook, got another glass of small ale to wash it down with.

He was really awfully tired of working in the stables. He'd saved up twenty-five pounds, mostly in tips, in two years. It would take ten times that to buy Mama a house. She might be dead by then. Why shouldn't he go and see this man, see if he was Ken? His twenty-five pounds would buy him a jade, good enough to get to Kent, not so very far away. And if it wasn't Ken at all, he'd just turn around and come back. No harm in that. He'd go at night so nobody would see him. Clare said he mustn't be seen, or they'd put him in gaol, maybe even hang him. He felt his neck, and wondered if he dared to go. He could write. But he couldn't write very well. He wouldn't want Lord Raiker to see what a messy fist he wrote. He'd buy a jade and go in person. Got Cook to wash his good shirt and give his good jacket and trousers a brushing off, and go to call on his half brother. He was so excited that night he hardly slept.

The next morning early he got up and did his chores, and went around to get Jemmie Sadler to take his job at the inn for a few days. He had the great luck of buying a horse, a little crippled but he could be nursed along, from a chap right at the inn. He'd ridden it in from Sussex and wanted to be rid of it now he was in the city. He was on the road home before ten o'clock, but there was no hurry. He daren't show his face in the village before it was pitch dark. He got nearly forty miles the first day, and would have got farther, but the nag gave out on him and he had to walk the last ten miles. My, he was tired. All he wanted to do was curl up by the side of the road and sleep, but he had to take better care of his clothes than that. He shouldn't have worn the good outfit. It was covered with dust. He slept in the stable of the inn at Maidstone and went on the next day with his horse making an even slower pace, but at least carrying him. There was no problem of arriving too early. He was afraid he'd get there too late to call at Raiker Hall. Of course Ken would be at Raiker Hall. Where else would Lord Raiker be staying?

When he got in front of the door, all nice and safe—not a soul had seen or recognized him—he was hesitant to knock. There were lights on. The man was home and up, but was he alone? Shouldn't he go around to the back and approach his half brother via the kitchen? That might be more respectful, and he didn't want to be lacking in respect. He walked around to the back and tapped timidly at the door, just as he used to when Papa was alive. He didn't recognize the fellow that let him in, but he was decked out in the Raiker livery right enough. He recognized that. Wouldn't that be a soft job, though? Walking around in fancy clothes answering doors and whatnot, and getting more for it likely than he got for tending horses. He said with the utmost deference that he'd like to see

189

Lord Raiker, please, if it wasn't too much trouble, and would he be so kind as to ask if he might go up.

"Lord Raiker don't live here, fellow. What do you want him for?"

"Business," Rutley mumbled. Not here? Where the deuce was he? He worded this question and was told Raiker was putting up at the inn, and that Lady Raiker was still in residence.

"Clare?" Rutley asked bluntly.

"Lady Raiker," the footman replied with a sneer. But the name had caused the footman to wonder if he hadn't better tell her ladyship about the person. With all the strange doings of late, it was as well to keep her ladyship informed, and a wide-awake fellow might very well replace old Wilkins, whom her ladyship didn't like above half. "Just step in and sit down," the footman said. "What's your name, eh?"

Here was a poser. He dare not give his name. There might be posters up proclaiming him for the villain he was. "Just say an old friend," he answered, and sat down. Clare would be angry as the devil he'd come, but no one had seen him, and she would help him. Clare had always liked him, had sympathized with his position. She was a lovely girl, Clare, and so dashed clever she'd know what he should do.

The footman had the ill luck to run into Wilkins on his way to her ladyship, and was told with a supercilious sneer that he would "see the person" himself. Wilkins was very careful about all his employer's doings these days. But before he had turned to go, Lady Raiker was in the hall demanding to know what was going on. Wilkins tried to dissuade her from seeing the man before he had seen him first, but she was adamant. With a leery look at Wilkins, she sent him off upstairs to close a window shutter she imagined to be banging before having the man admitted.

Her strange behaviour had raised Wilkins' suspicions to such a height that he hid at the top of the stairs to get a look at the person, and found the likelihood that he was Horace strong enough that he was at considerable pains to get a note off to the inn at once. It was difficult to do, but he had a working agreement with the stableboy, who was always glad to pick up a shilling. His next business was to

190

try to get his ear to the door to overhear what went on between Lady Raiker and her visitor, but she was not to be outwitted by her butler, and took Rutley into her private little study and closed the door. She never spoke above a whisper, either. Wilkins couldn't distinguish a single word from her, and she kept hushing up Rutley so that not enough came through the door to make any sense.

Clare didn't quite know whether she was relieved or dismayed to see Horace Rutley. That he was here was of course a giant nuisance, but only think if he had met Kenelm before herself! Here was one blessing. Then too, she had now the opportunity to be rid of him for good before Kenelm could find him. She immediately set about doing this.

"Horace, what brings you here? You know I told you you must *never* come here again."

"I see in the paper Kenelm is back. Bernard's dead. Kennie always seemed a friendly fellow, what little I seen of him. I'm hard up, Clare, with my allowance cut off."

She discovered by careful questiong and requestioning that no one knew he was here but herself, and with this satisfactory knowledge, she began her campaign. Fortunately Rutley still found her attractive. "It is lucky for you you found *me* here instead of Kenelm," she said. "The man is changed, Horace. He has been in India amongst the heathens for years, and has come back a hard man. He hates you—would certainly have you turned over to the authorities if he ever discovered you here."

"He can't know what I did, unless you told him, Clare," Rutley answered.

"Of course I didn't tell him. There have been all sorts of things going on. The gypsy was dug up, and they have found out all about your killing him."

"How could they know that? You were the only one there. I only did it to protect you. You shouldn't have been seeing him alone, Clare. It ain't proper."

"I told you why he was there. He wanted money. I owed him money for posing for me, and he was in a hurry to get it. His poor little daughter was ill."

"You were kissing him."

"No, Horace, *he* was kissing *me*. Forcing his attentions on me, after I was kind enough to meet him that night. You did right to shoot him."

"Then they shouldn't hang me for it. You could tell them the truth, Clare, that I did it to protect you."

"Dear Horace, we must protect the family name. *You* are a Raiker too—the best of them, in my opinion. How proud you must be of your connection with the family. We don't want the family name dragged through the mud. Lawsuits, and there is no saying the judge wouldn't decide against you, even if you did the right thing. Lord Raiker has taken you in such strong dislike . . . he is looking all over for you, Horace. He was here this very day telling me so."

"What does he want me for? I only killed the gypsy. How did they know he was a gypsy, Clare? You had me take off all his clothes and put on Ken's uniform so no one would think it was a gypsy."

"So much has happened I hardly know where to begin. The emerald necklace is missing. Someone stole it, the gypsies I expect, but Ken has taken the idea you took it. You didn't, did you?"

"I never knew anything about an emerald necklace."

"I never believed for a moment you stole it. *I* know you are not a thief, but Kenelm won't believe it. I expect he is jealous of you, if the truth were known."

"Ashamed, more like."

"He has become abominably proud," she said, changing tack neatly. "It annoys him that you are a living testimony to his father's straying. He would like nothing better than to get rid of you."

Rutley began feeling his neck again, and looking about the room for a hiding place should Lord Raiker come in.

"We must get you out of here at once," Clare said.

"I have no money, Clare. You've got to help me."

"Naturally I will give you all I have. All I can lay my hands on, but it isn't much. You must go away, Horace. Far away. Back to America would be best."

"I didn't like it in America, Clare. It's devilish hot in the summertime and perishing cold in the winter."

"America is a huge country. You wrote your mama from Boston. You should go farther west. Far enough away that Kenelm can never find you. He plans to kill you. He says it in so many words."

"I'll tell him what really happened. Tell him I didn't take the necklace."

Clare swallowed nervously. "He wouldn't believe a word of it. He is become positively deranged. What we must do is hide you. Get you out of here at once, tonight."

"I haven't been off the road for two whole days. I'm too tired to go on tonight, and my nag is winded too. I'll have to sleep here tonight. Oh, but I can't leave in the daylight. I'll hide tonight and tomorrow, and leave the next night after dark. How much money can you let me have?"

"Enough to see you on a boat to America, and something to get you started. I'll scrimp and save, do whatever I must to help you, Horace. It is hard to have to part with you so soon, but I must not be selfish. Your safety must come before anything else."

"I don't like America," he tried, hoping for a reprieve, since Clare seemed still to love him.

"You will like it better with some money in your pocket. Open an inn—that will be something for you, my dear. You are too good to be an ostler. You are a Raiker. You must be the proprietor."

Horace considered this with some satisfaction. "I suppose I could do that," he said at length, not happily, but resigned.

"I'll go to the stable to sleep, shall I?" he asked.

Clare was in a quandary as to what to do with Rutley in the immediate future. She dared not let him stay in the house, with Wilkins nosing around, and the stables were even more dangerous. He would be out of her surveillance completely there. But he must be kept on the premises. She needed a little time to collect sufficient money to get him packed off far away, and wanted to talk to him a good deal more—to impress on him the necessity of never returning, never writing his mother, never daring to return here. With the house full of servants, she didn't know where to conceal him.

"I'm famished," Horace remarked, in the middle of her deep thinking. Yet another problem. She didn't wish to arouse the servants' curiosity. They had already seen too much. Some story must be made to satisfy them. Glancing at Rutley, she doubted they would recognize him. The footman who brought him up had been with her only five years, but if Wilkins were to catch a glimpse, *he* might recognize the man. No, getting food was too risky. Horace must go hungry for one night. It wouldn't hurt him—he'd run to fat. With her mind darting a dozen ways, she suddenly recalled the mount Rutley had spoken of, even now in her stable. That too must be gotten rid of. Horace and the horse must both be sent off to some safe corner to hide, and in importance she didn't rate one much higher than the other, except as a nuisance. Somewhere Kenelm would not discover them. After a rapid calculation of her options, Clare decided on the abandoned shepherd's hut, a good two miles away from the house and the road. Bernard had gotten rid of the small herd; so far as she knew, the place was now sitting idle. Not so sheltered as she would like, but off the beaten track, with some trees that could hide the mount. Horace must not light a fire or in any way attract attention to his presence.

She impressed these facts on him several times, and finally sent him off, still clamouring for food. He was not to return. She would go to him tomorrow at dawn with food, return later with money. At his last objection that he was awfully hungry, she relented, not through pity, but for fear he would risk going into town for a meal. She asked for some bread and cheese for herself, and with this meager repast, Horace was made to do.

The taking of food delayed his departure; in all he was at the house for over an hour. Time for the stableboy to get to the inn, and to discover that Lord Raiker was not there. It was believed he was visiting the younger Lady Raiker. The boy considered the message urgent enough to deliver it to the Dower House without first consulting Wilkins. There too he drew a blank. Raiker had been there, but had left, presumably to return to the inn. Becoming panic-stricken, the boy left the message in all its detail—that Rutley was at the Hall—then returned to the inn. He had taken the short cut through the fields, and must have missed Raiker, who would have used the road back to the inn. Eventually, Kenelm was run to earth, and the news given.

"By God!" he said, laughing in delight. "A better piece of luck than I dared hope for. We'll see her squirm now. There's a handsome reward in this for you and your uncle, my lad." He immediately went to the inn stable and had his mount saddled up to gallop back to Raiker Hall.

There was no point in going to Clare. Raiker went instead to the back door to discover of Wilkins, lurking in readiness for him, that man and horse had been and were gone. Wilkins thought the bird was Rutley right enough, but gone to pot and seed, and looking a wretched enough fellow. He had set off to the northwest alone, and there was nothing there at all, unless he meant to go cross the country to Ashford, which made no sense to any of them. To Kenelm it indicated not Ashford but London, for Horace to lose himself in the crowded back alleys of that teeming city. He must overtake him before he got there, and he wasted not a minute in setting out in pursuit.

Chapter Nineteen

The minute the boy had left the Dower House after delivering his news, Malone took charge. She was highly perturbed, and secretly delighted. Words gushed out of her mouth, with little attention to accuracy, but much attempt at a vocabulary exalted enough to honour the occasion. "What we've got to do is get over to the Hall at once to be a collaboration of the testimony that Rutley is there. She'll do away with him in the batting of an eye. We'll be lucky if he ain't slaughtered already and stuck in a hole in the ground."

"Wilkins saw him, and Kenelm is on his way. There is no need for us to go," Marnie pointed out.

"We've no idea where Kenelm is, or if the moll-dawdling lad that was here will ever find him in time. We will look no-how come the dawn, if Rutley has slipped off into obscenity again, and not a one of us can take the stand and lay an affeydavey we saw him. It's imperious that at least one of us goes to see, and if you haven't the stomach for it, I'll go myself." This threat was delivered to Aurora, who was less anxious not to go than her sister.

"I think she's right," Rorie said.

"Of course I'm right, and there's not a second to waste. Get your jacket and let's be off. And we have to go quietly, too."

"Take a footman with you at least," Marnie cautioned.

"We don't want a whole brigade creeping up to the window. To take a peek and be sure it's him is all we're doing."

"You don't know him. You can't give an identification," Marnie pointed out.

"I can indemnify that the corpse Clare will have killed before morning is the selfsame one we're going to see through the windows, if we only hurry," Malone answered stoutly. "He won't last through the night. That's a foregone concussion. She'll swear on a stack of Bibles she never saw hide nor hair of the fellow before in her life, and get a dead man to vilify it. Time's wasting. Come on."

"I'll go," Rorie said, and jumped up.

Malone grabbed up her rolling pin as she hastened through the kitchen, and handed a meat cleaver to Aurora, who replaced it and seized a butcher knife instead. They did not arrive in time to see Rutley actually in conversation with Clare through a window, as Malone had intended. But they saw plain enough a large, dark man lead a dispirited horse from the stable and look carefully about him before striking off into the shadowy park.

"What do we do now?" Rorie asked in a whisper.

"Follow him. We must be able to tell Kenelm where to find him."

"He has a horse. Oh, why didn't I ride my mount?"

Rutley mounted his nag as they spoke, and in a flash Malone had taken her decision. "Steal one from the stable and follow him. I'll taggle along as fast as I can on foot. He ain't setting any hot pace. He'll end up carrying that nag before he's gone a mile if I know anything."

"There will be stableboys in the barn."

"No there won't. The lad that sleeps out is off looking for Ken. This is your chance to deserve Kenelm, my girl. Show him what you're made of."

With this bracing encouragement, Rorie slipped into the stable and untied Clare's mount. She didn't bother with a saddle, but put on the bit and bridle and mounted bareback, which necessitated her riding astride. Clare's mount was fast and strong, well able to outdistance the hack Rutley had. There was no fear of losing him, but as she crept along through the darkness with the eerie sounds of nocturnal animals magnified in the silence around, she felt other fears. A rag of cloud sailed over the moon,

197

momentarily increasing the blackness and her fear. She clutched at the butcher knife with one hand and the reins with the other, having some trouble to hold the horse back as far as she would have liked. Over her shoulder, she saw Malone running as fast as she could. She was highly visible, as her white apron flapped about her legs, with only her shoulders and chest covered by a dark shawl. She was a reassuring sight.

With Clare's warnings of the gibbet awaiting him should he be discovered, Rutley urged his animal on to a canter. Rorie followed at a safe distance, but as they wended their way through the park, Malone found her stamina didn't keep pace with her desire. She lost sight of them entirely, and stood undecided whether it was better to continue giving chase, returning for Kenelm, or calling out a posse. She decided to forge ahead, but had by this time no idea even in which direction the others were proceeding.

It seemed a long time she straggled on, cocking her ears forward and aft without hearing a thing but owls and night creatures. Rutley was keenly aware that he was in constant jeopardy while he was in the neighborhood. He took the notion he was even then being followed, and pulled in behind a bunch of bushes to look behind him. He thought he heard hoofbeats, then decided he was imagining it. He was about to go on, when he saw faintly in the darkness the outline of a horse. He felt it could be none other than Kenelm, already in some magical way on his scent, and he cowered behind the bushes, hoping with all his heart the rider would go on past him. By patting his nag in a comforting way, he kept it silent while the horse and rider passed by, then he saw that it was a woman. Wasn't that the mount he had seen in Clare's stable? It looked like it, and the rider was a woman. It must be Clare, come after him. "Clare. Clare, I'm here," he called. "What is it? What's happened?"

Rorie didn't recognize the voice, of course, but to her it sounded positively lethal. She trembled so she hardly knew what to do. Her instinct was to bolt, but this was her chance to help Kenelm. She must get a look at the man, so that she could identify him again. And he had called her Clare—that was some proof that it was the man the stableboy had spoken of. She turned her mount around, thinking she would just get a look at his face, then dash her mount back home. As she advanced, she gripped the knife under the fold of her pelisse. He'll have a gun, she thought, and her hands were trembling, but she kept going toward the man and horse and the bushes.

"Clare, I hope you brought some food, I'm—" Rutley cut his speech off abruptly. "You ain't Clare," he charged, frightened to death, but the sharp edge to his voice sounded like anger to his pursuer. "Who are you?" he demanded. He took a quick step forward and got hold of the horse's bridle before she could retreat. Whoever she was, she was just a young girl, and he had to silence her. At close range, he recognized Clare's horse from the stable. He had been right about that. He quickly concluded that Clare had sent a servant after him for some purpose. "Who are you? Why are you following me?" he asked, becoming more suspicious and frightened by the moment.

"I'm come from Clare," she said, hoping in this way to limit his wrath, and her own danger.

"What does she want?"

"Some proof that you are Rutley," Rorie said. She couldn't have said where this idea came from, but the words were suddenly being said, and as she heard them, they sounded not only plausible but downright clever. His reaction soon undeceived her.

"You're lying," he said. "Kenelm sent you." This dangerous villain was uppermost in his thoughts. He had assumed gargantuan proportions, till it seemed even the trees and bushes were spying for him.

"No," she said quickly, but already the man's hand was taking a tighter grip on the bridle, making her quick bolt impossible.

"You're lying. He sent you. I know he wants to kill me," Rutley said, his voice rising and becoming almost insane-sounding. He pulled roughly at Aurora's skirts, and she half fell from the animal's back, landing in a heap at Rutley's feet. Under her pelisse she still held the knife, and had fallen without quite putting it through herself, which seemed little short of a miracle. It must have cut her gown.

"He doesn't want to kill you. He only wants to find you," Rorie told him. "Why should he want to kill you?"

"Clare told me everything. I know what he's up to. You won't go running to him, telling him where I am." Oh, but how was he to stop her? Clare wouldn't want him to take a woman to the shepherd's hut. He wasn't supposed to let *anyone* see him, or know where he was. And he did not dare let her run to Kenelm and say she had seen him. It was an impossible puzzle, and he didn't have clever Clare there to solve it for him, as she had done in his other dilemma. He stood watching the girl, who had made no move to arise. He wished she would just stay there, quiet, but she suddenly arose.

"Don't move," he said, trying to think. Should he go back to Raiker Hall and tell Clare? But what if Kenelm was there? Clare had told him to leave at once, and not come back.

"Clare lied to you," Rorie said. "Kenelm doesn't want to hurt you."

Clearly this woman had come from Kenelm, was in league with him, and must be silenced. But he would never kill anyone again. Once was more than enough. He had stood by and seen Elmer Carson shoot a horse trader through the heart, and he had himself shot the gypsy in the back when he was attacking Clare, trying to make love to her. It was funny, though, that Clare hadn't been struggling more. But she had said, "Oh help me. Shoot him!" And he had shot him. "Be quiet!" he said. He couldn't think with the girl talking to him. He had to think.

Rorie obediently shut her mouth, and began tightening her grip on the knife handle. She wished it were Malone's rolling pin. She wouldn't hesitate to hit a man on the head with that, but she couldn't bring herself to stick a butcher knife into anyone, even if she could get the opportunity. At least he didn't seem to have a gun. The man noticed the movement of her arms, and grabbed at them. The knife rasped against her stomach, not hard enough to cut her, but enough to frighten her, and she let it fall. In an instant Rutley had seen it and picked it up. He held the wooden handle tightly in his hand, staring at the razor-sharp edge. "Kenelm sent you. You were going to kill me," he said. Clare was right. He had to let Clare know what had happened. Only clever Clare could save him. He grabbed Rorie by the two wrists and glowered at her, with the knife in one hand. She was sure she hadn't another second to live, and gave a desperate jerk to try to break away before she should feel cold steel enter her body.

Chapter Twenty

There was plenty of action in the park of Raiker Hall that night. Lord Raiker, having determined to head north and find the most direct route to London, was riding hell for leather with his eyes and ears alert for Rutley. Malone was huffing along, now reduced to a walk, which was interrupted every five steps to look over her shoulder for Kenelm. She heard him long before he saw her, and stood hooting and waving her hands. She was not hard to spot under these circumstances, and Raiker reined in impatiently. "Malone, what the devil are you doing here?"

"Following Rutley. He went that way." She pointed roughly ahead.

"Are you all alone?" Ken demanded, eager to get on now that he knew he was on the right trail.

"Rorie's gone after him on horseback. She won't let him out of sight."

"You didn't let her go alone! Who's with her?"

"Nobody, but she's armed."

"Does she know how to use a gun?"

"She hasn't got a gun. She has a knife."

"Oh my God! He'll use it against her. How long ago—"

"Not fifteen minutes. Hurry up and you'll catch them."

He didn't have to be told to kick his black stallion into another gallop. He was off while she still stood gasping with fatigue. Having come this far, she decided to plod on to the finish, but her pace could be slackened now. He thundered ahead, thinking a million useless thoughts. He didn't have a gun—should have got a gun from his room. What was Rutley doing here? What if he had got the knife from Rorie? What if he used it? No, don't think that. What was Clare up to? To the side he saw the clump of bushes, but Rutley and Rorie were concealed behind it. He nearly galloped past, then caught out of the corner of his eye the hindquarters and tail of a horse just as he approached. He reined to a sudden stop. Staring into the dark shadows, his blood turned cold. A very large man stood with a butcher knife at Aurora's neck, his other arm holding her against him. He thought his heart would stop.

The large man turned to him. "Get down," he said in a rough voice. Rutley. He thought it was Rutley.

"Let her go," Kenelm said, in a cold voice. He must be cool, reasonable. No time to give away to terror. He dismounted.

"Not bloody likely," the gruff voice answered, and he gripped her more tightly, pushed the knife a little closer against her neck, till she could feel the edge of the blade, cold and sharp. Her head, her whole body throbbed with fear, rational thought beyond her.

Rutley seemed to the others to have the advantage, but he saw no advantage to himself. What was he to do? Two of them now, one of them Kenelm Derwent, bent on killing him.

"Rutley, let her go!" Kenelm repeated, his voice becoming louder, losing its control as he saw her, eyes glazed with fear, her body rigid as death. She couldn't do a thing to help herself.

Rutley stood firm, not making a move, for he couldn't think of a single thing to do. The only outcome he could see was standing exactly as he was till morning. Till Clare in some manner discovered where he was, and what had happened.

"You don't want her. She has nothing to do with this," Kenelm began, persuasively now, controlling himself.

"She's your helper. She was going to kill me."

Kenelm took a tentative step, and Rutley gave a convulsive jerk in response. Rorie tried instinctively to stretch her neck away from the blade, but felt it follow her.

"Wait. We must talk," Kenelm said, watching the blade move, his heart in his mouth, as he tried to determine whether he could knock Rutley down without risking Rorie's life.

"No talking," Rutley shouted back. Talking bothered him. He couldn't think when people started talking. It confused him. He became perfectly still, completely at a loss as to what to do next, and stood so for a minute, which seemed an hour at least to everyone.

"We have no quarrel," Kenelm said at last, in a desperate voice, when he saw that the man apparently had no intention of speaking. And always he was watching, hawklike, for any sign of wavering, any slight lowering of the guard that might allow him to spring in.

There was a sound in the distance, and Rutley's head turned toward it. In a flash Kenelm leaped on him, going for the knife. His hand snatched at the hand holding the knife, wrenching it away from Rorie's neck. She squirmed free and knelt on the ground, gasping, unable even to crawl away from the battle area for several seconds. She looked up to see how Kenelm was faring, and saw Malone's flapping white skirts descending on her. It was her approach that Rutley had heard. When Rorie looked back to the two men, they were struggling over the knife, each with a hand on it. They seemed an even match. Rutley was bigger and had the better grip on the weapon, but he was slower to move. Kenelm suddenly let go of the knife and gave Rutley's hand a sharp knock that sent the knife flying through the air, to land with its point buried in the earth a yard from Malone. She didn't waste a second seizing it, with the full of intention of plunging it in Rutley's back. While she manoeuvered into the best position, Kenelm stood back and aimed a fist into Rutley's stomach, followed swiftly by another to his jaw, great driving punches with his full strength behind each. It was like hitting an ox. Rutley hardly budged, but neither did he make any move to return the blows. As soon as he had lost his knife, Rutley considered himself beaten. Raiker continued raining punches on the man till at last he fell to the ground. "Enough," Rutley moaned.

"Get up," Raiker said, panting.

Rutley rolled over on his stomach and lay immobile. Seeing he was beaten, Kenelm turned to Aurora, where she sat on the ground, unable to stand for shock and weakness from her fright. He went on his knees beside her and took her in his arms. He could feel her shivering, hear her short rapid breaths. "It's all right. It's all right, my dear. I'm here," he said, cradling her close, making soothing sounds of reassurance and patting her gently, till she was somewhat calmed.

Malone looked on with approval, then took up a stance above Rutley, rolling pin in one hand, knife in the other. After a few moments, Kenelm beckoned to her. She came and handed him the knife. "We have to get Aurora home," he said. "Can you take her? The two of you, on Clare's mount?"

"I've never been on a horse's back in my life, and ain't about to start now. I'll walk beside her. Can you look after that one?"

"Don't worry. I'll take care of him." He went to the man's side and turned him over with his foot. "Get up," he said. Rutley came to a sitting position, looking around the ground for the knife. Finding it in Kenelm's hand, he cowered back, but soon learned that his death was to be postponed. Rorie, too, was on her feet by this time, with Malone comforting her. After some discussion, Rorie got back on Clare's mount, Malone was talked into tackling Rutley's, which was winded enough not to be dangerous, and Kenelm walked back with Rutley, leading his own horse by the bridle. The women could hear them talking all along the way, but Malone was too tired and Rorie too distraught to add anything, or even to pay much attention. The talk was not angry, but reasonable. A discussion rather than an argument. They all went to the Dower House, as it was closer than the inn.

They went into the saloon and fell gratefully onto chairs, while Marnie poured wine and commiserated with her sister, with an occasional timid glance at Rutley.

"My brother is very hungry," Kenelm said, looking at Horace with pity. He was a gruesome sight, his face bruised and bloodied. He was sent to wash while some food was prepared for him. It was Malone who took the notion he wasn't to be trusted with the servants, and heaved her tired body from her chair to accompany him. Once she got him alone, she immediately demanded of him what he had done with the emeralds. He looked in dumb silence.

"Eh?" he asked at last.

"We know full well you sold them for Clare. Did you keep *all* the money yourself, or give her some? You might as well tell the truth. It'll go better for you."

She was at length convinced he meant to tell her nothing, and was eager to return to the saloon to let Kenelm beat the truth out of him. Kenelm had already discovered the gist of his half brother's story, and told it to the ladies, with an occasional correction from Rutley.

"When Horace left, it was not over the horse-trading business at all. It was Elmer Carson who killed the other man." Malone raised her eyebrows to her hairline, and Kenelm said, "I believe him. It was the same night that he went to Raiker Hall to discuss with my father, and his, what he should do about his involvement in it. It was not his intention to leave then, but he never saw Papa. Instead he saw Clare, with the gypsy. *She* says the man was attacking her, though what else she expected, meeting him alone in the conservatory at midnight, one can only wonder. It seems it was a rendezvous, and Horace stumbled on them unwittingly. Seeing him, Clare panicked and began shouting that the man was attacking her. Horace had his gun, which is unfortunate, but it seems to have been the custom with him those days, when he was with Elmer Carson. Anyway, Horace shot him."

"She told me to. 'Protect me! Shoot him!' she said. That's what she said," Rutley added. "And he was a big fellow, you know. Strong and wiry. He had a knife. He pulled it out, but Clare called to him and he turned around, and then she called to shoot, so I shot him."

"It was Horace who changed the man's clothing, stripping him to remove any evidence that he was a gypsy. She got my uniform to put on him. It would never be missed, as she had already got me packed off. I don't doubt for a second she had already taken my two rings for herself, and she put them on the corpse for the reason I told you earlier today. She felt the safest place for a body was the graveyard, and the least likely grave to be remarked upon was that of the Jenkins baby, which Father probably did intend moving. It is odd the child was ever buried there, with the family. And it wasn't sent to the next parish either, but buried right here in our local pauper's field, Horace tells me."

"Buried it myself. I can show you the spot," Horace added, nodding.

"Clare convinced Rutley he was a murderer, and gave him money to skip to America. Which he did, but he didn't care for it, and began saving money to return shortly after he arrived. He has been back in England two years, but was always afraid to come back here, as Clare had frightened him half to death. He read of my return in the papers and came to me for help, but thought I was at the Hall, so he fell into her clutches again. She was trying to convince him once more to dash to America, as *I* was out to kill him." He turned to Horace. "Now I don't quite understand how she convinced you of that, Horace. I never did you any harm."

"Said you was crazy as a loon after being in India for all those years," Rutley said simply. "Said you'd kill me if you got half a chance. Thought you meant to do it. I'd never have hurt the little lady," Rutley added with an apologetic glance toward Rorie, who found him still a fearsome sight with his battered face and bulky frame.

"Why was she so anxious to get Rutley shipped off again?" Malone asked. "You pretty well know the story. More or less what she told you last night."

"With the little detail of the emeralds changed. It is her story that Horace stole them."

"I never even *saw* any necklace. There was no necklace there," Rutley said.

"No, that may have been stolen earlier when *I* left, or she may only have taken it then. Nothing was said about it till father died."

"But why did she have to kill the gypsy?" Marnie asked.

"She must have been in a rare state when she got caught letting him make love to her," Ken answered. "She might have thought it was Papa coming into the conservatory. In the darkness she couldn't have been sure, I suppose. After having had to explain my attack on her only six months before, she may have doubted her powers of persuasion. Or she may have thought it was *me* come back. Only she could tell us, so we'll never know the truth. In any case, she was caught out by someone and would do anything to protect her fair name. I daresay she would have preferred it if Ferdinand had just run off and never showed his face again, but when he pulled out a knife—

206

well, it seems she was going to have a corpse of one kind or another on her hands. She had then only to get Horace to bury the body and persuade him to bolt, and she was clear, with the necklace thrown in as a reward. No one questioned Horace's flight, as he had been involved in that business with Elmer Carson, who also ran away."

"It's a great pity you men was all such greenhorns as to kick up your heels and leave the minute she told you to," Malone said. "*You*, Ken, when your papa saw her trying to make love to you. Why the dickens didn't you stand up like a man and say it was all her doing?"

"At sixteen, I felt it more important to be a *gentleman*. One of our duties is to protect ladies always. I wasn't yet wise enough to make the distinction between lady and— what Clare is. I felt sorry for Father, too. How would he have felt, his wife behaving so? He was still infatuated with her, would have believed her over me. She had lately given him a son, which endeared her to him. A very motherly sight she was, with her bundle tucked up in her arm for five minutes a day, to show Papa. I certainly couldn't go on living at home under such circumstances, and with her there to turn him against me, I had slim chances of ever inheriting anything. From that night on it was clear I had to make my own way in the world, and I wasn't all that sorry to get on with it. I had always wanted to travel. I didn't much care for India, but I didn't mind."

"What you should have done was write to Bernard," Marnie pointed out.

"I wrote once to Papa, and when he didn't answer, I felt Bernie had been told the version of the story that was passing at home. It seemed best not to upset the apple cart. I had no notion Clare had not shown my letter. There was nothing in it at all to incriminate her, only an apology to my father, but she feared perhaps that he would relent and ask me back home. He was always so good to us."

"I'm sure he would have, Ken," Marnie told him. "It seems the outside of enough to me that she should have tried to diddle you out of your rights after you did come back. How had she the nerve to tackle that?"

"She has the gall for anything. She had already made an ass of me once, and thought she could do it again. I had changed considerably in appearance, and her testimony would have as much weight as anyone's. Then too there

207

was the body so similar to mine buried in my outfit and rings. A coincidence, but a convincing one. And she didn't take much actual risk. All her testimony is only what father and assorted dead men told her. If she lost, she didn't lose much, only what she was bound to lose in any case when I took my place."

"I suppose it was worth the risk," Malone decided.

"If it weren't for *you*, Marnie, and my other friends and relatives who recognized me, she might have made it stick. I'm afraid I behaved rather badly, bending over backward to get everyone to accept me, flirting with all the girls, questioning the servants, using every trick to ingratiate myself with Dougall and the other local worthies, but when I saw her to be determined to oust me, I had to do it. It was all I could do to keep my hands off her neck. And she's turning Charlie against me. I wish I could get him away from her. She might let him go now he can't get her into Raiker Hall. A son no longer young will do her little credit at whatever spa she retires to make her next match."

"Surely the brazen creature will end up in prison where she belongs!" Malone exclaimed.

"On what charge?" Ken asked. "*She* hasn't killed anyone. As to her suppressing evidence and lying herself blue in the face—well, it was half a dozen dead men who told her false stories, and she will stick like glue to her story that she really thought me an impostor."

"Horace can tell how she put him up to killing the gypsy," Malone reminded him.

Ken glanced to Rutley, who was shrinking back at this suggestion. "But in that case, you see, it is Horace who will stand trial, not she, and I don't think the blame is his."

"I killed him," the man said simply.

"You pulled the trigger; she killed him," Ken contradicted. "But no one knows it except us, and no one will know it. The body in the grave must remain one of life's little mysteries."

"So she's to murder and steal and lie and adulterate herself and get an emerald necklace in reward! That's your justice for you," Malone said, big with indignation.

"She won't get the necklace," Ken said firmly. "That is the next piece of business. She'll get off with the rest of it, and for the small mercy that she won't drag our name

208

through the mud we can at least be thankful, but I mean to get the emeralds."

"How?" Malone asked.

"I've been giving that matter a lot of thought. I had Wilkins tell her there were prowlers in the house while she was away, and she'll have a pretty good notion the prowler was me, looking for the emeralds. I hoped that would cause her to get the emeralds out of the house, and to avoid the possibility that she conceal them on her own body, I had Cleary give Coons the hint that she might find herself faced with a writ for search at any moment. My hope is that she will have moved them outside the house, to some place where they might be thought to have been hidden by the gypsies, for instance. There are certain advantages in it for her. In that way, they can't be definitely traced to her. And if she is ejected suddenly, more suddenly than she thinks, she could get the necklace more easily. Hints of all this are being fed to her, if my people are doing their job as I instructed them."

"The estate is *huge*, though—five thousand acres. How will you ever find where she hid them?" Marnie asked.

"We can eliminate the four thousand that are being farmed. They aren't hidden under the haystack of any of the tenant farmers. They're right around the house, I fancy, some spot she can see from the windows, and not a heavily-trafficked spot either. But the area is still too large for us to find them. She must lead us to them. I mean to call on Mama tomorrow and pay Horace's respects to her. I'll tell her I think she was right to hide them outdoors, and watch to see if she doesn't make straight for them."

"She ain't that gullible," Malone warned.

"It won't do a bit of harm to try. In any case, I mean to be rid of her. I don't want her at the Dower House, and when she has to leave the area, she'll certainly take them with her. All I have to do is watch her twenty-four hours a day. I have Wilkins and the stable boy, and may have to take to winking at the house girls for some feminine help. Her dresser would be an inestimable aid, but unfortunately she is fifty, and not susceptible to a flirtation. Have you any ideas, Horace?"

Horace was well into a mutton chop, but lifted his head to think it over. "*I* used to meet her in the forest," he

209

answered quite shamelessly. "But the gypsies are there, and she wouldn't risk that. The conservatory, maybe."

"She likes the garden, spends a lot of time there, but that is a bit obvious. I imagine they're a little farther away than that. The gazebo, maybe. Did you ever meet her there?"

"No, it's in a bad spot where we couldn't see who was coming at all. Your own mother, Clare once told me, wanted it sheltered from the wind, and she had it built in a little valley. Nobody uses it much."

"Charlie plays there," Marnie said. "He and Mimi used often to go there."

"I don't imagine it's there then. Still, Mimi and Charlie don't play together these days, and it might be safe. We could talk all night and be no closer to the truth. I think we would all be better off in our beds. Come to the inn with me, Horace."

"Will I be safe? I did kill the gypsy."

"It would be better if you would stop saying that. You killed him in self-defence. You aren't a murderer. Come with me. There will have to be an inquest over that other business with Elmer Carson, but we'll come through all right. Just give your evidence; tell the truth. I'll do what I can to help. Dougall is not a hard magistrate," he promised, and the ladies exchanged a knowing glance, to hear who would be trying the case.

"Maybe you'd better pay a few more calls on Lady Alice," Rorie suggested, with a smile.

"Mind reader! You won't take into your head to be angry about it, will you?"

"Oh no, I am becoming quite accustomed to your carrying on."

"You're still in a state of shock." He arose, and Rutley too got up to go with him. When Kenelm lingered beside Rorie's chair as the others moved to the door, Malone took pity on him and ushered Marnie off on the way to bed and Rutley into the hallway, where she kept an eye glued on him to see he didn't escape. While she questioned him about America, Kenelm turned to Aurora. "Are you all right?" he asked.

"I'm fine now, but I was frightened half to death. I'm not cut out for this reckless life you lead."

"Why did you do it?" he asked. "You're supposed to be
210

the sane member of the family. You shortened my life by ten years, to see you with that knife lodged against your throat. Don't *ever* do anything like that to me again, understand?"

"I was trying to help."

"I know. That's what made it so hard. *I* led you into it. I shouldn't even have proposed to you yet. I should have straightened out my life first, and not involved you in this mess. But Sally kept hinting that Hanley and you were interested in each other, and I was afraid if I waited he'd beat me to you. I'm a bit impatient anyway—you may have noticed," he said, with a smile, glancing to the hallway where Malone could be overheard quizzing Rutley.

He put out his hands and drew her to her feet, then put his arms around her. "You're still trembling. Malaprop only allows us sixty seconds. We've wasted about fifty-nine. Don't do anything else foolish. My conscience is burdened enough. I don't want you on it too."

"You're just saving me for your funeral pyre."

"That's right. We'll go up in one glorious blaze together when I die, but first I want to live—with you. I want it very much. Now, don't waste our valuable second—kiss me."

Unaccustomed to taking any initiative in her romance, Rorie looked startled, but as he stood waiting, she stood on her tiptoes and kissed his cheek.

"Oh, really!" he said in exasperation, and turning his head to find her lips, he did the thing properly. "And now don't you think it high time you tell me you love me?" he asked. "You have let me kiss you, and let me tell you I love you. There is usually some form of reciprocity existing between friendly nations."

"I wouldn't be agreeing to marry you if I didn't."

"Do they call that sort of hedged comment making love in England nowadays?" he asked, dissatisfied. "While you are teaching me manners, I see I shall have a few things to teach you too. But not with Malone listening in the hallway." They walked together to the door.

"Don't forget to take Clare's horse back to the stable," Malone reminded him.

"We'll do it on the way to the inn," Ken replied. "You young ladies had better get to bed. You're looking peaky,

Malone. I want to see the roses back in your cheeks tomorrow, hear?"

Both the command and the "young ladies" sat well with her. She emitted a sound that was not far from a giggle. "Go on with you then. What does an old thorn like me want with roses in her cheeks?"

"Selfish creature! What about *my* pleasure? I like to see all my women looking hearty."

"Shameless philanthropist!" she charged happily.

"You're a treasure, you know," he told her. "I give you fair warning, Malone, *you* are going to end up in my harem."

"Hindustani! There'll be no harems for me. I'm a monopolist."

"So am I. I mean to monopolize all lovely women. Come along, Horace."

They left, and Malone, her cheeks pink as peonies, ushered Aurora off to bed, condemning her fiancé as a terrible flirt every step of the way.

Chapter Twenty-One

At Raiker Hall, Clare went to the stables early in the morning, with food purloined from her own larder for Rutley. She was full of misgivings about his reappearance, but felt he would follow her orders. Kenelm was proving intractable, but he would never expose his own father's wife to criminal proceedings. She had come to feel she must indeed own up to having been "mistaken" as to his identity—a pity—but nothing was lost after all. She was by no means despondent. She was worried to see no mount at the shepherd's hut, and when she entered to find no signs of the place's having been recently occupied, with the dust all undisturbed, she fell into serious alarm. Where had that stupid Rutley gone? She looked about sharply on the way home for signs of his straying, but in her heart she felt he had fallen into Kenelm's hands. This could be her undoing.

She was hardly surprised at all when her butler announced at ten o'clock that Lord Raiker wished to see her. Her first thought was to deny him entry, but curiosity was rampant and she had him admitted.

"Good morning, Mama," he said with a wicked grin. Any last sprout of hope withered and died within her, but even as she looked at him with hatred, she was aware of what a fine, strapping fellow he was, what a satisfactory lover he would have made.

"Good morning, Raiker. You come with news of your brother, I collect?"

"That's right, Mama. I have brother safe and sound. And you are finished. He's told all. Your little *à suivi* flirtation with him, and with Ferdinand, your order to kill Ferdinand, your giving Horace the uniform and rings. In short, Clare, you're against the wall. It will be uphill work to convince anyone you're innocent after this if he ever takes the stand."

"*He* is the one who pulled the trigger—your brother. He's no kin to me. I doubt you will want to see him deported, or hung."

"Very true. I have no quarrel with Rutley. My revenge is all for you, Mama. I am come to wreak my revenge." He advanced toward her, staring at her with a baleful eye.

"Kenelm!" she sat up, frightened. "What do you mean— what is it?" She clutched at her skirts.

"I want my necklace, Mama," he said in a menacing voice.

"I don't have it!"

"I want it, *now*."

"It's not here, I tell you."

"Get it, Clare. I know it is not here in the house. I know you decided to conceal it outside of the house. Get it."

Her eyes narrowed, and she glanced at him with a question. "Oh yes, I have a fair idea where it is," he went on. "I have worked out the approximate location, but it might take me three or four hours to find it. It will go better for you if you return it voluntarily. Otherwise— well, really, it would be too degrading to have one's own stepmama hauled before the courts for thieving."

"I don't have it, Ken. I—I *did* have it."

"You still have."

"No. Your papa sold it, to pay his debts when he was dying. He had it sold in Europe—Holland I think, or Austria."

"*C'est à vous*," he said with a shrug. "If that's today's story, then so be it, but I'll have my necklace before this day is out. And before the week is out, I will have my home. Goodbye, Mama." He turned and left the room.

"Kennie!" she called after him, but he was already in

214

the hall, exchanging a wink with Wilkins, who knew his duties to the letter.

When Clare rushed to her room and grabbed a pelisse, Wilkins nipped into the study and waved his handkerchief once toward the shrubbery to indicate that her ladyship had gone into the rose garden by the parlour door. Kenelm circuited the house, staying behind shrubberies when he got to the other side, but Clare had done no more than set up her easel to sketch the peacock, strutting on the lawn with his insignificant mate tagging behind him. Charles was already there, reading a book.

For about ten minutes Clare sketched, occasionally directing a few comments to her son. She never once glanced about her, yet Kenelm was sure she must suspect she was being watched. She painted on, the only movement of her eye from peacock to easel. She called Charles to her side, looking at his book, explaining some matter to him.

Charles put the book down and said, "I'm going to play, Mama."

"Don't stray far, dear. The gypsies are still here."

"I'll go to the gazebo," he said, and darted off.

"Don't be long."

She resumed her work, putting on a wonderful act. It was only the tense set of her shoulders and the peeps in the direction of the gazebo that gave any indication of strain. Kenelm stood on, watching, finding it hard to believe she would sit idly painting while her emeralds, *his* emeralds, were in peril. He had been sure she would go off after them. But then she was up to anything. She might have sent some person she trusted, her dresser or one of her own servants, to get the jewels while she acted as a lure to hold him here. Ken looked to the window chosen by Wilkins as their communications point, to see Wilkins shaking his head, indicating no one else in the house had made a hasty exit. There was only Clare and Charlie out. Would she use her own son? He quickly decided she'd use her mother if necessary, and went dashing off after Charlie.

He was surprised to find him climbing up one of the struts of the gazebo, for he was not a very athletic fellow. Kenelm stood quietly watching him, with his heart racing to see what the boy was doing. He appeared to know

215

exactly what he was about. There was an abandoned swallow's nest in the corner of the building, its gray saucer of twigs and mud clinging to the corner where the strut met the roof. Charlie was feeling in it, for eggs, he supposed. He had done the same thing himself twenty years ago. Charlie reached up from the hand railing, steadying himself with one hand on the corner beam, in some danger of falling. Ken waited, wondering whether he shouldn't be back at the rose garden, and wondering too after a moment whether it was eggs or emeralds the boy fished for. A small brown packet was pulled from the nest. Charlie jiggled it and smiled, balanced himself on the hand railing, then scrambled down.

"Oh, you found Mama's necklace!" Ken said, walking forward and speaking in a normal voice.

"Ah, you weren't supposed to know!" Charlie said. "Mama said it was a joke on you, and I shouldn't tell. Grown-ups are no fun to play with."

"Maybe we'd better just look and see if it's still in the bag," Ken suggested, tousling the boy's hair with his fingers.

"It was right where she said," Charlie told him, and obediently opened the bag, shaking the necklace out on to his palm. It glowed a deep fire-green, catching the sun in its faceted gems.

Kenelm lifted it up and admired it. "I'll take it to Mama for you," he said. Charlie accompanied him to the rose garden.

Clare rose to her feet when she saw the two of them approach across the lawn. Her face was rigid with anger, but she was fighting to assume a look of either surprise or merriment, so he assumed he was to be treated to another farce.

"We found it, Mama," Charlie said.

"Found what, dear?"

"Your necklace. Ken already knows. Didn't you tell him?"

"I guessed," Ken explained to his half brother.

"It was right where you said, Mama. Only fancy the magpies stealing it from your dresser, and hiding it in the swallows' nest."

"Those pies are up to anything," Ken said, smiling at Clare. "Only fancy their being crafty enough to know it

216

was tucked up in this little leather bag. They'll be picking our locks next, and emptying our safes. Why don't you run back and see if they have anything else hidden in that nest, Charlie?"

Charlie, seeing the game was ruined, ran back to the gazebo to do more investigating. Clare watched him go, then turned to Ken. "After speaking to you, it struck me the magpies might have taken it, for they once flew off with a collar stud of your papa's, Ken. The necklace was left on my dresser for a few moments the last time I wore it."

"Would that be before or after Papa sold it?"

"I thought he said he had sold it. . . . But really you know, his mind was straying a little at the end."

"More laxity on the part of the dear departed. I had a strong inkling a dead man would feature in the story. No matter. I have it now."

"It must be handed over with the rest of the heirlooms till the matter of your claim is settled."

"That won't be long, and in the meanwhile, I'll keep it in safekeeping from the pies myself."

"We don't know how long it will take. I still think—"

"Think again. I have Ghizlaine, who will report on the disappearance of Ferdinand the night Rutley disappeared; I have Rutley, who will testify that you directed him to shoot Ferdinand; and now *we* have Charles, who will say you directed him to the emeralds. Every neighbour for miles around is ready to swear I am Lord Raiker. Know when the odds are against you, Mama. A discreet retreat is your best bet—your only bet, now. *You* find you were mistaken in my identity, Rutley forgets the night you had him shoot Ferdinand, we 'find' the emeralds in the bottom of a chest in Papa's coat pocket—the one he was wearing the last night you wore the necklace would be less incredible than any other means, I think."

Clare quickly ran over her choices, really only a resume of mental work already done a dozen times. She had no wish to darken her own character by an ugly scandal involving a love affair with a gypsy—and what a lover he had been! She had no hope of getting the necklace back now, no wish to antagonize Lord Raiker, who was very fond of her son, and might quite possibly do something in

217

that quarter when she made a new match. She smiled a sweet smile of capitulation.

"You win! How clever you are, Kennie. What hope has a poor woman against you? Now how should we best proceed? Rutley, I think, ought to be shipped off to America. We don't want him gabbling some story of his own."

"Rutley stays. He needs a sharp eye kept on him to keep him out of trouble. Who better to do it than his brother? I will buy him a fishing boat, and his grandfather will introduce him to the business. He tells me he's becoming tired of horses."

"I don't think that's a good plan, Ken."

"Don't you? I do. He stays."

"I won't be comfortable with him around, never knowing what he will say or do. And he bothers me, you know. He always used to be here, trying to flirt with me."

"Poor you. I can well imagine how distasteful that was to one of your high principles."

"Ah Ken, you misunderstand. Because I encouraged *you* a little, you think there were others, but there never were. I never gave him a bit of encouragement."

"It was your meeting him in the forest at night that led him astray in his thinking, I expect. But he's not at all clever, Clare, and misunderstood your total lack of interest. You are quite right to foresee difficulties in remaining here, however. As Marnie is to marry soon—"

"What a lack of respect to your poor brother! Bernard hardly dead a year and already she is to be married again."

"Yes, as I was saying, that will leave the Dower House free, and at your disposal. I will be happy to pay you a fair sum in lieu of your taking occupancy. Sufficient to let you hire a house at Tunbridge Wells."

"Tunbridge Wells! No one goes there anymore. I had thought of Brighton."

Raiker looked her up and down in an insolent manner. "It's not far enough away to suit me, but then, it's where the rackety set are idling these days, so it might be your best bid. With luck you'll get yourself attached to someone before the year's out. All right, Brighton. I'll have to supplement your income. Pray don't consider it as a reward for your behaviour, but only as pure eagerness to see the last of you. You still have a few good years. With

218

luck, you'll make another catch. Remember what I said about Charles."

"I could never part with my son. He is the world to me."

"Yes, yes, I know how fond you are of him, but he isn't Lord Raikor, Clare, and will not likely ever be, as I don't plan to waste any time in setting up my own nursery. You might find your fondness for him diminishes when you marry. Especially if your husband has a handsome son. If—say, when—Charles becomes an encumbrance, send him to me. I will be very happy to have him."

"I don't know how you can be so cruel!" she said, with a large tear forming in the corner of her eye.

"Neither do I. I amaze myself. Still, he is over eleven. Soon he'll be ready for Eton, and it isn't cheap sending a boy to school."

"True," she said, blinking the tear over her lid so that it slid down her cheek slowly. "I have nearly lost him. He is nearly grown up. One of these days I must let him go away to school."

"*Expensive* school. Now, I think you should call Coons and have him take those steps necessary to indicate your withdrawal of Charles's claim to my title. You will be eager to get up to Brighton and look over a house. A good season for it. I'll give you a thousand a year in lieu of occupying the Dower House, roughly twice what it's worth. Along with your jointure, it is sufficient to set you up in respectable style. Of course, on your marriage, payments stop."

"I would prefer a lump sum."

"I wouldn't mind having it over and done with myself."

"Say ten thousand."

"Say five, and not a penny more."

"Oh well, if you're going to be clutch-fisted about it, I'll take the thousand a year."

"Fine. Of course, unless you remain as a widow for over five years you're making a bad bargain, but it is hardly in my interest to point it out, I suppose."

"Well, I'll take the five, then, but if I'm still not married in five years, I'll come back."

"No. Five thousand to clear all claim by you on the property. Take it or leave it."

"I don't know how I'm expected to provide a home for myself and Charles on such a pittance."

"You were contriving one for yourself on one hundred and fifty a year when you met Papa, and doing it very well too," he pointed out.

She sniffed. "Marnie has put you up to this. Let me tell you, it looks very odd to see you chasing her, offering to buy her the Gypperfield mansion."

"Yes, the neighbours are more accustomed to see Lady Raiker chase *me*. You know which Lady Raiker I refer to, Clare? But you needn't fear Marnie. John is as strict as a Methodist. Only dances on one foot, as they say."

"I suppose you and Lady Alice will be announcing the banns once I am got rid of, as you speak of setting up your nursery."

"*I* plan to. I don't know about Sally."

She looked up quickly. "What do you mean?"

"Read the newspapers, Mama. I'm afraid you won't be receiving an invitation to the nuptials. Now I'm off. I'll see my banker and arrange the settlement. I'll see you again before you go. You were very foolish, Clare. I am pretty well to grass now and had intended being more generous with my stepmother. Why did you do it—set on this course that you must have known would lead to nothing but trouble?"

She examined him with cold, unblinking eyes. "You loved me once. You told me you'd do anything for me. But men are all alike—self-interested."

He shook his head and smiled ruefully. "I was certainly a fool, wasn't I? You told me you'd do anything for me too, Clare. But when father caught you in my room trying to corner me, it was *I* who kept my promise. I defended you, let my own father think *I* was the one at fault, and you stood without saying a word while he ordered me from the house as a rake and unnatural son. Not so much as one word in my defence. You didn't even show him my letter of apology, and there was nothing in it to incriminate you. I went off with my tail between my legs and protected your name for all those years, and this was the thanks I got for it. You pretended not to know me when I returned, and to add insult to infamy, you concocted that story about my beating my father, and his shooting me in the back. You *would* do anything, but for no one but yourself. Thank God women are not all alike! It doesn't seem right to turn you

220

loose on the unsuspecting world. I can only hope you find someone who deserves you."

"Don't worry. I will."

"You're going to the right place for it in all events. Happy hunting, Mama." He bowed and left, walking at a jaunty gait, the matter already drifting from his mind as he went out the door to head to the Dower House.

Clare walked to the mirror, fluffed out her curls and examined the corners of her eyes for crows'-feet. Five thousand and her income. She would do very well in Brighton. Now, who could provide her an entrée to the Prince's pavilion?

Epilogue

The younger Lady Raiker postponed her nuptials to John Berrigan till her brother-in-law was duly installed in Raiker Hall, so that she might have her reception there. It was a very grand reception; everyone came. Everyone except the dowager Lady Raiker, who was too busy contriving her entrée to the Prince's pavilion to waste a second. Not that she was invited, though she did receive a notice of the wedding that she would have used as an invitation had she desired to do so. She had caught the eye of an infamous nobleman who was negotiating with her for some service in return for the desired invitation to the pavilion, and she would not dream of leaving at such a crucial moment.

The Berrigans decided against Brighton as a honeymoon spot when they considered whom they might be apt to encounter there. They went to the Isle of Wight instead, and Malone and Rorie stayed on at the Dower House to mind Mimi till they returned. Lord Raiker was very happy with his trio of a harem, pointing out to a delighted Malone that he had girls of all ages, just as he liked. Rather than have the Falkners make two trips to Kent, they stayed visiting with Raiker till the three weeks that saw Marnie and John back home.

The interval was a busy one, with a second wedding in

preparation and many visits back and forth between the two houses and into the village to be made. There was as well a quiet inquest held into the death of a horse dealer, with Mr. Horace Rutley the only witness. Lord Dougall was not at all difficult in the matter, and Mr. Rutley was allowed out on suspension under the guardianship of his half brother and friend, Lord Raiker. He took to the fishing business very well, and his mother came all the way from Hampshire to visit him when she learned he was alive. As she disliked the journey so much, she never returned, nor intends to. She says philosophically that her husband knows where to find her if he wants her, but there has been no intimation that he does, and she goes on very happily tending her chickens and flowers.

Malone has her capable hands full finding a bride for Rutley, which she declares is all he needs to turn into a halfway respectable fellow. "Millie is the one ought to nab him, for she don't much care who she associates with, a gypsy or a murderer, it's all one and the same to her."

"Now take care, Malaprop," Kenelm says sternly. "You're foraging in my harem there. *I* had first bid on Millie."

"I'll have you know I'm as well propped up as anyone, and if you don't believe me I'll lift my skirts and give you a view of my ankles. Beef to the heels, like a Muenster heifer."

To keep him in line she threatens to go over to the Berrigan household, "for there'll be a babe in the basket there before the year's out, or I'll know why not. Her well past thirty, and never a son produced yet."

"In that case, I shall have to bring an ayah in from India for *our* children," he replies, ever inventive.

"There'll be no Hindustani servants in *my* house!" she decrees firmly, revealing unconsciously that she has already claimed Raiker Hall as her own.

Kenelm tries hard to restore some dignity to the family name. He maintains that as his father had no wits, his stepmama no morals and Marnie no propriety in remarrying thirteen months after her widowhood, he must establish a regime of decorum. It is to this end that he goes in a sedate dark jacket to the village and bows formally to everyone. Till he gets to the sweet shop, he does quite well. But a bag of sugarplums detracts greatly from his reserve, particularly as he cannot keep his hands from them till he

223

gets home. His lips become unsteady as he views the sugar bowls on the heads of Beckstead's customers, and to tell the whole dreadful truth, his eyes misbehave as well when a pretty young girl strolls by. But as Malone says, "He was derived of English girls entirely in India, and the Angel Gabriel hisself might be forgiven for *looking*."

She suspects his bride has a little more than looking to forgive him, and so keeps busy running to the door ten times a minute to see that the Hindustani doesn't get out of hand before the wedding. It plays havoc with his love-making and his patience.

"Well, dearest heart," he says with a wary eye to the door and an arm creeping about her shoulders, "I think I just heard Malaprop dash upstairs. Don't you think we should take advantage of the next five minutes?"

"Yes, Kenelm, I want to ask if you managed to get Marnie's engagement ring back from Clare. I have been meaning to do it."

"No, I didn't," he says, moving closer to her and tightening his hold.

"She will be disappointed," she says, eying her own diamond contentedly.

"We'll buy her one." He kisses her ear, her chin.

"John won't like it."

"To hell with John." Kisses are bestowed on her cheek, the edge of her lips.

"Gentlemen don't swear in front of ladies."

He kisses her on the lips, ignoring his instructions. "I love you. I don't think I can wait three whole days for our wedding. Couldn't we get hold of the reverend tonight?"

"No, you'll have to wait till Marnie and John get home. And I doubt very much if gentlemen spend every spare moment alone with their brides trying to make love to them."

"Indians do," he says, undismayed, and proceeds to kiss her again, with his ears cocked and his eyes frequently flying to the door for fear of Malaprop, who already rules his roost.